The Wayward Muse

The Wayward Muse

by

Brian Stableford

A Black Coat Press Book

Acknowledgements: Earlier versions of "The Secret Exhibition" and "The Incubus of the Rose" appeared respectively in *Weird Tales* Nos. 317 (Fall 1999) and 321 (Fall 2000). "The Arms of Morpheus" is original to this volume.

Visit our website at www.blackcoatpress.com

ISBN 1-932983-45-7. First Printing. September 2005. Published by Black Coat Press, an imprint of Hollywood Comics.com, LLC, P.O. Box 17270, Encino, CA 91416. Printed in the United States of America.

Table of Contents

Introduction

The ultimate origin of this book was an invitation I received to submit some stories to an anthology that Stefan Dziemianowicz was co-editing for Barnes and Noble, which was to be a horror fiction "book of days" containing 365 stories, each one less than 750 words in length. Stefan said that I could submit as many stories as I wished, so I sketched out plans for four when I had a spare moment, and sat down to write them on a Wednesday morning.

Because they were so short, I had finished all four by lunchtime, so I while I was eating my customary sandwich, I planned out four more to write in the afternoon. As I was still having fun, I did another eight the day after and four more on the Friday morning–by which time I had run through all the adaptable synopses in my ideas file and all those I could produce off the top of my head. I printed them all off and put them in the post.

Unfortunately, Stefan and his co-editors only accepted nine items out of the 20–perhaps feeling that many of them were not really horror stories at all–which left me with 11 ultra-short stories on my hands. I set about rewriting the ones that were expandable, adjusting them to more easily marketable lengths. "The Secret Exhibition" is the second one that eventually became the basis of a book, by virtue of providing the foundation-stone for a story series. (The first was "When Molly Met Elvis," which ultimately became *Year Zero.*)

The note in my file of story ideas that gave birth to the 750-word version of "The Secret Exhibition" had been made while I was translating Jean Lorrain's decadent novel *Monsieur de Phocas* (1901) for Dedalus. *Monsieur de Phocas* is a transfigurative compendium of a number of short stories and newspaper articles that Lorrain had written over the previous decade, reformulated as a phantasmagoric account of the relentless exaggeration towards madness of the peculiar state of mind that the Decadents called spleen. There is a key episode in the novel in which the protagonist, the Duc de Fréneuse, visits his nemesis, the artist Claudius Ethal, in his studio. Ethal shows the Duc three portraits he has done of beautiful women, offering a scathing commentary on the personalities and careers of his three sitters. Ethal's scabrous remarks outrage the Duc, proving to be the final straw in his long-drawn-out psychological struggle, and he stabs the artist to death. My variation on the theme transformed the motivation of the characters, in order to generate a markedly different outcome of a broadly similar scene.

(Most writers, when asked where they get their ideas from, are carefully evasive; I generally come clean and admit that I steal them, although I take some pride in being honest enough to pervert them considerably as I do so.)

When I expanded "The Secret Exhibition" for resubmission, I filled in the back stories of the two key characters and elaborated the setting of the story slightly, placing it in an "artists' colony" of the kind that has figured in a number of conspicuously decadent science fiction series since J. G. Ballard transfigured Sunset Boulevard into Vermilion Sands. Because it was a copy taken from a standard template, I referred to it simply as "the Island" and placed it off the shore of "the Empire" without giving much thought to the specifics of the world in which the story was set. Once the story had appeared in *Weird Tales*, I began considering the possibility of extrapolating it into a series, in which the narrator's cynically unorthodox voice could address other themes situated at the porous interface between artistic inspiration and the supernatural.

The initial inspiration of "The Incubus of the Rose" owed as much to the 1946 movie of *The Specter of the Rose*–scripted by Ben Hecht, author of one of the finest examples of American decadent prose, *Fantazius Mallare*–as to the notorious Nijinsky ballet on which the movie was based, but it is conscientiously perverted according to my usual strategy. The version that appeared in *Weird Tales* had to be cut by 3,000 words or so because Darrell Schweitzer thought the introductory phase far too languid and self-indulgent, but I restored the missing text to this version before beginning a final edit.

"The Arms of Morpheus" was begun in response to a note from Darrell to the effect that *Weird Tales* was planning to start running novellas as two-part serials, inviting me to submit something of that sort. When I started out, I was aiming for 20,000 words or so, but recklessly introduced too many complications into the dual-stranded plot, and soon had to give up any attempt to restrain the word length. Alas, letting the story run to what seemed to be its natural length produced something far too long for magazine publication and far too short for publication in the commercial sector of the book market.

(When I began my career back in the late 1960s, I was forbidden by my publisher to write less than 50,000 words or more than 65,000 words, so "The Arms of Morpheus" would have been ideal back then–lengthwise, if not in terms of its subject-matter–but now that British and American books are expected to be as obese as British and American children, nothing less than 100,000 words will suffice.)

Even as a long novella, "The Arms of Morpheus" required a more detailed backcloth than either of its predecessors, so I was forced to devote some more attention to the where and when of its proceedings. It was obvious, though not specifically stated, that the earlier stories took place in some kind of parallel world, which featured an Empire even more decadent than any in our own turbulent history. It was also tacitly obvious that the technological and cultural background of the stories, like their aesthetic sensibility, was approximately similar to that of the heyday of the Decadent Movement–the late 19th century, not a million miles away from Jean Lorrain's Paris.

Aesthetic logic seemed to demand that, if a decadent Empire were to be located in an era of that sort, the perfect candidate would be the ultimate faded relic of the grandeur that had once been Rome–a Rome that had never actually fallen to the barbarians, even though it had doubtless gone through many slightly-less-drastic phases of transformation as it expanded to occupy the entire Western world, both Old and New.

The territory occupied in our world's political geography by France would, in this world–nominally, at least–be a mere province, with an ethnic mix very different from the one imposed by Frankish and Norse invasions. Aesthetic logic also encouraged the notion that there was no reason why the heterocosmic physical geography of the story need be identical to that of our world, so there was no need to make the island–now named Mnemosyne, in honor of the mother of the Muses–identical to one or other of the Channel Islands that exist in our world.

The world of the story told in "The Arms of Morpheus" is, therefore, one that has a Classical heritage very similar to ours, its history having diverged some time in the first or second century A.D. (although the years are not named in that fashion, because Christianity, in the world of the text, never produced an all-consuming Christendom), but whose history has been markedly divergent for nearly two millennia.

Should the series continue, I shall doubtless add further detail to this vague scheme, filling in details as and when they may become useful or desirable in narrative terms. Although it seems improbable that the patterns of genealogical descent in the world of the story would have produced any individuals parallel to the individuals of our world, it is not beyond the possibility that parallels of a sort might exist, so some scope is conserved for exercises of the kind to which this book's publisher is fondly devoted.

If any such series does unfold further, I shall of course have to address various issues raised in the first three stories in the form of dark and tantalizing hints. I shall, for instance, have to explain at some point how old their protagonist really is, and why he is so much older than he looks. Aesthetic logic requires him to have a complex personal history, inclusive of many interesting events, and I shall have to do my best to fill in that currently blank canvas, should the Muse demand it. In the meantime, though, this is the story so far.

In adapting the first two items to take their place alongside "The Arms of Morpheus," I added in a little more background detail, including the island's name and something of its history. I also added a few incidental references to characters and locations that play significant roles in "The Arms of Morpheus" but had not been thought of when I penned the earlier pieces, so as to increase the apparent coherency of the whole. The ultimate result of all the amendments is that the versions of "The Secret Exhibition" and "The Incubus of the Rose" featured here are each a few thousand words longer than their magazine versions.

None of the characters in the stories is based on any living person (alas!); the opinions of the protagonist are not necessarily those of the author, who is merely trying them out for size and has not yet made a final decision as to what, if anything, he believes.

The Secret Exhibition

Claudius Jaseph came to the island of Mnemosyne in the 14th year of the present Emperor's reign. He arrived in early June with the last fleet of summer migrants, borne by one of those freak tides of fashion that catch up the idle rich, albeit in a far more gentle manner than they afflict the slaves of the Muse. His advent was, however, anticipated for some days beforehand, the news of his intention having traveled ahead of him by courtesy of his champions and his agent.

Given that more than half the island's permanent population consisted by that time of writers, composers, players, painters, necromancers, mystics and similar recipients of unsteady aristocratic patronage, the last thing it required its seasonal visitors to bring was *more* writers, composers, players, painters, necromancers and mystics, but wealth inevitably nurtures an addiction to novelty. Were the rich ever to become content with what they already have, they would no longer be able to spend the dividends of their capital; the entire Imperial economy would then lurch towards collapse–or so the patient Physiocrats assure us. True artists know that true art is timeless, and that they are collaborators in a great endeavor rather than competitors for transient fame and fortune, but so-called patrons of the arts see things very differently.

I was not at all distressed by news of Jaseph's impending arrival, and found it very difficult to muster any sentiment but indifference–but others would not let me be content in my carelessness. Even some few of my friends and admirers probably thought me incandescent with envious anticipation, but artists often conceive of one another as uncontainable whirlwinds of child-like emotion. Almost every one of us believes that he–or she–is clever enough to play the role without actually fitting it, although few of us actually are. I am, of course, the rarest of the rare exceptions, as befits a man who has been resident on Mnemosyne longer than anyone else can remember.

I suppose that I made a few acidic remarks in advance of Jaseph's arrival, but only because it was expected of me; appearances have to be kept up when our patrons are watching expectantly, no matter how wearisome the work becomes. Privately, I did not expect the fuss to last long. I had seen other portraitists sail in on a wayward tide with a thousand eyes watching, and become *passé* long before they moved on to some comfortable city full of aspirant burghers and desperate matrons. I had no reason to think, when June began, that Claudius Jaseph would be any different.

"This one will offer you real competition, Axel," Hecate Rain assured me, as we lounged on the terrace of the *Sprite* in the mid-day heat, looking out over the harbor. She was drinking absinthe but there was iced water in my own glass; I had work to do that afternoon. "They say that his brushwork is superb and his accuracy uncanny. More to the point, he makes a fetish of painting beautiful women, just as you have always done. They say that he plays them off against one another with consummate cruelty: the wives whose beauty is beginning to fade, anxious to be captured on canvas one last time, while they are still desirable; the daughters just coming into their inheritance of pulchritude, intoxicated and deranged by a magnetism they cannot yet control. Those have always been your favorite victims, have they not?"

"Victims?" I echoed, with ostentatious alarm. "Are my subjects *victims*? You have posed for me yourself, on more than one occasion. Did you feel victimized?"

"My vanity is less vulnerable than some," she told me, closing her eyes against the sunlight as she leaned backward languidly, "but even I have felt a certain sting in your analytical eye. There are others whose souls have been more deeply penetrated."

"There is all the difference in the world," I pointed out, "between a painter whose brush reaches tenderly into the soul of a sitter in order to bring something precious to the surface of his canvas, and an assassin who puts away his palette when darkness falls in order to don a black domino and ply a gleaming dagger like some metropolitan bravo."

"Your analogy is uncommonly poetic," Hecate observed. She was a poet by vocation, although she had been given a necromantic name by a careless parent. "Do you really imagine your work as a kind of mining? Others might represent it quite differently. By day, they say, you regard your sitters with a cool and clinical eye, impassively noting their flaws and cleverly erasing them from the images that appear by degrees upon your canvas—but after dark, your face changes completely; your gaze becomes avid and your lips are reddened with lust. I do not speak for myself, of course, but the summer visitors do not see you as I do. Your reputation has its darker aspect."

"Of course it does," I told her, gesturing to the waiter as he passed by to request fresh ice. "I cultivate it very carefully."

"But you cannot entirely control what others think. Rumor-mongers exaggerate. You may think of yourself as a gentle seducer, a lover whose artistry compensates more than adequately for your lack of attention to conventional morality, but there are some who say that, in your heart of hearts, you despise your subjects with a fervor you could never admit."

"It is a silly slander," I said. "You know it."

"I do, and I defend you—but the summer visitors bring anxieties, jealousies and resentments to Mnemosyne that we permanent residents have long-since banished from our lives. There are some, even among your patrons, who believe that your habit of seducing your sitters is a kind of predation. They are not poetically inclined, for the most part, but they would not be unfavorable to the analogy of your driving a metaphorical dagger deep into the bodies of your clients' wives and daughters, ripping their respectability to shreds."

"It is because the rich have no souls to be ripped," I opined, wearily, "that they speak of *respectability*. It is all nonsense. Why are we wasting our time with it?"

"Because it affects the way that your impending competition with Claudius Jaseph will be seen—and there will be a competition, no matter how you might try to avoid it. Everyone expects it: not merely the visitors but the permanent residents. You've ruled this little roost of ours for a long time, and there are a great many people who'd like to see you knocked off your perch, if only to stir things up a bit. Jaseph is the man who can do it, it's said. He plays your game, but with the flair and fervor of a younger man."

I looked around for the ice, but the waiter was nowhere to be seen. I shook my head, and looked out over the water instead, towards the Devil's Rocks and Nicodemus Rham's lighthouse, which stood guard over them.

Hecate knew perfectly well how insulting her reference to my "game" was, but she was not speaking for herself; she was trying to explain the curious excitement that had been generated on the island by the news of Claudius Jaseph's impending arrival. I was not at all sure that I wanted to be bothered with it, not because I feared competition but because I was impatient with the popular misrepresentation of my character and ambition.

"As I understand it," I said, "there has only been a single exhibition of this upstart's work, in a gallery where my own work has been shown a dozen times."

"In a gallery that you have never visited," Hecate pointed out, "despite all of Myrica Mavor's entreaties. I understand that your refusal to leave the island is the keystone of your carefully cultivated eccentricity, but there are people on the mainland who see it as simple rudeness. Claudius Jaseph is by no means a polite man, it's said, let alone an unctuous one, but he's willing to put in an appearance–and a single exhibition is more than enough to whip up a sensation nowadays. We're approaching the Empire's 20th century, after all. In ten years we'll be celebrating the second millennium of Divine Caesar's birth."

"Yes," I agreed, "but a further 56 will pass before those who come after us are forced to celebrate the actual inauguration of the Everlasting Empire. How different the world would be had Caesar's would-be assassins succeeded! But I don't understand why you're so insistent on using the violent imagery of daggers and whips. Surely no one is expecting a competition between painters to extend as far as dueling?"

"Some might be hoping for that," Hecate said, "but most seem to be anticipating a contest of metaphorical daggers, relishing the thought that as a much younger man, his might be a good deal straighter and more durable than yours. They say that he is one of those rare men who really does *love* women, although he never flatters them, by day or by night. He is honest, and he knows how precious they truly are. Myrica told me herself–so mournfully I had to believe her–that he would not lend her his very best work to show in his first public exhibition. There are those among his creations, it seems, which he adores so absolutely that he consigns them to a secret exhibition which none but he and a favored few may ever view. He refuses to accept his fee in such cases, because he believes that the portraits have souls of their own, which ought never to be sold."

I thought, on hearing this, that Jaseph seemed to have discovered an entirely new way of breaking hearts. What woman, hearing the rumor that Hecate had just quoted–even knowing that it came from the artist's agent–could resist the temptation to commission a portrait, quietly hoping that it might acquire a soul of its own and thus prove worthy to be retained in the secret exhibition? What woman, in pursuit of that aim, would not offer herself to the artist with exceptional abandon, hoping to prove her worthiness by the luxury of her surrender? And what woman, told in the end that her portrait was, after all, to be shown in Myrica's gallery or returned to her husband or father in exchange for the contracted price, would not suffer a disappointment far greater than any that I could ever have contrived to inflict?

Even so, I was not at all jealous of the newcomer. Hecate had misjudged me, as poets are so often wont to misjudge their one-time lovers. I never despised my sitters, and there was nothing cynical about the manner in which I flattered them with my art, when I did elect to flatter them. I did make love to those who were willing–and how many women sit for a portrait who are not willing, once they understand what his artistry can accomplish?–but I took nothing from them but trivial affection. No woman had ever killed herself for me.

That, alas, was the next rumor to reach Hecate's avid ears and she spared no time in spreading it. By the time Claudius Jaseph actually stepped on to the shore, following Lady Hintermann and the Marquis of Caissot along the gangplank of Ramon Rabirio's yacht, even the Sisters of Shalimar knew the record of his power, and certainly had not divined it in their skrying-glasses.

No less than three of the sitters whose portraits had made their appearance on Myrica Mavor's hallowed walls were now dead, it seemed. Naomi Lynhurst, daughter of the Marquis of Castelle, had thrown herself into the city's least-known river, not even from a bridge but through an iron-capped manhole in the steel-sprung pavement that had reduced it to the status of a sewer. Sarah, Lady Generoix had hanged herself with a bell-rope in the Temple of Minerva. Worst of all, Roxane, the elder daughter of the Duke of Alectryon, had opened a vein in her arm with a barber's surgical razor, cutting all the way from the shoulder to the wrist with a single imperious sweep.

I had painted Roxane myself, and might have made love to her had I not feared the wrath and malice of her father. Given time, I would probably have painted Naomi and Sarah had they lived to be a little older, for they would surely have come to visit Mnemosyne eventually.

Not one of the three had attained 20 years of age before dying; Naomi had been barely 17.

One such death might have been regarded as tragic happenstance, even two might have been dismissed as macabre coincidence, but three looked uncommonly like the Devil's work, at least to everyone who believed in the Devil.

And what effect did this seeming Devil's work have on Claudius Jaseph and his reputation? According to what Myrica had told Hecate, the man was devastated by grief, but relied upon the feverish expertise of his art to pull him through—and he had so many commissions impending that he was receiving bribes for preferential treatment higher than the price I usually asked for my paintings.

I suspected, even before Rabirio's yacht set down its anchor, that the summer would be an unprecedentedly profitable season for the island's magicians.

As chance would have it, it was at a séance rather than a party that I first met the man that my peers had appointed my arch-rival. I am not a necrophile by habit or inclination, but when Vashti Savage told me that Alectryon's distraught wife had demanded that she summon the spirit of her dear departed daughter, and that she could not do it without a full coven of 13 persons who had some firm connection with the dead girl, I immediately agreed to lend my hands to the circle. How could I possibly have refused?

Perhaps it was disingenuous of me not to ask who else would be there, and stupid of me not to realize that Jaseph might still be regarded as a friend by the bereaved matron rather than the agent of the family's misery. Suffice it to say that he was there, with Myrica Mavor dancing attendance on him. The only man who cast a hateful glance in his direction was the Duke—and even he was forced to be discreet, because Alectryon, for all that he had served as a general and won at least three battles, was always circumspect in the face of his wife's determination.

Myrica, who made what attempt she could to serve as his shield, was the only woman not vying for Jaseph's attention. Even Hecate–who must have known that she had several too many wrinkles by now to catch the eye of an accurate artist– was reduced to using her elbows on the opposition, to no avail whatever. I was amazed by the brazen manner in which the opposition in question was led and effortlessly outclassed by Alectryon's surviving daughter Dian, but sibling rivalry can be a terrible thing.

Jaseph was everything that had been said of him: not merely handsome but boldly handsome. His hair was raven-black, but not in the least shiny; it seemed to soak up all the light that fell upon it. His eyes were so darkly violet as to be hardly less than black themselves, but his skin was remarkably pale. The island's summer Sun had not yet made the slightest impression upon his complexion, although I judged that the wide-brimmed hat he wore–also black, of course–would not protect him as fully as he expected, given the whiteness of our pavements and the tendency of light to reflect. His black silk shirt had all the gloss that his hair lacked, and seemed to have leaked more than a little to his leather trews, which were worn tight enough to exaggerate his leanness and display the sinuous movement of his hips as he swayed on the spot or crossed a room.

I was very glad that I had dressed myself in burgundy and twilight grey–mercifully, I never wear black to séances, because so many other people do–and could not possibly be thought by anyone there to have entered into a sartorial competition. I was not nearly so glad that Jaseph made unreasonable haste to brush off his admiring coterie–his brushwork was good–in order that he might introduce himself to me.

He seemed, as he crossed the room, to be deeply relieved to have shaken off his lovely admirers. Indeed, he seemed every inch the haunted man, too distracted by sorrow to pay attention to female wiles–but I assumed that it was an act, contrived to suit the occasion.

"I see your work everywhere I go in the capital, Master Rathenius," he said, after telling me what a privilege it was to meet me. "How is it that you are never there yourself?"

"I fear that I've been so long becalmed on the island that I've taken root," I lamented, trying hard to make my insincerity glaring. "I simply can't abide the bitter winters on the mainland, nor the awful stink that summer liberates from the culverts and alleys of cities. Fortunately, the island's summer visitors are kind enough to keep me busy, even though I'm so far away and generous enough to display my work on their walls. I fear that I have not seen any of your work, although I hear that Myrica is selling it as fast as she can lay her hands on it."

"I'm barely starting out," he told me. "I hardly dare to hope that my work will be as generously distributed as yours when I reach your age." In retrospect, I suppose he must have meant it as a mere observation, with no insult intended, but I had lived too long as a true artist among artists less than true. I construed the phrase "generously distributed" as a calculated euphemism for "commonplace," or even "cheap."

"Generosity has always been a fault of mine," I assured him. "It allows me to paint older women extraordinarily well, often favoring the cherished memory over the vulgar fact. I fear that I'm no longer capable of the brutality that determined accuracy demands." A shadow of anguish passed over his face as he glimpsed the cruel implication, but I was unrepentant.

"I have never been brutal in my art," he said, in a low tone. "Nor in my life, no matter what anyone may think."

"Existence itself is brutal to blossoms that emerge in the spring," I said, with a softness that could easily have been taken for consolation. "Delicate flowers too tender to bear the glare of maturity shrivel before their time. Parents always hold themselves responsible, but they should not seek solace in necromancy; forgiveness from beyond the grave is always hollow."

21

"You're not a believer, then?" Jaseph said, raising an eyebrow in faint surprise. "Does Madame Vashti know that you doubt her honesty?"

"She knows that I do not," I told him. "She forgives me my conviction that she is mistaken in her interpretation of what she sees with her mind's eye and hears with her inner ear."

"I firmly believe," he said—and if his sincerity was feigned, he was a consummate actor—"that the souls of the dead outlive the wasting of the flesh. I am convinced, too, that the survival of intelligence is not the whole of it. Either the ancient Egyptians were right to say that we have several souls, or...." He was interrupted then by the ever-efficient Vashti, calling us to order and demanding that we take our seats.

Like any unbeliever, I have little patience with the extravagance of folly, and I forgot what Claudius Jaseph had been saying as soon as I took my allotted place between Hecate Rain and the Lady Dian. Had I remembered it, and taken the trouble to pursue it when I had the chance, I might have gained access to the secret exhibition earlier than I did. No matter what the gossips were saying, Jaseph evidently reckoned me an artist, and he must have seen the merit in my own portrait of the Lady Roxane. He would surely have talked to me as one true artist to another had I only given him the chance—but my carelessness prevented me from realizing that.

As I took Dian's little hand in mine, I felt her shiver, but I am sure it was excitement rather than fear. Even at 17, she had no fear. She was not one of the tender ones, destined to shrivel early in the oppressive heat of maturity; she was one of those who would turn the brutality of the world back upon itself, hurting others at least as much as she herself was hurt.

I thought that a good thing while I held the girl's hand at Vashti's table—and I think so still, in spite of the fact that a little of her echoed brutality was to exact its pain from me.

Vashti never dressed her séances with overmuch trumpery. That is one of the reasons I considered her honest: an authentic artist rather than a shallow cheat. There was no shrieking and groaning about her performance. She did not wail, nor did she command; she simply slipped into her trance and waited for inspiration to come.

It came, in the beginning, in the form of a whole sequence of persons who impressed their own dubious individuality upon hers. They claimed, as they always did, to have lived in the pre-imperial era of Odysseus or Alexander, or in the turbulent times of the Empire's heroic victories against Attila, Theoderic and Saladin. They claimed to have been great captains, beautiful courtesans or the catamites of emperors. Every voice was eager to sell its secrets for an ounce of attention—which is, alas, less than the sum of their so-called secrets was worth.

The task of calling Lady Roxane had been delegated to Hecate, who executed the duty with all due dignity, although I was not certain at that time whether she really believed in the power of magic or not.

And in the end, it seemed, the Lady Roxane deigned to present herself.

Whether Alectryon's wife had come in search of reassurance as to the Lady Roxane's fate in the world beyond the world—as she was bound to pretend—or in search of some signal that she need not hold herself at all responsible for her daughter's suicide, she was to be disappointed.

"Do not mourn for me," said the girl's voice, emitted from the versatile throat of Vashti Savage. "I did what needed to be done, carefully and without impairment of my reason. I desired to be dead, and I am."

"Have you found Paradise?" Hecate asked, as she had doubtless been instructed to do.

"I have not looked for it," replied the voice from beyond. "I did not die in the hope of finding bliss, any more than I feared to die for dread of eternal torment. In truth, I have not the capacity for either state. All warmth is in the flesh, be it

23

love or pain; there is none in the soul. Do not grieve for me; I have left suffering far behind."

Had Hecate not been occupied I would have whispered in her ear, saying that this was not the news Vashti's spirits usually brought, and that it seemed to contradict the testimony of her other voices. As things were, however, I felt compelled to remain silent. Hecate's hand was quite steady within my own, but the Lady Dian's was still tremulous, and she had to clasp my fingers a little too hard in order to suppress the *frisson*.

"Why did you choose to depart when your life was hardly begun?" asked Hecate, with frank curiosity.

"I did not," said the other. "My life was finished. I had business elsewhere."

"Business! What business?" The interruption, inevitably, came from the Duke; I imagined the Duchess' painted and pointed fingernails digging into his hand by way of complaint.

"Something finer than commerce or the provincial court, father," the voice replied, as freely as any daughter might who was beyond the reach of parental displeasure. "Finer by far, and richer too–but not in any currency you would understand. There is metal more precious than gold, and light far brighter than the glow of Elysium."

I was interested by that, not as a revelation of what might await me beyond death, but as a revelation of hitherto unsuspected subtleties in Vashti Savage. Who, I wondered, could have put such heretical notions in her head?

I guessed the answer, of course: Claudius Jaseph. Vashti had been using her elbows too, in that undignified scrimmage for the man's attention, but she had already seen him privately, by way of preparation for her séance. Had she, I wondered, nursed the ludicrous hope that he might express the desire to paint her, even though she could not pay a twentieth of the kind of fee that the Duke of Alectryon could lay out, let alone the kind of bribe that would claim the artist's immediate attention? Was this strange performance for *his* sake?

The candlelight was far from bright, but my eyes were well enough adjusted to pick out the lines of Jaseph's pallid face. I could no longer believe that his haunted look was feigned; his eyes were wide with anguish, and he was listening as if with avid terror, fearful to miss a single word and yet fearful of what each and every word might declare.

I expected the next question to be raised by the impatient Duchess, but it came instead from her impertinent daughter. "What can you tell me of my future, Roxane? What lies in store for us all?" I assumed that the second element was added by way of apology for the selfishness of the first.

"Your future is your own to make, little sister," said the voice. "You might make it with courage, or with love–but not, I think, with both."

Dian's hand tightened again when she heard that, but I judged the force as petulance rather than gratitude or anxiety.

"Why?" asked the Duchess, at last. "For the love of Heaven, Roxane, *why did you do it*?"

I wondered how many of the 13 people joined in Vashti's circle had already taken it for granted that the answer to the question was: *Not for love of Heaven but for love of Claudius Jaseph, who would not place my image in his secret exhibition, discarding all others.*

What the supposed spirit actually said was: "Because it was necessary, under the tyranny of reason."

My unbelief remained unshaken, but I thought it brave of Vashti Savage as well as cunning to place the word *tyranny* in the mouth of a lost soul. In a world like ours, where we must always speak of our *beloved* Emperor and the *nobility* of his myriad dukes and barons, *tyranny* is not a word that trips lightly from the tongues of the unentranced.

The Duchess felt that she had not had a proper answer to her question, but the spirit disagreed. The Lady Roxane, if she had indeed come to give account of herself, had no more to tell us.

When the circle had broken, the nine females present soon gravitated to their momentary Sun, leaving the remainder of the males a trifle bereft. Jaseph seemed even less grateful for their attentions now than he had before, but that only made them press in upon him all the harder, competing to soothe his evident distress with their kindness and sympathy.

In such circumstances as that, fate may make strange bedfellows. I am certain that the Duke of Alectryon acted on the spur of the moment, driven towards me by the sight of his wife and daughter dancing attendance on a man he had reason enough to hate.

"Master Rathenius," he said, as he set himself abruptly before me. They were the first words he had addressed to me since his steward had paid me for the portrait of Roxane I had completed 20 months before.

"Lord Alectryon," I replied, with a sober bow. "I am deeply sorry for your loss."

He was not interested in my condolences. "I want you to paint my daughter," he said, unceremoniously. "Whatever you have on your easel, put it away. You must start tomorrow. Take as long as you like."

If the first of these sentences was surprising, the last was astounding. The words were innocuous enough in themselves, but the implication of the poor man's eyes was positively tortured. I wondered if he knew what he was saying, and whether I dared to take the inference that impressed itself upon my startled mind.

Most of the men who have commissioned me to paint portraits of their wives, sisters and daughters have thought my reputation as a lecher exaggerated, as artists' reputations usually are. Even those who have taken it seriously have always considered it irrelevant to themselves; the well-born have an inbred tendency to believe that they are utterly immune to the misfortunes that descend upon the less fortunate, and this often gives them an unbreakable faith in the exceptional virtue of their own womenfolk. Alectryon was not so stupid. He knew what I was, and I knew that he knew—which was why I had made no effort to press myself on the Lady Roxane while she sat for me. I had known that I was under threat because of the Duke's insistence on keeping very careful account of the time his daughter spent in my studio, negotiating minutes and hours with as much attention to detail as his steward lavished upon the calculation of my expenses. He had used that means to inform me, subtly, that any extra time I might lavish upon his daughter would be just as minutely assessed.

Now, by contrast, he was inviting me to spend *as long as I liked* with his younger–and recently his only–daughter.

I looked hard at Alectryon before I lowered my head again to acknowledge my acceptance of the commission. Then I looked hard at Dian and her mother, fawning upon the unhappy Claudius Jaseph in the far corner of the room, and understood that *her* time was already half-pledged to another.

I realized that Alectryon was making a desperate attempt to head off trouble, and that he could not have been certain himself how far he was prepared to go in that cause.

Had the commissioning of Dian's portrait been a military matter, the Duke would undoubtedly have brought his *manoeuvre* to a successful conclusion–but this was peace-time, and summer, and Mnemosyne is even further from the Empire's heart than Alectryon's estates. Dian wanted Claudius Jaseph to paint her, and her mother wanted Claudius Jaseph to paint her, and in the end the only way that the luckless Duke could preserve his will was to let them have theirs.

Absurdly, but perhaps inevitably, the agreement was made that Dian was to sit for two portraits. In the mornings, she would go to Claudius Jaseph; in the afternoons, to me.

It was not, of course, a formal contest. In the undeclared thoughts of everyone on the island, however, it would be a confrontation whose like had not been seen since Thorold of Lamry had cast a gauntlet before the self-styled black magician Herod Ojas and cut him to ribbons with his saber, only to die three days afterwards from a trivial self-inflicted cut that became septic and turned his blood to bile.

I did not need to consult Hecate Rain's inbuilt barometer to know that the island's opinion-makers would set the odds against my making the better painting at three to one, and the odds against my making the better seduction at 30 to one. It would have done me no good to protest that the contest was not of my making. The fact was that it had been made–and that I had been appointed to the uncomfortable situation of Alectryon's champion.

The only consolation I could find, at the time, was that I was certain to collect my fee, whereas Jaseph–if his reputation was deserved–might choose to forgo his if the margin of his victory was as great as popular opinion believed. That, I knew, was what the Lady Dian must crave, as her sister must have craved it before her, however absurd the ambition might be.

"What kind of a world do we live in," I lamented to an absinthe-befuddled Hecate, as I kindly put her to bed before taking myself off to my own home, "when those who believe in souls have no desire more ardent than to have them stolen by a painter?"

"Axel," she said, severely–and very inaccurately–"you have no romance in your own soul, and will never understand it in others."

I slept well, unintimidated by the thought of the odds stacked against me, and spent the first two hours of the following morning making my studio fit to receive a sitter of the highest rank. This required a great deal of tidying up–but not, alas, the unceremonious removal from my easel of some half-accomplished masterpiece.

When everything had been made ready, I went to see Myrica Mavor in the quayside cottage that served as her summer residence.

"You're wasting your time, Axel," she told me, immediately. "I have none of Claudius's paintings here to show you. Those that were on loan were returned; those that were for sale were sold. If you are too stubborn–or too frightened–to go to Alectryon's house on the mainland to compare his portrait of Roxane with yours, you might go to Caissots' house, or the Hintermanns' lodge. I believe they brought their trophies with them this summer, to bear witness to the excellence of their lucky find."

"I am not here to measure Jaseph's abilities as a draughtsman," I told her, suppressing my resentment of her accusation of cowardice. "If you have judged him a fine artist, he is a fine artist; I do not need to see for myself how expert his brushwork is. But why, given that he *is* a fine artist, have you gone to the trouble of trying to boost his reputation with silly rumors?"

"Axel!" she complained, feigning injury. "Can you possibly think...?"

"Of course I can think," I told her, with calculated rudeness. "Now, what is all this nonsense about a secret exhibition? What on Earth made you think of it? Could you not imagine the effect it might have on his sitters?"

"Of course I could imagine," she retorted, coldly. "That is why I would never have invented a story as pernicious as some of those that are now flying around the island–and I am even willing to admit, now, that I may have been wrong to encourage the dissemination of any one of them. On the other hand, the first trickle of whispers certainly inflated the prices he commands. As you've doubtless heard, they're greater than any I've ever obtained for one of your portraits, although I could have done a great deal better for you if you'd actually condescend to show your face at one of your shows."

"Better still, no doubt," I observed, "if I'd contrived to drive a few of my sitters to suicide with the aid of a rumor. How could you, Myrica?"

"How could I have prevented it? In lending what brief assistance I did to its flow, I was merely capitulating with the inevitable. For what it may be worth, though, my opinion is that the particular rumor you cited wasn't the cause of the suicides but their result. It was probably inevitable that jealous and ignorant people–whose numbers are by no means few in the city–should begin to whisper suspicion that the deaths were connected by more than coincidence. I don't know who invented this tale of a collection of portraits never placed on

29

public exhibition, kept locked away in a windowless vault, but I imagine that it was a matter of petty malice born of jealousy. If Claudius has kept some portraits from public view, it is for his own reasons, not because the portraits contain the captive souls of the women who had posed for them. What, exactly, was it that you've heard? I can hardly keep up with the transformations of the tale."

"Only that three young women died of disappointment, because they were not thought worthy of this ridiculous secret exhibition," I told her. "Is there worse?"

"Oh yes," Myrica said, bitterly. "There's talk of black magic, especially now that Vashti's séance is today's fresh news. The malicious fools cannot make up their minds. Does Claudius steal souls from his victims, or disappoint them by refusing to steal their souls? They seek to damn him either way, and they do so by piling new infamies upon the old. I've said it a hundred times and I'll say it a thousand more, if necessary: *Claudius has committed no crime, and he is guilty of no sin*. His work is sublime, and the Devil hates sublimity; that is the sole cause of his bad luck."

Her indignation seemed real enough. I judged that if she *had* made up the tale of the secret exhibition to promote her protegé she had long since repented of it. Alas, it is in the nature of rumors that the ones that do not wither and die in infancy are amplified and embellished with the passage of time; further decoration is the nourishment that sustains them. The rumor of Jaseph's secret legacy had taken root, and its monstrousness must have grown far beyond its inventor's original intention.

"What further infamies have been added to the mixture?" I asked her, as gently as I could.

Myrica hesitated, but she knew my reputation as an unbeliever. "In the capital," she said, "it is apparently now being whispered that the souls trapped within the portraits were perverted by their unnatural imprisonment, and turned to evil. Denied whatever sustenance souls require from flesh, they are reputed to have become exceedingly hungry, acquiring a kind of will that permits them to leech the soul-stuff from anyone who saw them. Not only have their losers been driven to despair and suicide, it is now said, but any unsuspecting art-lover who might be allowed access to the secret vault where Jaseph kept the paintings will be in dire danger of a similar fate. The same calumnies are being whispered on the island even as we speak. Preposterous, is it not?"

"Preposterous," I agreed.

Myrica sighed. "The air is far cleaner here on Mnemosyne than it is in the capital," she said, "and even rumors cannot reek so offensively as they do in narrow metropolitan streets–but the boat that brought the new tale to my ears will nevertheless pollute the entire port."

"I fear that it will not be sufficient to dissuade the Lady Dian and her mother," I told her, soberly. "What effect do you think this silly competition will have on the girl?"

Myrica shrugged her shoulders. "If you fear involvement in a tragedy," she said, skeptical as to the honesty of my concern for the girl's welfare, "you have only to withdraw from your commission."

"And deny Alectryon? He might forgive me for failing, but he would never forgive me for not trying, since he has commanded me to do so. Unfortunately, I do not think he knows himself what license he has given me–and whatever I decide, I shall probably be blamed for the outcome."

Myrica raised an eyebrow at that. "If I were you," she said, skeptically, "I'd content myself with painting. I shall do everything in my power to make sure that Claudius does the same. It would be best for everyone if the young lady's emotions remained uninvolved, or at least unexasperated. If you came here for reassurance, you have all that I can give."

I wished that she had sounded more confident that she had any power at all over Claudius Jaseph's ambitions, but I had indeed come for reassurance, and I did indeed have all that she could give. I went back to my own house, to keep my appointment and begin my work.

The uglier rumors that had now crossed the calm summer sea were soon common knowledge, from Aidan's Head to the Devil's Rocks. The account of Claudius Jaseph's secret exhibition had grown even further while the infection spread.

Those who were not true aesthetes, it was now said, were immune to the vampiric predation of the ensouled portraits–but anyone capable of perceiving the genius that had gone into their creation would be lost as soon as he beheld them. The souls of the sensitive would be sucked out of them, shredded and parceled out among the avid images while the baleful ringmaster of the sinister circus, Claudius Jaseph, looked on and laughed.

No artist or aristocrat could ever believe such wild tales, of course, but that did not prevent them being passed on. Nor, alas, could it prevent their adding to the dark glamour of their subject. Although Claudius Jaseph certainly did not seem to revel in his notoriety, he made no constructive attempt to refute the charges laid against him. Instead, he hid himself away in the cottage that Myrica Mavor had procured for him, which was set alone on the topmost height of the promontory which extended to the broken rocks of Poseidon's Point.

The Lady Dian proved to be a good sitter, far less impatient than her sister had been, even though she came to my house having already posed for Jaseph for three hours and more. She arrived in clean clothes, with her auburn hair very neatly groomed. It was only to be expected that she would change between sessions, given that she would not want to appear identically clad in two different portraits, but I could not help wondering what she wore for Jaseph. What she wore for me was a gown of white silk trimmed with crimson, pinned with enameled brooches; the sleeves were ruffled and the neckline very moderate. It seemed to me that she was trying to appear younger than she was–which immediately suggested that when she sat for Jaseph she tried to appear older.

Roxane had been the more beautiful of the two sisters— there had been an admirable *hauteur* about her, and she was longer in the limbs–but Dian was the more robust. At first sight, she gave the impression that she might bruise easily enough, but I had already begun to penetrate that illusion at Vashti's stance. When I brought my artist's sight to bear, it was perfectly obvious that her porcelain surface hid a curious combination of her father's cynicism and her mother's determination. She had no imperious *hauteur* because she had no vanity; she was less inclined than her long-limbed sister to overestimate her reach, and thus better able to make her grasp secure.

I realized, too, that the thought of sitting for two portraits at the same time had begun to amuse her tremendously once she had given it due consideration. It had occurred to her that the implicit competition would drive both artists to excel themselves, and that the extra effort Jaseph and I were required to invest would work to her advantage, and perhaps to her glory. She must have calculated, too, that if Jaseph were foolish enough to sustain his myth by refusing to deliver his portrait, she would have the best of both worlds. She would be part of the notorious secret exhibition as well as taking pride of place in Alectryon's manse.

I was kind to her during her first few sittings, but I made not the slightest attempt to make love to her. I had decided that Myrica Mavor's advice was sound, and that it was dangerous to take advantage of an implication that the Duke might easily refuse to admit that he had ever made.

It had sometimes been my policy to begin my amorous advances as soon as a painting had begun, with a little scolding counterbalanced by more than a little flattery. On such occasions, I would use my hands to tilt the face of the sitter one way and another, to smooth the cloth upon her bosom, to caress her wrists as if by way of encouragement or thanks. Slowly but surely, as the portrait took shape, my words would grow more affectionate, my hands more adventurous, building a crescendo of emotional response that could only have one conclusion. With Dian, however, I was careful to strike an exact balance between instruction and apology, and I kept my hands strictly to myself.

The inevitable result of this unaccustomed self-restraint was, of course, that the desire I sought to set aside was amplified by frustration. My determination to make sure that the girl did not fall in love with me was translated by perversity into a process by which I found myself falling headlong in love with her.

By the time the Lady Dian had spent four afternoons with me, I could not get her out of my head; every time I closed my eyes her face confronted me, strangely compounded out of flesh and paint, half-person and half-portrait. As the face on the canvas gradually took shape and became clearer, so did the haunting image.

I knew and understood what was happening. I never lost my sense of perspective—but my understanding could not diminish the intensity of my feelings. I berated myself mercilessly, but scolding only served to inflame the unrepentant emotion. Everything I did, everything I thought, added to my confusion.

Then, for the first time, I did become jealous of Claudius Jaseph—and my jealousy added further fuel to the fire. Then, and only then, was the competition between us joined in deadly earnest—and despite that I was still a committed unbeliever, I began to feel that it might indeed be a competition for the Lady's very soul.

By the fifth day, I could see that Dian was changing before my expert eyes. Her skin grew gradually paler, her hair gradually wilder, her eyes more hollow and more feverish. The white silk that lay upon her bosom seemed shadowed, if not actually tarnished. She was haunted—and not by the ghost of her unlucky sister.

I knew that Jaseph was the cause of Dian's gradual metamorphosis, but I was uncertain as to the precise nature of the leverage. Had Myrica prevailed upon him to be as cold and businesslike as I had determined to be, and was his coldness distressing her? Was she pining for him as I was for her? Or had he rudely rejected Myrica's advice and set out upon a course of seduction that was confusing and draining her? Was she wilting beneath the assault of his flatteries and demands?

I could not tell–and she could not enlighten me.

On the morning of the sixth day, while Dian was with Jaseph, Alectryon came to see me. "You pose as a reasonable man," he said to me, without preamble. "You deny the very existence of the soul–but you always do so in your accursed artist's fashion, all sarcasm and theatricality. I want to know the truth of your beliefs, Rathenius. Do you believe that souls can be stolen, or made captive?"

"Not in any literal sense, my Lord," I told him, sincerely. "But, with all due respect to the military precision of your thinking, there is such a thing as poetic truth. Matter is obedient to the laws of nature; your artillerists can calculate the flight of a cannonball, the range of a musket-shot, the blast of a petard. Mind is different; it is compounded out of our hopes, fears and beliefs. We are what we pretend to be, and if we care to insist that we have souls, we can and do ensoul ourselves. The hope that our souls survive our death is insufficient to establish the fact, but it is sufficient to establish the appearance–and beyond the mere appearances of mind, there is insufficient substance to repair the error. If a believer in the soul were to be convinced that her soul had been stolen, the loss would be tangible enough."

"Damn you!" he said, radiating wrath. "I wanted a straight and simple answer, not one of your fancy speeches."

"The world would be a far less confusing place," I told him, as temperately as I could, "if the straight and simple answers were also the true ones. Alas, they are not."

He did not want to believe me, but he could not deny that the world was sorely confused. "Can you stop Jaseph?" he said, shortly. "Can you prevent him destroying Dian as he destroyed Roxane?"

The straight and simple answer was that whatever Jaseph might have done, he had not destroyed Roxane. The straight and simple truth was that Roxane had destroyed herself, with Jaseph serving as a catalyst at most–but I could not tell Alectryon that. Seen straightforwardly and simply, the truth was that Dian had more backbone than her sister, and would likely survive no matter what, even if she were slightly bruised in body and mind–but I could not tell him that, either.

"I will try, my Lord," was what I actually said. "I do not know whether I can succeed, but you have my solemn word that I will try."

"Do what you have to," he said, his eyes dark and his cheekbones outstanding. "If you can't, I might have to–and I don't want that."

Whatever cynics may think about the corruption and decadence of our aristocracy, the myth of its intrinsic nobility is not without its force–or perhaps even the straight-thinking Alectryon understood that, if Claudius Jaseph were struck down by a masked assassin, he would lose his daughter just as surely as he would if Jaseph had his wicked way with her.

I spent the afternoon making plans while I painted, but I do not remember what they were. They were driven from my mind as soon as events took a turn that I had not anticipated–a turn that I had not even considered possible.

When I laid down my brush, a little earlier than usual, and signaled to Dian that she could relax her pose, she stood up and came directly to her feet. I thought that she had come to measure my progress, and I stood aside–I am not one of those artists who refuse to let unfinished work be seen–but she did not even glance at the canvas.

"Master Rathenius," she said, "will you make love to me?"

I was speechless.

"You have a reputation as a lover," she added, as if by way of explanation, and only paused for a moment before adding: "but you did not make love to my sister. She thought that society had misjudged you–but I told her even then that you were simply afraid of my father. Was that true?"

"Yes, my Lady," I said, simply and frankly, "and I still am."

She smiled rather than say out loud that she did not believe me. "You have never seen the portrait which Claudius made of Roxane, have you?" she said. "It hangs side by side with your own, in one of the drawing-rooms in our ancestral home, still beribboned in black."

"I have never seen any of his paintings," I told her. "The reports I have had claim that his version is the better of the two–more neatly done, more accurate and more revealing."

"It is," she said, brutally. "But his present work is not as good. Something is holding him back. Whereas you..." At last she condescended to glance at the canvas, approvingly.

She honestly thought that she was paying me a compliment. What she was actually saying was that Claudius needed more encouragement to do his best work–the work that would outshine my best. She wanted to excite his jealousy!

Perhaps, if the world were a simpler place, I would have begun to love her less when she displayed her true colors. Perhaps, if I were a better man, my stomach would have revolted against the notion of being used. In the event, the world is no better than it is, and nor am I. What good would it have done, in any case, to harden my heart and my face and say: *I cannot make love to you*?

I took her face in my hands and kissed it. I kissed her hands. I abandoned myself to my wonderful, wayward emotions. I feel the muse within me when I make love, just as I feel her within me when I paint; she is equally imperious in either case, and equally inventive.

I remembered what Hecate Rain had told me about the general impression of my lustful character, but I knew perfectly well that it was an empty slander. I loved Dian with all my heart, and everything I did with her, I did for love. All the fear in the world could not have prevented me, nor all the *conventional morality*. I am not an amoral man, but I have a healthy loathing for convention.

Loving Dian was, in any case, a mere extension into a different kind of action of all the care and genius I had already lavished upon her painting. They are not *entirely* wrong who claim that art is a form of lust, and portraiture a kind of possession. There is no penetration more intimate than that achieved by an artist's eye; the engagement of the flesh is no more than confirmation. That is why artists cannot marry, cannot be faithful, and cannot even linger long over their affairs; it is in the nature of artwork that the artist must always be moving on, from one portrait, poem or composition to another, and from one infatuation, lustful desire or soulful affection to another.

If only Claudius Jaseph had understood that, he might have made a great artist as well as a true one. He had the eye, and he had the hand, but he believed in the soul and *more than the soul*, and that proved to be his damnation. Whatever the world may think and whatever rumor may say, it was fidelity that destroyed him.

I am, of course, entirely true after my own particular fashion. While I made love to the Lady Dian, I was as utterly committed to her flesh as I was to her appearance. While I stroked her warm skin, she was the universe that contained my sense of touch; space and time had lost their empire. While I looked into her eyes, into the darkest depths of her pupils, she was the shell of my imagination, the only host of my desire. I was hers, and she knew it. Whatever she had expected, and however meanly she had sought to dispose of herself, she was everything to me... for as long as the moment lasted.

I think she realized–although she could not yet bring herself to admit the fact–that no matter how clever his hands might be, Claudius Jaseph had not the means to match me in the art of making love. I think she realized that, for all his delicacy and all his accuracy, there was something lacking in him.

Although I did not know it yet, the truth was that he could never have lost himself in her as I could lose myself, because something of him was already lost, and irredeemably committed.

When we had finished, and dressed ourselves, languidly reveling in our calmness and satisfaction, she said: "Will you let him know, or shall I?" She did not mean, of course, that either of us would ever be so vulgar as to tell him.

"Leave it to me," I said, as I was bound to do. "That way, if anyone else is hurt, it will be me."

Jaseph was, of course, astonished to see me. He was a young man and he was new to the island. He did not know me and he did not know my world. He probably felt that I had snubbed him when I had made no effort to pick up the threads of the conversation he had initiated at Vashti Savage's séance. He had probably begun to take the gossip about our competition more seriously than it needed to be taken–or perhaps less seriously.

"What do you want from me, Master Rathenius?" he said, without even offering to pour me a glass of the wine that he was drinking.

"It happened that I was passing," I lied–transparently, for I could not possibly have been bound for the rocks at Poseidon's Point–"and I remembered that I had not yet bid you a proper welcome. We met for the first time in such awkward circumstances–necromancy inevitably casts a pall over professional courtesy. We are artists, after all, and rivals. We ought to be friends, even though we should never admit to the world that we are anything but deadly enemies."

"I never thought you were my enemy!" he protested.

"Of course not," I said, serenely. "Even the world knows, deep down, that we are not. But we must put on a flamboyant show, for both our sakes. Rivalry is good for business. While we are deadly enemies, who would dare to insult either one of us by offering a fee conspicuously lower than the other commands? I am deeply indebted to you for the masterly way in which you handled Alectryon and his wife. It will make both our fortunes!"

"The contest was none of my making," he assured me.

"You are far too modest," I assured him in return. "If you paint half as well as you manufacture rumors, you will be summoned to the heart of the world in no time, installed in a tower in the Imperial Palace. You will paint the greatest ladies in the world, and Alectryon will bathe in the glory of having found you."

"I do not manufacture rumors," he said, coldly. "If my words are twisted by others, exaggerated to ludicrous effect, and soiled by the filth of common gossip, that is the malice of the world at work—and my misfortune." I noticed his admission that the seed of the rumors had been sown by his own words.

"Misfortune!" I echoed, sardonically. "Do you mean the misfortune that forced Alectryon to pay the highest price ever paid for a painting made on the island? Do you mean the misfortune that delivers the loveliest girl in the land to your door every morning, so that you might have the privilege of her inspiration? I can assure you that I count none of that misfortune, even though I have by far the lesser share."

"Are you drunk, Master Rathenius?" Jaseph asked, looking at me as if he believed that it might be true.

"Not a drop of wine has passed my lips today," I informed him, merrily, "nor have I partaken of absinthe. Dear Hecate loves the disorder it brings to her mind, but that is the kind of poet she is; I dislike the disorder it brings to my hand, because that is the kind of artist I am." I looked pointedly at the glass in his own hand, but he was not about to be offended by such an empty slight.

"Well, I am glad to have brought you such good fortune," he said, with a bitterness that seemed rather premature, "and sorry that you seem to be anticipating a reversal in that fortune when I leave. In truth, though, I have no plans to visit the Empire's heart. I am quite at home in the provinces—in their capitals, at least. I am not sure that I could learn to love the island as much as you do."

"No doubt you'll return to the city in the autumn," I said. "Alectryon always does–and he'll be doubly determined to make sure that his daughter goes with him."

"I would rather have avoided this commission," he said, bluntly. "If anything were to happen to Dian, in the wake of what happened to her sister..."

"But you did not love her sister," I said–implying, of course, that he might love Dian.

He stared at me as if I were a snake that had formerly kept its fangs concealed.

"I see her every day," I reminded him. "I see the light in her eye, the shadow on her cheek. She is in love with you, if only because her sister was. She is very enthusiastic to out-shine her sister. It must be terribly difficult, don't you think, for a girl to grow to womanhood knowing that her sister is just a little more beautiful as well as just a little older? Young women are so ruthless, are they not? They take their rivalries so much more seriously than you and I."

"I am not in love with her," Jaseph said, pronouncing each word with the utmost care–partly because he wanted to be believed and partly because he did not know what I was trying to accomplish.

"I fear that she will not rest until you are," I said, with a sigh. "She longs to be part of your legendary secret exhibition, in order that she might prove once and for all which was the better of Alectryon's daughters. She is old enough to know that it will be her last chance, for her rival has placed herself beyond the reach of age and misfortune. Roxane will be as young and lovely forever as she is in the portraits that hang side by side in Alectryon's house."

Jaseph's expression was becoming ugly now. It is aston-ishing how ugly a handsome face can become, if one can only irritate it cleverly enough. "I am not in love with Lady Dian," he repeated, with the air of one trying to convince himself.

"She has made up her mind that you shall be," I re-minded him, "and she is her father's daughter. She will stop at nothing. It is a pity the rumors of your secret exhibition have been so wildly magnified. This time next year, hardly anyone will remember them–but for the moment... will you take some advice, Claudius, from a fellow artist?"

The straight and simple answer would have been *no*, but he had curiosity enough to ask: "What advice?"

"If you really do have paintings which you will not show to the world, at least show them to Dian. If they really are locked in a vault on the mainland, fetch them here. Demystify them."

He laughed. I do not think he intended the laughter as an insult, but it certainly hurt me, although there was a raw note in it that suggested that it hurt him too. "*Demystify them!*" he repeated, as if it were the most ludicrous suggestion he had ever heard. "If only I could! For the love of Heaven, man, you have not begun to understand–and you call yourself an artist! You stupid, sordid flatterer!"

The flagrant insult hurt less than the subtler one, as flagrant insults usually do. "Bravo!" I said, stoutly. "You seem to be getting the hang of the politics of rivalry."

He stood up abruptly and hurled his wine glass at the wall, the way petty lordlings sometimes do when they want to put on a show of camaraderie, or emotion, or any similar affectation.

It shattered, of course. Wine glasses obey the laws of matter, not the perversities of mind.

"Do you want to look at my secret exhibition?" he demanded, implying by his tone that I had been angling for exactly such an invitation. "Do you dare, having heard what they say of it?"

"Is it here?" I asked, mildly.

"Do you think I could go anywhere without it? Could I leave my shadow in a mainland vault, or my soul? The lock that secures it is the prison of my heart. In the city, to be sure, I keep it in a cellar; but on the island, I make do with a little room. You know what they have begun to say, do you not? That if you are a tasteless fool, you have nothing to fear–but

42

that if you are a true artist, they will steal your soul through your rapt gaze."

"I thought you were not responsible for the rumors," I said, still speaking with conscientious gentleness. "Are they not the malice of the world, and your misfortune?"

He beckoned me, as imperiously as Alectryon might have. I followed as meekly as I would have had he been our beloved Emperor himself. I was curious. How could I have done otherwise, even if I had thought that there really was a risk?

I stepped into Claudius Jaseph's little room without the least hint of trepidation, not doubting for a moment that I would remain in a fit state to come out again, and not fearing for an instant that my capability might demonstrate my aesthetic imbecility.

I had underestimated the risk–but I was right not to be afraid. I was equal to the challenge, and more than equal.

There were three paintings in the room, each one covered by a linen cloth deeply stained by generations of paint and turpentine. Jaseph whipped the protective coverings away, one by one, to reveal the faces beneath.

I recognized each face the instant it was displayed. The first was Naomi Lynhurst, daughter of the Marquis of Castelle. The second was Sarah, Lady Generoix. The third was Roxane, the elder daughter of the Duke of Alectryon,

The criminal stupidity of rumor is that it always seems to omit the most telling detail of all. Even Myrica Mavor had observed the crucial uncertainty in silly stories that were being bruited about. Had the sitters killed themselves because their souls had been stolen, or because their souls had been deemed unworthy of theft? In truth, the hidden treasure trove whose existence had sparked so much speculation did not consist of paintings that Claudius Jaseph had refused to deliver to their commissioners, but paintings he had made alongside the ones that he *had* delivered. Whatever had compelled the young women to commit suicide, it was certainly not Claudius Jaseph's refusal to admit them to his secret exhibition.

I now understood why Jaseph had laughed at my suggestion that he show the Lady Dian the secret exhibition. Roxane was a part of it and Jaseph was determined that her sister would not be added to it. In fact, he was determined that no one else would ever be added to it, if he could possibly help it.

You will recall that I had not seen any of Jaseph's paintings before I stepped into that room. I saw half a dozen afterwards, of course, but I did not need any such standard of comparison to know that the paintings comprising the secret exhibition were unlike any that had ever been painted before, even by Claudius Jaseph. The works that Myrica Mavor had exhibited had been complimented for their brushwork and their accuracy, but no one would have noticed such mere matters of detail had Myrica's paintings had the quality that these works had.

I had told the Duke of Alectryon the truth, although he could not find the intelligence to understand what I had said. I am a materialist. I do not believe in the soul as an objective entity obedient to natural law—but I do believe that we provide the light in which we see our inner selves, and that if we decide to see our inner selves as souls, our decision is not without real effect.

Claudius Jaseph believed in the soul, and he was an artist. When he painted, he painted what he saw, what he felt, and what he believed in. I saw, now, that I had been utterly wrong. He *had* loved the Lady Roxane, with a fervor that had defied his intention to be faithful to Sarah, Lady Generoix, just as the love he had discovered for Sarah had defied his intention to be faithful to Naomi Lynhurst. There is, alas, only so much destruction of that kind that a man can take.

Each of the three paintings was infected by a lust so powerful as to be tangible in the warm and sullen air. No one could have looked at them without response, a true artist least of all.

I looked at them, one by one, and was possessed–not by any demon, even in poetic truth, but by a passion so raw that it cut into me like a dagger. Perhaps a lesser man would have felt less, but no man ever lived who was so devoid of aesthetic sensibility as to be incapable of feeling the frank and flamboyant eroticism of those images. Perhaps it was an illusion, a mere fantasy–but it was real enough to rake my heart and leave me more breathless than any passion I had ever spent on my own account... even the passion I had spent that very afternoon, with the lovely Lady Dian.

Anyone will tell you that the eyes of a good portrait have life enough for its gaze to follow you around a room, and any artist will tell you how simple it is to work that trick–but the eyes of Naomi Lynhurst looked into mine with so much life that I might have drowned in the tide of her hunger. She looked at me with love: commanding, undeniable, irresistible love.

We pretend that when we say "I love you" we are describing an emotion, and we are not entirely dishonest in saying so–but what the lover also means, above and beyond that, is that he or she is determined to place the other under a moral obligation to submit to the lover's will. Naomi Lynhurst had no voice, but her eyes spoke of a love much fiercer than any ever signified by mere spoken words.

Alas, she was not alone. Beside her was Sarah, Lady Generoix, who had come after her, and had been forced to break down a barrier of love already pledged, emotion already exhausted. Her lust was less colored by illusion, the force of her gaze more brutal and more cynical, but not one whit less powerful. Her image might have been a masterpiece, were it not set next to the portrait of Roxane, daughter of Alectryon. Roxane had a kind of *hauteur* that neither of the others had ever possessed; it magnified and purified her lust into something that would have been literally demonic, if there really were literal demons to tempt and plague us. Because there are not, I knew that what the portrait embodied was purely human, even child-like–a prospect which I found more frightening by far.

While I stared at Roxane, who had been forced to displace Sarah even as Sarah had displaced Naomi, she seduced me with her painted eyes–and the force of her seduction was implacable as well as intoxicating, adamantine as well as irresistible.

Claudius Jaseph whispered in my ear: "Now do you understand, you petty flatterer? Can you see what a man who loves women sees when he is honestly beguiled? Do you see now why the spirit of the Lady Roxane cares neither for Heaven nor for Hell? Can you see what has been stolen from her soul, to leave her the mere shell that she is, even beyond the grave? Can you see what art really is, what power it really has, when it is the province of a true artist? *Have you ever before seen love, or felt lust, isolated from all confusion?*"

He meant to imply that the answer was no. He meant to imply that whatever I had called love before, and lust too, was something merely superficial–and that I was not and never would be a *true* artist. He was wrong, of course.

"They are good," I said, but not because I hoped to damn them with faint praise. The word *good* has as many meanings as it has inflections. "Your skill is growing by leaps and bounds. A lesser man would have reached his limit before this sequence was even started, as lesser men always have before, but I can see that you are not done yet."

Whatever he had expected, it was not that. That is the beauty of competition–one always has that last slim chance to surprise the adversary, to set him on the wrong foot.

"*Not done yet?*" he whispered. "What in Heaven's name do you mean by that, Rathenius?"

He was mad, of course. Had he been only mad, he might have made better use of his talent, but he was moral too. The combination is deadly.

I was still held captive by Roxane's stare, but I had a voice and she had not–and I had no soul to be stolen. "I can hardly wait to see the square completed," I said. "Your portrait of Dian will be even better than these, of course. She loves you so intensely, and yet so cleverly. You must have captured that cleverness in your canvas, and it will give your work the one quality it still lacks: maturity. That is the curse of the young, is it not? However fierce the passion naïve and immature sitters might inspire, one always feels slightly silly taking advantage of them. Dian will help you overcome that. She is quite unique, is she not?"

I was improvising, of course. Had I had time to prepare, I might have made the lie less transparent, the nonsense less confused–but my audience was exceptionally uncritical. The paintings had no intelligence of their own, of course, even by his own account–the one thing seemingly left to the insipid spectre summoned by Vashti Savage was intelligence–but in Claudius Jaseph's eyes, the love and lust that they made captive were no mere artifice of the artist's brush. To him, the paintings' souls were literal, and they had the power to move matter as well as mind–and because he believed that, it was so, at least in the effect they were able to have on him. The claws they used to rake my heart were metaphorical; they drew no blood. The claws with which the furies from the heart of Hell reached out for him sent him cowering, fearful for his flesh.

Anyone will tell you that a good portrait can appear to be looking at every one of its observers simultaneously, and that the only way to escape its gaze is to cover it up or leave the room. Claudius Jaseph did neither. Instead, he sank to his knees and begged for mercy, while the fever of Roxane's jealousy scoured his inner being, supported and amplified by the wrath of those he had already betrayed.

Jaseph bled from his nose and his mouth–and, finally, from his eyes. He bled, but he did not die. They did not intend to let him escape as easily as that; they knew too much about the world beyond the world to think it punishment enough for him.

I should like to think, of course, that there was a little jealousy of his own in the brainstorm that wrecked his mind, but I shall never be sure. I had tried to let him know that Dian had offered herself to me, and that I had accepted her offer gladly and triumphantly, but he might have been too distracted to take the hint. He had wrapped himself so tightly in his own fantasies of love and duty that he had almost ceased to care about the precise facts of life.

I covered the paintings one by one, leaving Roxane till last. Then, I carried Claudius Jaseph from the room and laid him tenderly upon his bed. I wiped the blood and tears from his face, and gave him wine to drink. He drank it gluttonously.

By the time I left him alone, he was as well as could be expected.

Claudius Jaseph fled the island that night. He did not return to the city. Rumors spread soon enough, saying that he was seen in one of the northern provinces a year later, but nothing was heard of him thereafter. No one knew what became of the extraordinary product of his erotic obsessions that gossips called *the secret exhibition*. I sometimes drop dark hints to the effect that I was not only the last person to see it, but was also privy to the secret of its fate, but in truth I can do no more than guess.

Perhaps my guess is correct–but I make so many, and I can never decide which one is most likely. My favorite account is that Claudius took a bright dagger to the portraits, ripping them to shreds one by one–saving Roxane for last, of course–in the hope that he might liberate the dream-stuff he had stolen from their souls. On the other hand, he might equally well have burned them, or thrown them over the side of whatever boat it was that carried him away from the island. It is even possible he has them still: his three demonic brides, who love him as angrily and as faithfully as he loves them.

He might, of course, have destroyed two before he even left the island, taking one and one alone away with him, in the hope that the one might forgive him everything, in exchange for a devotion so utter and absolute that he would never touch a brush again, nor look at anyone or anything with an artist's appraising eye. That, I believe, is what many poets would call a happy ending–but I would not agree. Nor, I hope, would my beloved Hecate Rain.

As Hecate and I sat on the terrace outside the *Sprite* in late July, shielding ourselves from the harsh rays of the midday Sun with huge white hats, while she drank absinthe and I drank iced water, she said: "I always knew that you would win, of course. Claudius had the greater talent, but he was temperamentally unsound. If you were not so ridiculously lazy, you might turn out work of that quality far more often, but given that you are what you are, I fear that you will never again produce anything half as good as your portrait of Lady Dian."

"You misjudge me," I said. "Everyone does. Alectryon has quite forgotten that he asked me for my help, and lets it be known to anyone who cares to listen that I am a dirty scoundrel. Even Dian believes that I took unfair advantage of her when she was exceptionally vulnerable–but I love her still, just as I love you. I always will."

"Those who murder in the name of art always pretend to love their victims," she informed me–or perhaps it was the absinthe speaking, in its usual disordered fashion.

"No one I have painted has ever felt the need to kill herself," I reminded her, "or even to kill anyone else. If that makes me less of an artist, or less of a lover, I am content to be diminished."

The Incubus of the Rose

All artists thrive on love, but there are different ways in which they draw its nourishment. Some feed on piquant challenge, some on the joyous zest of first consummation, some on the heady riot of intense engagement, some on the fierce pain of parting and some on the mellow melancholy of remembered loss.

On the mainland, it is said, there are long-established artists who have drawn inspiration from the same love-match for decades, but on the island of Mnemosyne, nearly 2000 years after the birth of the Divine Caesar, there was not a single artist worthy of the name who did not follow the pattern of the seasons or the vagaries of the mercurial winds, counting lovers by the handful if not by the dozen as their work matures.

By the time that 190th decade began, I had lived on Mnemosyne longer than any of its other inhabitants could remember: more than long enough to have attained the reputation of a fickle and shallow seducer who never really loved at all... but I was misunderstood. Younger men made a bold show of intensity and incapacity when they drink, because they have not learned to savor the subtler stages of intoxication, but I had always been a connoisseur of fine flesh as well as good liquor, and intoxication and I had no secrets from one another.

My expertise also made me a good observer of other men's romantic follies. Some were foolish enough to think me a good adviser, but as an artist, I only ever offered advice in the cause of art. The last thing I would ever have done was to urge a fellow man to follow the dictates of reason and common sense, especially if I saw an opportunity to add fuel to the flames of an intriguing psychodrama.

I presume that Conrad Othman brought his troubles to me because he supposed that I had some special insight into the mental state of Dorothea Rosa, with whom he had become unluckily besotted. The supposition was, of course, entirely correct, but he might have been better pleased in the short term had he obtained more orthodox counsel from one of Dorothea's female acquaintances–Hecate Rain, perhaps–or from a neutral source like the Sisters of Shalimar. When the events I am about to relate were concluded, Conrad affected to hate me, although I expected that his resentment would ebb with time, and surely would have, had he remained on the island. Wherever he went, I hope that he had grown wise enough by the time he lay upon his deathbed for a second time not merely to forgive me, but to thank me for my kindness.

Conrad had been living on Mnemosyne for four years before the bitter winter came that served as a backcloth to my story. He was a composer of music for strings and woodwind. Few of his compositions required more than four instrumentalists–a useful economy on the island, especially in winter–and many were duets that sought to use the contrasting temperaments of two instruments that were not conventionally required to play in harness to generate productive tension. His work was too ethereal, some might say too eerie, to be popular with the island's aristocratic patrons, but its quality was valued by the cognoscenti. Whenever one of his pieces made its debut, the audience would make up in appreciative expertise what it lacked in numbers.

Conrad always played the leading wind instrument himself at such debuts, although he was a little way short of first rate as a flautist or panpiper. He always had difficulty finding string-players, because he rarely wrote for the violin or cello, preferring to use the guitar, the lyre and the harp. Harps posed a particular problem because there were so few performers available, but Conrad was too attentive to the dictates of his muse to let the pattern of his compositions be guided by the ready availability of players. If one or more harps would suit his inspiration best, then he would write for one or more harps. He would not even begin to worry about the shortage of harpists until the piece was done.

Afterwards, of course, he was compelled to worry–and the pressures of practicality inevitably had a cumulative effect.

Dorothea Rosa was universally recognized as the best harpist on the island, but she preferred to operate as a soloist. Her concerts would have been better received had she confined herself to playing the compositions of others, but she always insisted on interspersing her renditions of the classics with markedly second-rate pieces of her own. It is possible that her reluctance to lend her services to Conrad owed something to envy of the fact that he was a better composer for her own instrument of choice than she could ever be, although the fact that she was an exclusive lesbian also had something to do with it.

I do not know when Conrad first invited Dorothea to play one of his pieces, or how gradually his polite requests intensified into urgent pleas, but I suppose she must have refused him at least a dozen times before she finally agreed, reluctantly, to accompany him. He had, in the end, to win her agreement by the only means possible: by producing a piece so cunningly adapted to her tastes and talents that she would be avid to play it. He used other instruments of seduction as well, of course–he flattered her outrageously, sent her expensive bouquets of her favorite moss roses and procured rare books from the mainland that she needed for her library–but all that would have been in vain had he not eventually been able to lay before her a score that accomplished everything she had been striving for, unsuccessfully, in her own compositions. She would doubtless have liked it better had it been a solo, but she had wit enough to recognize as soon as she understood the manner in which the harp and the flute combined and contested their effects that the composition was a perfect duet.

I was, of course, present at the first performance of the *Rose Duet*, as were such diehard Othman aficionados as the physician Fion Commonal and the funeral director Emmaus Partibus. I was exceptionally glad to be there, because there was a rare relief in being able to escape my studio. My current commission was to paint the twin sons of the Duke of Dellacrusca, whose unsupervised journey to the island had provided their first experience of freedom from direct supervision. They had already raised six kinds of merry hell and would doubtless have been delighted to discover a seventh if and when the opportunity presented itself. They were the most restless sitters I had ever encountered, continually breaking their poses in order to squabble.

Hecate Rain was also at Othman's that night, although her presence owed more to her friendship with Dorothea than her appreciation of music. As a word-obsessed poet, Hecate preferred her music accompanied by lyrics. I recall that I took her to task on this point while we were sipping white wine before the performance.

"I know how hard it is for one who formulates all her own inspirations in words to set that kind of thought aside," I told her, "but you really must try. Music is the purest of all the arts because it has no content apart from its form. Its representations speak directly to the emotions, unfiltered by the cruder kinds of artifice that you and I employ."

"What nonsense you talk, Axel," she replied. "You're not even consistent. Have I not heard you insist that our emotions would be deaf, blind and stupid were they not trained by poets and painters to entertain meanings and possibilities? Are you not fond of reminding Romantics and Mystics alike that there is nothing natural about the manner in which music calls forth emotional echoes, and nothing magical either. It is something we learn–an ordinary element of our sentimental education."

"All that is true, of course," I said, with a sigh, "but you mistake its import. The point is that once we are properly educated, aesthetically and morally as well as sentimentally, music flows smoothly and efficiently to the core of our being, without requiring us to pause and consider, as a poem or painting still must. I dare say that you will see a clear demonstration of that tonight. Whether he is fully aware of it or not, Conrad has conceived this piece as a means of seducing Dorothea Rosa to perform for him. It succeeded in that even while it was naught but a series of ink-blots on paper, and its success has doubtless been further emphasized by practice and rehearsal–but only performance can complete the process. Tomorrow, the two of them will be in love."

"Don't be ridiculous," said Hecate. "Dorothea never takes male lovers. She has a powerful distaste for conventional intercourse."

"I do not say that she will admit him to her bed," I told her, "although I do predict that his desire to be admitted will be magnified tenfold within the next two hours. Dorothea uses her affections in a rather different way, but they are no less strong for that. When she has played his duet properly, she will be in love with Conrad, and however she chooses to express that love, it will possess her utterly for as long as it lasts. She might be rid of it in a fortnight or a month, but while it has her, she will be quite unable to escape it, no matter how she seeks to transform or pervert its power."

"Well, we shall see," was all that Hecate had time to say before we were ushered to our places.

Even if I were a poet and not a painter it would be difficult to describe the duet that Conrad Othman and Dorothea Rosa played that evening. If we had a language adequate to convey the effects of music we would not need music. Technical description is all very well for the purposes of mere analysis, but is the polar opposite of the direct and immediate emotional effect that I had been trying to explain to Hecate Rain. Lay readers might obtain a far better sense of the composition if I try, however clumsily, to say something about the resonance it struck within its players and hearers alike.

It is easy enough for humans to conceive of themselves as divided beings, in whom the dictates of reason and emotion are constantly in conflict. Our scrupulous "higher selves" often seem to be under threat from the urges of our "baser instincts." As an artist, of course, I understand the limitations of such crude commonplaces, but they are not without their uses. All of Conrad's compositions tended to reproduce some such division in their opposition of strings to woodwinds, and they were clearest of all in his duets. He always cast his woodwinds in the nobler role, as representatives of more conscientious yearnings, while the fulsome harps or guitars against which their questing pipings were set always played an earthier and more voluptuous part. The piece Conrad had written in order to seduce Dorothea Rosa to play for and with him exaggerated this distinction to a new limit.

As Hecate had observed, Dorothea found the male body repulsive, and had not the least attraction to the ordinary transactions of male and female flesh. Exactly how this repulsion had first arisen I have no idea, but, whether it was the result of an innate inclination or an exceptionally effective education in femininity, it had grown with time to become a literal horror. Dorothea relied on other women for erotic stimulation and was apparently quite content to do so. Her own music gave no indication of dissatisfaction with this state of affairs–there was nothing about it that voiced frustration or a lack of completion–but she had insufficient talent to translate the particular spectrum of her feelings into wholly effective musical terms, and she knew full well when she played pieces by other composers that they were expressing quite different spectra. No matter how brilliant they were, or how cleverly she played them, they remained slightly maladapted to her own idiosyncrasies.

The harp part in Conrad Othman's *Rose Duet* had been conceived with Dorothea firmly and centrally in mind. Although Conrad cannot have made the slightest attempt to decode or psychoanalyze the sequence of sounds, he had the kind of genius that allowed him to transmute her emotional landscape into music more effectively than she had ever been able to do herself. What Dorothea played that night–with consummate skill and total absorption–was a truer representation of the complexity of her own eroticism than she had ever found before. Like any great composition, it was both powerful and plaintive, because it rejoiced in the discovery of the self even while it yearned for evolution, and also because it recognized that while imperfect humanity is only capable of limited achievement, the human imagination is more than capable of desiring the impossible. The world is full of music that reflects some such general awareness, but the harp part of Conrad Othman's *Rose Duet* reflected Dorothea's particular consciousness more accurately than anything she had ever played before.

It was, however, a duet; her part was entwined and intimately bound with his–and his was something else.

Conrad's instincts had doubtless informed him–though not, of course, in words–that he might spoil the seductive effect of his duet if he put too much of himself into his own part. When all was said and done, though, it was his composition. He was writing it for himself first, and for Dorothea second. He wanted her to play for him because she was the best harpist on the island, not because she meant more to him than he did himself. He wanted the totality of the piece to be his own reflection as well as Dorothea's, and he wanted his own reflection to be paramount. He knew that he must avoid writing a woodwind part that would be in any way offensive or upsetting to her, but the real point of the exercise was to add her part to another in such a way that the whole would be greater than the sum. He set out, therefore, to produce a flute part that was like none ever heard before: a flute part whose strangeness would be its most obvious aspect.

I have already described Conrad's music as "ethereal" and "eerie" but neither word is adequate to convey the import of the flute's contribution to the *Rose Duet*. The harp part was voluptuous in a frankly exceptional fashion, but the flute part was so far beyond the commonplace complements of voluptuousness as to have forsaken all recognition of the flesh. It was an escapade of pure spirit, of that hopeful part of human consciousness that cannot believe that it will die, conceiving of itself entirely in terms of immortality, irrepressibility and incorruptibility. Its tone, perhaps paradoxically, was one of lamentation, but it was a kind of lamentation that no mere grief in the face of death could ever have inspired. It was the lamentation of something much more profound: the ultimate extinction of the stars, perhaps, or any matter of comparable suggestive magnitude.

There was no implication in the flute part of the *Rose Duet* to offend the sensibilities of Dorothea Rosa, but the measure of Conrad Othman's accomplishment was that it actually exerted an attractive force upon them. The flute part was not in the least disconnected from the harpist's part; it seemed, in fact, to be a kind of completion that the harp part required, even if that part lacked the intelligence to express a yearning for it. The strength of the whole piece was in the synergy of the two instruments and the sinews of their interplay. If Dorothea was privileged to play a part that she could never have written for herself, and yet was hers as well as his, Conrad was even more privileged to play a part that he had written for himself, and yet was all the more his for being alloyed with something distinct and different.

As the players gave themselves to the music, in the wholehearted way that is only possible in real performance, they could not help but be transformed by it, if only for a little while. In time, the effect would have worn off, as all effects do–we are only human, after all–but in the immediate aftermath of their playing, it formed a kind of bond between Conrad and Dorothea that neither of them had known nor conceived of before.

Eight days had passed before Conrad sought me out in my favorite covert in the *Sprite*, where I was sipping absinthe–as I occasionally did in winter, while I was not engaged in composition.

"That stuff will be the death of you, Master Rathenius," he observed. "You'd have done better to stick to iced water."

"I have built up an impressive tolerance," I assured him. "My body has made its peace with wormwood, and would now be quite desolate to be permanently without it. In summer, of course, it makes concessions. Are we no longer on first name terms, Conrad? I did not know that I had offended you."

The depth of the sigh he let loose as he sat beside me informed me that it was embarrassment that had prompted his thoughtless formality. "I beg your pardon, Axel," he said. "My mind is so agitated that even my habits are confused. I have fallen victim to an absurd infatuation."

"Why absurd?" I asked, although I already knew.

"Absurd," he said, "because I allowed it to grow out of all proportion. I have been wooing the Lady with presents and compliments for months, having fooled myself into thinking that I only wanted her to play for me. Doubly absurd because I knew all along that she prefers the company of her own sex, and would never allow a man to make love to her."

It would have been a waste of time to offer conventional commiserations or to ask him why he had brought his problem to me.

"The question you have to ask," I told him, "is whether that preference is the greater of two attractions or the lesser of two repulsions."

"What difference does it make?" he retorted. Even great artists can be unsubtle in matters unconnected to their art.

"If it were the greater of two attractions," I said, "the task before you would be to discover an even greater attraction, and to equip yourself with it–but you have already done that, I think, and it has only served to complicate the issue. Am I right in supposing that the problem is not that Dorothea does not reciprocate your love, but that she feels unable to consummate it despite her reciprocation?"

He stared at me as if I were a magician, although I had not said anything that was less than obvious.

"She swears that since we performed the *Rose Duet* she loves me with an intensity she never thought to feel for anyone," he confirmed. "She insists, however, that what she loves is my genius, my soul and my intelligence. It is, she claims, a purified emotion far finer than any mere matter of the flesh. She says that what she feels for me could only be sullied and spoiled by bodily intercourse. All nonsense, of course–but she believes it. How can I persuade her that she is sublimating an affection which is solidly rooted in the material, and which demands material satisfaction?"

"With great difficulty," I told him, "given that you have already done your utmost to persuade her of the opposite."

"She has heard no such argument from me, I can assure you!"

"Of course not," I said. "Had she heard it as an argument it would probably have sounded fatuous. The problem is that she heard it in a far more immediate–and hence far more persuasive–form. She heard it in the dialogue between your flute and her harp: a dialogue unconfined by mere matters of language and anatomy. You took care to incorporate a certain unusual voluptuousness into her part, but your own part set echoes of the flesh firmly aside. That aspect of you with which she fell in love is not something which demands material satisfaction but something which comes perilously close to denying any such possibility."

He hesitated, with furrowed brow, before answering. "That was not my intention," he said, finally.

"Not consciously," I admitted. "But you did it very well. There is no higher achievement in art than to communicate a keen sense of the impossible, and the tragedy of its unattainability. I was near to tears myself."

"But that is not what I felt," he insisted. "It was, I admit, the music that transformed my inchoate desire into aching lust, but it is certainly not lust for anything extraordinary, let alone anything impossible of attainment."

"That is because you identified yourself too fully with the flute part, thus creating a sense in which you could only listen to the harp. As a member of the audience, I could only play the eavesdropper, hearing both. Dorothea, on the other hand, identified herself completely with the harp, and she could only listen to the flute. While you fell in love with her voluptuousness, she fell in love with your lack of it." I could have pointed out that the simplest way out of his predicament was to wait until both effects were dulled by time, but that would not have been the best advice to offer *for art's sake*; it would merely have been the advice most likely to minimize the cumulative sum of Conrad's misery.

Conrad thought about my analysis for a few moments, and then said: "I still don't understand the distinction between the lady's preferences being the greater of two attractions or the lesser of two repulsions."

"Because the former would give you no chance of success, given that you have already found the greater attraction and laid it before her. Mercifully, Dorothea's lesbianism is a matter of peculiar fastidiousness rather than animal magnetism. She is not powerfully attracted to women in a sexual sense–she merely finds their material attentions more easily bearable than those of men. Were there another subspecies even more bearable, she would readily accept the advances of its members–not very avidly, I dare say, but as gladly as she can."

"But there is no such subspecies," Conrad said, "and if there were, I would not be a member of it." He was not an unimaginative man, but he could not exercise his imagination in other than musical terms.

"What there is, and what you are, need not trouble us overmuch," I said. "Even Dorothea's firm and long-held beliefs need not enter the equation. The question is: what illusion can she be made to accept, however tentatively, for a little while?"

"What *illusion*?" he echoed, and then repeated the question with the emphasis differently laid. "Well, then, what illusion might she be persuaded to accept?"

"Whatever illusion already haunts her dreams," I said. "Whatever illusion her unconscious mind attaches to the lusts that disturb her in spite of her fastidiousness."

"And how are we supposed to find that out?" he wanted to know.

"We have already found it in your music," I said, "which has answered her unadmitted desires more successfully than her own. You have said yourself that she loves your genius, your soul, your intelligence. We have only to confront her with what she believes to be your disembodied spirit, and she will surrender to you utterly."

"You mean," he said, slowly, "that I have to convince her that I am a ghost. How on Earth am I to do that?"

"Not so much a ghost," I said, "as an incubus. As for the means, you must appear to have died. Such things can be arranged, if you know the right people. Fion Commonal and Emmaus Partibus, for instance."

Conrad had never been one of the many residents of the island who entertained doubts about my greatness as a painter, but it was a delight nevertheless to see him look at me with a new expression on his face: the humble expression of a clever man who realizes that he is confronted by superhuman ingenuity.

"There are some on Mnemosyne who think you're a wizard, Axel," he observed. "There are some who think you're the Devil himself. At times like this, I could almost believe them."

"I've lived a long time," I told him, "and made the most of my experience. If I'm a magician, it's only because I commands the magic of art. And if I were the Devil–" my eyes shifted as I spoke to the Devil's Rocks outside the harbor–"I'd be the living proof that the adversary of mankind is sorely misunderstood, in his motivation and his manners... though not, perhaps, his mischievous whim."

Given that there are so few prescriptions that actually work in more than a morale-boosting way, all physicians must be artists first and artisans second. Having practiced so long on Mnemosyne, Fion Commonal was as far removed from the rudely mechanical as any doctor in the province, and perhaps the entire Empire. He was also the attending physician at the World's Stage Theatre, where his duties had forced him to become a master of dramatic artifice. When I explained to him that we must contrive a swift but artful apparent death for Conrad Othman, he was only too willing to agree.

"We might have him run through in a duel," he suggested. "I have been experimenting with several new kinds of blood, and no one fakes a belly-wound better than I. On the other hand, I have an excellent concoction that will bring on a very real but perfectly safe fever. Used in connection with a salve for turning healthy skin pallid it provides a perfect facsimile of the point of death. Which would you prefer?"

"Both," I said, without hesitation. "But the wound should not be in the belly. It should be to the left of the heart, as if the thrust had been turned aside by the ribs, and it should be gangrenous as well as bloody. That will allow it to serve as the ostensible cause of the fever."

"We would need another duelist," Commonal mused. "It will not be easy to find a volunteer. To be the killer of Conrad Othman, if only for a little while, would attract a great deal of opprobrium on the island."

"A hired killer might be better," I agreed. "A mysterious masked man. No one would hire a professional assassin to kill a master musician, of course, so Conrad must be hurt while coming to the aid of a more plausible victim. It would add to the poignancy of the occasion if the man he saves were to be some high-born but utterly unworthy rapscallion. You can safely leave the casting of the assassin and his intended victim—or victims—to me."

63

Commonal nodded understandingly at my substitution of the plural for the singular. "The Dellacrusca brats!" he said, his tone expressing his satisfaction with the choice.

"The Dellacrusca twins," I confirmed, "will be only too delighted to be assisted in the discovery of a new kind of mischief. In any event, surviving an assassination attempt might serve as useful practice for them in later life."

Genius does not pause when inspiration commands. Within 24 hours, the entire island was abuzz with the alarming news that a hired assassin had been dispatched from the provincial capital to murder the elder of Dellacrusca's twin sons, in order to carry forward some half-forgotten blood feud, and had caught up with the boy on the balcony of the *Sprite*. The younger son would have been the heir apparent if the thrust had struck home, but the great composer Conrad Othman had made a bold attempt to disarm the masked man. Thwarted in his purpose, the killer had disappeared after the mysterious fashion of his kind, but the dagger must have been poisoned, for the glancing blow that Conrad had suffered had not been as lucky as it first appeared. He had been carried to his bed, and the question of whether he would survive the night was not yet settled.

Although it was only November, that winter was too cold to allow bad news to flow with its usual celerity. Commonal and I had to wait a full 30 minutes longer than I had anticipated before Dorothea Rosa came hammering at the door of Conrad's house, demanding to be allowed to see him.

At first, Commonal refused, telling her that Conrad was too sick to recognize his visitors, let alone converse with them, and that the infection in his wound created a danger of contagion. Dorothea had to plead with him very ardently–which she did most affectingly, considering that her flooding tears rendered her all-but-helpless, and by the time she was finally let in, she was in no condition to detect any imposture.

Conrad's part was by no means difficult–dying is easy, as any tragedian will tell you–but he played it superbly. He babbled a little, refused to recognize Dorothea for a full five minutes, while she sobbed hysterically, and then put on a show of clearing his senses. For just a moment, his wildly wandering eyes fixed upon her face, and he whispered her name once before collapsing upon his pillows in a moderately convincing faint.

It was then that I took Dorothea by the shoulders and steered her gently from the room.

"He knew me!" she exclaimed. "Even in the extremity of his distress, he knew me!"

"Pray that you have given him the strength to live," I said, as I hustled her through the door and closed it behind us. "He loves you with all the passion he can muster. That might just be enough to pull him through."

"And I refused him!" she mourned. "Oh, if I had but known! What is my niceness compared to the suffering of a man like that! If he lives, I swear that he shall have me. If he lives, I shall deny him nothing."

"Shhh!" I said, urgently, pretending that it was for her sake. The last thing I wanted was to put the idea into Conrad Othman's mind that he need not see my little drama through to its intended conclusion. "Go home, Dorothea, and try to sleep. I shall sit up with him all night, and I will keep Commonal to his task. I will bring you news in the morning myself. You have my promise."

"Thank you, Master Rathenius," she said. "If you can only tell me that he is saved, I shall be in your debt forever."

Artistry is much rarer among funeral directors than among physicians, but as the island's principal practitioner, Emmaus Partibus had perforce to specialize in arranging the funerals of artists and he was well used to rising to such occasions. The service, procession, interment and wake that we planned together was mostly of my own devising, but he added a few professional touches which rounded off my script to perfection.

Instead of lilies, we decided that the flowers accompanying the coffin must be roses: the moss roses that were

Dorothea's favorite. I, of course, would provide the principal oration, offering a fulsome tribute to Conrad's achievements and an intimate account of his last days. There would be two others, both poetic–classic pieces only, both to be delivered by male mourners. This decision annoyed Hecate Rain, who would have loved an opportunity to read one of her own elegies, but I did not want Dorothea's attention to be in any way distracted and Hecate can be heart-rendingly attractive when she is in an elegiac mood.

The most important aspect of any musician's funeral is the music. Instead of the conventional hymns and dirges, convention demanded that the music played during the service must be Conrad's finest pieces, but here I intruded one of my most delicate strokes of genius. I decreed that each piece should be performed without the part that Conrad would ordinarily have played, so that their incompleteness would demonstrate his absence more obviously and more sensitively than any mere appearance could ever have contrived. The climax of this eccentric concert was, of course, to be provided by Dorothea Rosa performing the *Rose Duet*, for once and once only, as a solo.

The whole affair went off very well, but from my own viewpoint, everything that followed Dorothea's performance at the church was anti-climactic. The procession was tedious, the interment as empty of effect as the coffin, and I was so quiet at the wake that I almost spoiled my reputation by engendering the suspicion that I must, after all, have a soft heart. Perhaps I could have roused more enthusiasm for my own part had Dorothea not played hers to such perfection, but she was magnificent–so unexpectedly clever, in fact, that I felt quite unable to take the whole credit for her work, even though I had contrived the situation. While I listened to her, I was convinced that she would never play better.

Under normal circumstances, there is a profound dissatisfaction in listening to a piece played without one of the instruments for which it was designed. The fact that I had heard the *Rose Duet* played as it was meant to be played only a few days earlier should have made Dorothea's rendering of the harp part seem even more jejune, but these were not normal circumstances. Had I believed–as Dorothea and almost all her fellow mourners did–that Conrad was really dead, I honestly believe that I would have been able to hear that half-duet as a work of genius in its own right, all the more wonderful for the fact that its context could never be reproduced. Even as things were, I could see that it was uniquely brilliant.

I often close my eyes when listening to music, thus alleviating the risk of being distracted by any haphazard glimpse of something beautiful. As a painter, I am unusually vulnerable to visual distraction. While Dorothea played her solo version of the *Rose Duet*, however, I kept my eyes firmly fixed on her face. I watched the grief and sadness that had marked her features ever since I took her news of Conrad's death deepen by degrees as she transported herself into a private realm where she could not help but feel the force of Conrad's absence more keenly than anyone in her audience. Then, I watched her expression change, becoming calmer and strangely joyous, and I knew that in her mind she could hear the missing part, perhaps more clearly than she could have heard it if it had really vibrated the air around her. I watched her forge a new link with Conrad in spite of his absence: a new union. It was a marriage truly made in Heaven, even though there is no Heaven, save for the idea that haunts the human imagination.

I have wrought this miracle, I said to myself–but I could not quite believe it. I knew that I had merely been the facilitator, and that Dorothea alone had wrought the miracle, because Dorothea alone had the will and the art to do it. I had to remind myself, instead, that my plan was unfolding as neatly as I could possibly have expected.

Perhaps I should have worried that it was proceeding a little *too* well, and remembered how fate delights in cheating us when we are at our most confident, but I was too self-satisfied for that. I thought, once the empty coffin had been laid in the waiting grave, that the difficult part of the scheme was concluded and that its momentum was now unstoppable.

I was absolutely right, of course–more absolutely, as it turned out, than I had anticipated or thought possible.

As soon as Dorothea was ready to leave Conrad's wake, I volunteered to see her home. It was not late, but the winter dark always falls too eagerly for comfort; she was grateful for the offer.

"I believe I have misjudged you, Master Rathenius," she said, as we walked. "I never believed that you could be so deeply affected by the death of a mere acquaintance."

"There was nothing *mere* about Conrad Othman," I assured her.

"True," she agreed. "He was the finest man I knew–the only one, I think, whose finer qualities transcended his fleshly manhood. I wish that I had known him more intimately than time and pride permitted."

"Life is too short," I observed. "No matter what we achieve, we all die with an infinity of experience untasted. You and I must be thankful that we are artists. The majority, I think, die too contentedly, with that infinity of lost experience not merely untasted but unsuspected."

"Should we be thankful for that?" she asked. "Is not ignorance bliss? Would we not be happier if we did not know the true measure of our loss?"

"Of course we would," I said. "But what have you and I to do with that vulgar kind of happiness? Should the blind be glad that they have been spared the sight of the world's misfortunes? We should be grateful for every glimpse imagination gives us of possibilities unrealized and potentials unfulfilled, for they are a more precious form of wealth than any mere coin or completed achievement. We are artists, Dorothea. We are the true humans, the hope and soul of the race. The extremity of your grief may be tearing you apart, but so it should–and you should be delighted to be torn, for that is the measure of your sensitivity and the measure of Conrad Othman's worth as musician and man."

"As musician and man!" she echoed, plaintively. "I only loved the musician, no matter how he strove to make me love the man. What a miser I am! What a pusillanimous, uncharitable soul is mine! I have been a fool, Axel: a self-protective fool."

"I do not believe it," I lied. "I heard you play today, and I watched you too. I heard and I saw what you really are, and I know your true capacity. You are no miser, Dorothea, and no coward either. Conrad Othman may have died before making that discovery, but if his dying helped you to make it, he did not die in vain. Here is your house–I should bid you farewell."

I did not, of course. I let her invite me in–and when she gave way to her distress and sank down upon a couch, I volunteered to show myself out, Having reconnoitered very carefully when I visited her to bring her news of Conrad's death, I knew exactly which window to unlock and exactly where to hide once I had loudly closed the door without actually passing through it. We are fortunate on the island not to have been reached by the new fashions in decoration that have all-but-banished screens and tapestries from the capital in favor of padded wallpaper; I had no difficulty in making my way back to the room where she had cast herself down–the same room in which her servants had re-established her harp, having carried it back from the church–and secreting myself behind a screen.

I knew that I would have to be patient, but I also knew that my wait would not be in vain. For an hour, she could not move, and when she could, her first thought was to revive herself with brandy. Had I thought it necessary, I might have contrived to have the brandy drugged, but I had faith in her artistic temperament. I knew that there was no danger of her lacking imagination–alas, I had not seen the contrary danger that she might possess too much.

I knew that Dorothea would fret for a while and weep for a while, that she would flutter aimlessly around the room twice or thrice, and throw herself down on her couch at least twice or thrice more. I knew that she would consume not less than three glasses of brandy, that she would strike her breast and worry the hem of her black gown, that she would sob and mutter and bite her lip—but I knew that all such gestures would be a mere tuning up. I knew that she would torture herself only by way of preparation, and that there was only one way in which her frustration and self-abuse could eventually find proper expression.

In the end, two hours after midnight, she went to the harp. At the darkest hour of her distress, she went to play her part of the *Rose Duet*.

As soon as she sat down, she was listening. As soon as her fingers touched the strings, she was reaching out with every fiber of her being into the great unknown, hoping to hear the complementary voice of the flute.

And she heard it. From the very beginning, she was playing a duet—although I, the audience, could only hear the harp.

I had given Conrad very strict instructions as to the precise moment when he should begin to play outside Dorothea's window, adding a real instrument to the one that was already sounding in her imagination. I thought that I had judged the moment to perfection, and I was annoyed at first when the flute joined in some seven minutes early—but as the piece proceeded, I came to understand that I had been wrong. I am a painter by vocation, and although I consider myself a connoisseur of half a dozen other arts I have not the special expertise of a great player or a great composer. I realized, once the duet was halfway through, that the flautist had added the audible to the imaginary at a moment even more appropriate than the one I had identified, and I was generous enough to extend my honest congratulation to the unseen player.

I had expected to see Dorothea start slightly when the notes she heard in her mind were supplemented by something more robust, but she gave no sign of any awareness of change.

She continued playing quite seamlessly, She played no better than she had in the church, but she played more intently, as musicians tend to do when they believe that they are playing for themselves alone. Now that I could hear both instruments instead of only one, I was able to savor the *Rose Duet* as it was meant to be savored, and I had no doubt that this was a stronger and more sincere performance than the one I had heard at the debut–but I could not help comparing it slightly unfavorably with the incomplete performance I had heard in the Church. The new performance was deeply moving and perfectly executed, but there is sometimes a superabundance in emotional harmony and perfection: a saturation which is not entirely to be preferred to the best kind of tragic breakage. I had to tell myself that what I was hearing was best regarded as the second movement of a collective whose first had been played in the church.

When it was finished, it was all that I could do to quiet the reflex which bade my hands applaud–but it had to be sup- pressed, for the third movement was yet to be played, and the true climax of my collaborative composition still remained to be achieved.

I was sufficiently captivated by the magic of the moment not to be anxious when I did not hear the slightest creak from the window I had carefully unlocked. I was not surprised when it seemed as if the incubus that had been Conrad Othman really had materialized out of the shadows behind the couch on which Dorothea had lain down before she began to play.

She ran towards him as soon as she saw him, and gladly admired the way he glided around the couch, so that he could meet her in front of it and topple her into its tender embrace.

Although my vantage was good, too many candles had guttered and died while Dorothea played to allow me to see very clearly what was happening on the couch. I did not mind; too much light would have lent their performance a suggestion of cheap pornography, while the shadows helped to ennoble their intercourse far above that level. I could hear perfectly well, and I was left in not the slightest doubt that the intercourse in question was munificently material and exceedingly earthy.

Whatever Dorothea's previous proclivities might have been, and however they had been inspired, I knew that there was nothing for her in this experience but ecstasy. She believed—had I not given her every reason to believe?—that her playing had summoned a response even from beyond the grave, and that Conrad Othman had been allowed to return to Earth for a single hour in order to complete that which had been left incomplete before. And if she believed it, was it not true *for her*? Was she not artist enough to be an authentic creator? Had she not genius enough to make the impossible real, if only for a moment? And was I not privileged to have had a part in the making of such an artwork? Was I not entitled to congratulate myself as the true author of the drama that I had already titled, if only privately, *The Incubus of the Rose*?

Yes, yes, yes, yes and yes. All of that, and more.

What material difference does it make, after all, that the incubus she summoned was not Conrad Othman at all? What material difference does it make that Conrad Othman—the living Conrad Othman—had been unable to take up his position outside Dorothea Rosa's window, because he had been rudely seized and detained by the secret spies whom the Duke of Dellacrusca had set to watch over his twin sons during their first experience of apparent freedom, who were very anxious to know exactly how and why the younger had been persuaded to put on a mask and make a very convincing pretence of trying to assassinate the elder?

I must emphasize at this juncture that it was no part of my plan that anyone should suffer any serious injury. I did not expect Dorothea Rosa to be grateful to me when she discovered that Conrad had been introduced to her bed by a cunning ruse, and I did not suppose that she would easily forgive Conrad, but I had faith in her as an artist. I sincerely believed that when her immediate anger had abated, she would realize that I had, after all, gifted her with a unique experience of considerable value. Even if she refused to entertain the idea that her new sexual experience had advanced her sentimental education considerably, I felt sure that her memory of those two remarkable performances of the incomplete *Rose Duet* would be infinitely precious.

I had, of course, envisaged that Conrad would remain with her after completing his deceptive seduction, and would soon reveal to her that he was, in fact, still alive. I was surprised when he disappeared, leaving Dorothea alone on the couch–and surprised, too, that I had somehow failed to notice his withdrawal–but it did not seem to be so terrible a violation of my script. I assumed that he had been temporarily overcome by the enormity of his own experience and that he would return as soon as he had composed himself.

I, of course, stole quietly away, using the window that I had unlocked for Conrad. I went stealthily, because I had carefully omitted to mention to Conrad that I intended to watch his performance, and I did not want him to catch me descending from the sill. I was glad that he was not there, because I knew no better.

It was not until he roused me from my own bed, two hours after dawn, to show me his bruises and complain bitterly at the manner in which Dellacrusca's bully-boys had interrogated him, that I belatedly realized that my scheme had gone awry.

I was so starved of sleep that I nearly blurted out a demand to know who *had* played the flute outside Dorothea's window and then made love to her, if he had not, but I remembered just in time that he was not supposed to know that I had remained in the house after seeing Dorothea home. It is hardly surprising, though, that while I kept silent that very question possessed my brain like an irresistible fever.

I am, of course, a thoroughgoing materialist. I know full well that there is no world beyond the grave–neither Heaven, nor Hell, nor Purgatory–and I have never believed for an instant that ghosts routinely walk the Earth, or that incubi and succubi are anything but the product of dream-driven appetite.

On the other hand, I do believe in the force of the human imagination and the capacity of art to communicate that force.

It did not astonish me to learn that Dorothea Rosa had the ability to conjure up a phantom of Conrad Othman, even though Conrad Othman was not actually dead, and then to play the *Rose Duet* with the phantom's accompaniment, and even to enjoy physical intercourse with the phantom. I will admit that it did surprise me, a little, to discover that she also had the ability to make me see and hear the phantom too, but when I had time to reflect, I could see that it made sense. I heard her playing, and was as conscious as she was of the absence implied by her playing alone. I am a painter, well used to the employment of my mind's eye in seeing the possible within and beyond the actual. If the *Incubus of the Rose* was a folly, it had every right and reason to be a *folie à deux*. If it could be material to Dorothea's ear and eye and touch, there was no reason why it should not be equally material to mine.

Although I am a great artist, I am–alas!–only human. It took time for me to work all this out, and while I was making the calculation, I did not have time or space in my thoughts for anything else. I simply had no opportunity to address the next question, which was: what would Dorothea do next, in the circumstances as I now understood them?

Perhaps I would have guessed, and perhaps not. It makes no difference now, and would have made none then.

In the event, Fion Commonal came hammering at my door two hours after Conrad Othman–while Conrad was still with me–to bring us the news that minutes after waking on her couch and beholding the cold grey light of the winter dawn, Dorothea Rosa had swallowed a draught of poison strong enough to kill a horse.

It was not such a terrible tragedy as everyone seemed to think. Dorothea was in her thirties. Not only had her looks begun to fade but–more importantly–her talent had already peaked. Had it not been for my little drama, she might never have played as well as she had on the day and night of Conrad's false funeral, and she would certainly never have played so well again. She killed herself because she felt that there was nothing left for her on Earth, and because she wanted to enjoin herself for all eternity with the phantom she had conjured from the vast deep.

In that, I presume, she succeeded, insofar as any success was possible. I do not say that she was not to be pitied or mourned, and I would certainly have been glad to see her appear alive and well the day after her funeral to declare that it had all been a joke designed in reprisal–but I still insist that if there are ways to die that are better than others, then Dorothea Rosa's was far from the worst.

Nobody agreed with me then, of course, and the lapse of time has not yet persuaded anyone to change sides. Emmaus Partibus was not grateful for the opportunity to stage two of the finest funerals that the island has ever seen within a single week, and Conrad Othman was not grateful for the opportunity to excel himself at Dorothea's funeral service almost to the extent that she had excelled herself at his. Hecate Rain was not grateful for the opportunity to make up for being omitted from the list of orators at Conrad's funeral by presenting the primary oration at Dorothea's. The twin sons of the Duke of Dellacrusca were not grateful to discover that their ostensible lack of supervision had been deceptive, and that their clandestine watchers would be reporting every detail of their bad behavior to the Duke.

All in all, I walked abroad in a distinctly frosty atmosphere for months, and not only because the winter turned out to be exceptionally harsh. But what else could I have done, given that my only loyalty was and always will be to the cause of art?

All artists thrive on love, but there are different ways in which they draw its nourishment. Some feed on piquant challenge, some on the joyous zest of first consummation, some on the heady riot of intense engagement, some on the fierce pain of parting and some on the mellow melancholy of remembered loss. Rare indeed is the opportunity for any artist to make a singular banquet of all those nutriments, but Dorothea Rosa achieved it–and if Conrad Othman did not, the *Incubus of the Rose* more than made up for his omission.

The Arms of Morpheus

1

"It's no good asking Axel," said Ragan Barling, the antiquary. "He never takes these things seriously. He's as likely to give us a lecture on the fine art of murder or rumor-mongering as he is to tell us what he really thinks."

I hardly heard him. I had detached myself from the discussion some minutes before, partly because it was so tedious, partly because the smoke from Morloc Hyat's pipe was irritating my eyes and partly because I had been studying Hecate Rain's mournful face, wondering why she was even more distracted than I was.

We were indoors at the *Sprite*, because the air surrounding our customary table on the balcony was too cold and damp to be comfortable, but Hecate was sitting next to the leaded window, staring out through the diamond-shaped panes over the waters of the harbor. She seemed quite desolate. I had painted Hecate five times, and had thought that I had captured all the emotion she had that bore the stamp of true artistry, but there was a depth of sadness in her eyes now that I had not seen before. It made me want to paint her one last time, even though the luminosity of her lost youth had faded entirely to grey.

"I'm sorry, Ragan," I said, in belated reply to the antiquary's sarcastic observation. "I seem to have drifted off for a few moments. What subject is it on which my opinion is being sought?"

Ragan Barling only laughed, with a sly smirk on his face–presumably at the thought of having caught me out. It was Fion Commonal, the physician and recently appointed chairman of the island's Winter Council, who replied. "No need to worry, Master Rathenius," he said. "It's merely the hoary old chestnut about which of the arts is the purest. These young people don't realize how often this discussion has taken place before in this vicinity."

These young people were the three individuals who completed our ill-assorted company of seven. The violinist Tybalt Sphendon wasn't really young–he might well have been older than Hecate–but he was a relatively recent arrival on the island, having been part of our little colony for less than five years; that gave him three years' advantage of the harpsichord-player Davida Amalek and the lyricist Morloc Hyat, who really were in their twenties. The relationship between the three was fraught just now. Tybalt had taken Davida under his wing when she first arrived on the island–in return, of course, for the usual sexual favors–but she had recently shown signs of an independence to match her greater talent, and was now engaged in a hectic, if rather shallow, love-affair with Morloc. All three of them were, of course, highly ambitious, impatient to present their most recent compositions to the audiences that would form when the summer visitors arrived.

In a good year, the first of the seasonal visitors would have begun to arrive on Mnemosyne by now, but the spring had been unseasonably cold and violent and the miserable weather showed little sign of breaking. The passage from the mainland is not really dangerous, but it can be unpleasant when sudden squalls materialize without warning–as they often do when spring is in its capricious phase–and the aristocrats who come to enjoy the balm of the sea air and the fruits of our artistic genius are not at all tolerant of discomfort. The fact that our best harbor–the one overlooked by the *Sprite*–is so very close to the tiny archipelago of the Devil's Rocks adds to the trepidation of visitors, although the rocks' reputation is greatly inflated. That particular spring, it had been inflated far beyond the norm because we were within a fortnight of the centenary of the worst disaster ever to take place there: the wreck of the *Haemon Redondo*. In the fashion that such rumors sometimes have, gossip about the possible return of the vengeful ghosts of the *Redondo*'s dead had been flying around the isle for the last month, and had almost certainly reached the sensation-starved mainland by now.

I didn't care one way or the other whether the advent of the migrant aristocrats and their hangers-on might be delayed for a week or so; I was no longer dependent in any way on the gold they dispensed by way of commissions, and I was in no particular need of a new source of social or psychological stimulation. My companions, understandably, were of a different mind.

Boredom and impatience had crept into the discussion from which I had absented myself, aggravating rather than canceling one another out, and the argument had become more heated than its stale subject matter warranted. It was rare for such a silly debate as the hoary and pointless argument about which of the various arts could lay claim to be the "purest" to arouse passion in the *Sprite*, but the fretfulness of the season had been augmented by the defection of Davida's affections from Tybalt to Morloc. Inevitably, Tybalt was refusing to concede the contest and was taking every opportunity that arose to demonstrate his intellectual superiority over his opponent. Under normal circumstances, the others would have attempted to soothe the situation as best they could, but it seemed that no one could be bothered. Ragan Barling seemed to be intent on extracting what amusement he could from the conflict, and Hecate was so distracted by her own concerns as to have abstracted herself entirely from the group.

"I'm sorry," I said, not very sincerely. "I fear that you'll have to fill me in on the argument so far, if you need my expert opinion."

Ragan cackled again, but Fion–who seemed to feel that his responsibilities as Council chairman extended even to the taproom of the *Sprite*–was quick to respond.

"Morloc has been arguing that music cannot be reckoned the purest of the arts," the physician said, "because it is so obviously improved by the addition of words. Words, he says, are the primary substance of thought, and thus of human existence. For this reason, lyric poetry–which fuses the intellectualism of thought with the musicality of emotion–has to be reckoned purer than the artistry of sound alone.

"Tybalt has been pouring scorn on Morloc's notion of what the word *pure* might imply. Words, and the thoughts they represent, have in his opinion to be reckoned impurities in an artistic context. The whole purpose of art, he claims, is to soothe away the oppressions of thought in order to bring the human mind back to a purer form of consciousness and existence, which is entirely emotional. Because music in isolation consists of harmonious form unpolluted by mere content, he deems it infinitely purer than music overlain and complicated by meddlesome words.

"It seems to me, on the other hand, that music and lyric poetry are both alike in appealing to the ear rather than to the eye. In humans, unlike bats, sight is the dominant and definitive sense. The purer form of musical augmentation, in my opinion, is dance–not merely for the dancer who internalizes the rhythm of the music but also for the audience, who can see its interpretation..."

"*Interpretation*!" Tybalt broke in, as if he were spitting out something disgusting. "That's exactly my point, Master Commonal–although I suppose that a mere dilettante like you could hardly be expected to appreciate it. Interpretation is complication and impurification. Any kind of augmentation is superfluous. Any appeal to the sophisticated eye is superfluous, precisely because the sense of sight is so dominant, so cerebral. The ear is primitive, elementary...."

"Not nearly so primitive or elementary as the sense of touch," Fion riposted, testily. "It is in dance that the *physicality* of music becomes manifest...."

"Rubbish!" Tybalt declared. "Hearing *is* a kind of touch, and by far the purest kind of touch, infinitely more refined than any mere sensation of heat or pain, or any artless *groping*..."

Tybalt's eyes were fixed on Morloc as he pronounced the final word, and his nose was wrinkled in distaste–although that might have been the effect of Morloc's awful pipe. It was Morloc who struck back while Fion Commonal was momentarily hesitant.

"The wordsmith does not need to grope," Morloc said. "The wordsmith does not scratch away at the four strings of an instrument with taut catgut. The wordsmith's tools are infinitely more refined and delicate, whose infinite potential is the truest form of purity–at least in any sensible definition of the term."

"You can see, Master Rathenius, why we need the opinion of a wise man and a true genius," Davida Amalek put in, raising a coquettish eyebrow as she spoke. She wasn't trying to flatter or seduce me, although it wasn't for lack of confidence in her beauty or her talent; she was merely trying to lighten the tone.

"I shall give the matter some thought," I said. "Please carry on the debate for a few minutes more, while I deliberate."

Ragan Barling was grinning broadly, and even Davida smiled, thinking that I was being jokily condescending. Actually, I wanted to have a quiet word with Hecate while the combatants' loud voices provided cover. Tybalt, obligingly, took up his own argument in stentorian tones.

"Your definition of purity," he informed his ex-lover's new favorite, "is so far from sensible, so utterly corrupt, as to be..."

I moved back from the table, then moved my chair closer to Hecate Rain's station by the window. "What's wrong, Hecate?" I murmured. "You look as if you've seen a ghost."

She turned her tragic eyes on me, and they captured my gaze so completely that I no longer saw the marks of age upon her face. I had seen her grieve, but I had never seen her haunted. I had not thought it possible, given that her long friendship with the necromantically-inclined Vashti Savage had never infected her with the slightest fear of ghosts or shadows.

"As a matter of fact, Axel, I have," she replied, in a sour and slightly sarcastic tone that was ill-fitted to her doleful expression. She did not elaborate–which was most unusual for her. Because the rest of us had been following the popular trend in joking about the allegedly-imminent return of the dead crewmen and passengers of the *Haemon Redondo* less than an hour before, I made the natural connection.

"Out there beyond the Crooked Finger?" I queried. "Have the long-dead seamen begun their march across the Knuckle already, to make their centennial protest 13 days ahead of time?" I knew as I spoke that my jocular tone was ill-calculated–the expression of hurt on her face was sufficient to make me repent of it.

"No," said Hecate, dully. "The ghost I saw was on a boat, heading in the opposite direction." Again, infuriatingly, she left it there, unwilling to explain until I consented to take her plaint more seriously.

I moved my chair closer to hers, and put on my best apologetic expression. "I'm sorry, Hecate," I said. "You mean, of course, that you saw a real person–someone you haven't seen for a long time. Someone who meant a great deal to you, in the distant past. Who was it?"

I felt that I ought to have been able to guess, and was slightly troubled by the fact that I couldn't. Hecate had often spoken to me of her life before she came to the island, when she lived in the great port of Ormaux 60 kilometers to the southwest of the island, but she had never told me about any lover whose loss had been sufficiently devastating to cause her present state of distress.

"You're right, of course, Axel," Hecate said, waspishly. "You always are, aren't you? Yes, it was a ghost of a purely figurative kind. Poetic license! Not so much the ghost of a man as the man of a ghost–not dead at all, but capable nevertheless of haunting me."

She hadn't answered my question, and might have been laboring under the delusion that she didn't want to–but I felt compelled to probe, for her sake as well as mine.

"An old lover, I suppose?" I said, by way of provocation. I saw in her wonderfully dark and anguished eyes that the indefinite article was ill-chosen: it had not been *an* old lover at all, but *the amour* whose defection had shaped her spirit and darkened her life, in her own estimation. I had never known that Hecate had that kind of a shadow in her past, and I scolded myself for having left the discovery so long. The kind of affection that she and I had for one another had never entailed confessing our inmost secrets, but I had always prided myself on my ability to perceive such secrets whether they were told or not. A painter of genius is supposed to be able to see into his sitters' souls, and Hecate had been more than a model to me.

"I'm sorry," I said, again, when the only reply she made to my ill-judged remark was a deepening of the resentment implicit in her silence. "The poor weather must be affecting my judgment." I knew that I had to make up for my carelessness, and set my mind to work on the puzzle with full concentration.

I recalled that Ragan Barling's recent chatter about the impending centenary had included mention of the fact that Nicodemus Rham, the keeper of the Lucifer's Light–situated on the largest of the Devil's Rocks–had elected to retire a fortnight short of the day on which the *Haemon Redondo* had gone down, slyly implying as he let the news slip that fear of clamorous phantoms had spurred Rham's decision. I happened to know that Ragan was wrong, because I was one of the few men on the island who ever risked the old causeway to Lucifer when the tide was unusually low, and I had talked to the old man on more than one occasion about his planned retirement. If Hecate had seen a boat in the harbor that was not there now, though, it might have been the ferry that was taking the new lighthouse-keeper to his post, which would have called in *en route* to pick up additional supplies of fresh food and water for the lighthouse stores.

"Can you possibly mean the new lighthouse-keeper?" I guessed, heroically.

At least I managed to startle her. "Do you know him too?" she asked. "How? Has he...?" She broke off, realizing that I had only been guessing.

"I know his name," I admitted. "Fion mentioned it to me. Phelim Kracy. From Ormaux. According to Fion, his family has been connected with sea trades for many years, although he's recently fallen on hard times. Friends nominated him for the position, in spite of his lack of experience. He wanted to come here because he has... what was the phrase?... *artistic sympathies*."

Hecate laughed at that, bitterly.

"Do you suppose that his real reason for applying to keep Lucifer's Light was to be close to you?" I asked.

Her gaze lost none of its poignant darkness, but it took on a certain medusal quality–although I dare say that she was in more danger of being turned to stone than I was. She had always been a profoundly self-regarding person.

"I doubt that very much," she said, coldly. "In any case, he will be unable to leave his post, so it hardly matters how near I am."

I laid my hand gently upon her wrist to inform her that my interest was tender as well as polite, and that I was anxious to help her if I could. "The keeper of the Lucifer's Light may be unable to come to the *Sprite*," I pointed out, "but there's nothing to prevent you from going to him. The ferryman who keeps the lighthouse supplied with provisions–Hillbeck is his name–will take you out, if you care to ask him. When the tide

reaches its lowest ebb, which it does on several occasions before and after every full or new Moon, you can walk across the
old causeway from the Knuckle. One has to be careful, even in
daylight, but it's not unduly difficult or dangerous; I've done it
often. I'll take you across myself if you like."

"Phelim will not expect me," was her bleak reply, "and
he would not be glad to see me. I shall not go, whatever the
state of the Moon may be." She didn't mean it; I could see
very clearly that she could not possibly let the matter rest, no
matter how hard she might try. Her world had been suddenly
turned upside-down, and would have to be righted again.

I wanted to help. We were friends, after all–and now that
I knew that there was still something in her worth capturing on
canvas, I wasn't about to let it escape.

2

I wanted to probe more deeply into Hecate Rain's intriguing
distress, but the immediate opportunity was denied to me. Fion
Commonal, having tired of the increasingly fractious temper
of the artists' petty quarrel, appealed to me again to pour a
little oil on the troubled waters.

"Surely you have an opinion of your own in this matter,
Master Rathenius," the physician said. "There are more arts
than are contained in words, music and dance, after all. Won't
you make a stand on behalf of the visual image: the art which
asks of the eye only that it sees, rather than obliging it to
function as a deciphering machine, as printed text must?"

I hesitated. The temptation was there to make a calculat-
edly absurd case on behalf of some trivial activity not usually
considered an art at all, but Ragan Barling had already scoffed
at that tactic. Given that I had not, as I had vaguely promised,
been thinking about the matter, I had to improvise–and even I
am not above considering, *in extremis*, the possibility of tell-

ing the truth. I caught sight of a hostile expression in Tybalt Sphendon's eyes as he turned his gaze upon me, and thought I saw a slight hint of contempt in it–which I could hardly be expected to tolerate, given that he was the only participant in the debate who had said anything at all with which I could agree.

"I certainly couldn't argue that painting is the *purest* of the arts, Fion," I said, feigning negligence, "nor would I want it to be. Unlike Tybalt, I prefer my art impure–rich, complex, full of nuances. But the discussion thus far has, I fear, been quite fatuous. The purest of the arts, without any possibility of dispute, is morpheomorphism."

I like to stop a conversation in its tracks, precipitating a silence born of amazement at my presumption. Alas, Davida Amalek was the only one of my listeners who seemed willing to believe that I was serious in what I said. This time, Ragan Barling wasn't the only one to pretend amusement.

"What on Earth is morpheomorphism?" Morloc Hyat asked. He was not only the youngest person present, but also the least learned.

Tybalt's lip curled. He couldn't resist the opportunity to score another point off his upstart rival by showing off his superior knowledge, no matter how incautious the display might be.

"It's not art at all," he said. "It's quackery. It's the work of charlatans who claim the ability to shape dreams by occult influence, in order to heal or to predict the future." He might have stopped there, but he was too firmly in the grip of his foul mood, which had set him temporarily against the whole world. "It isn't even a legitimate coinage," he added. "If such a thing were really possible, the correct term would be *oneiromorphism*. Morpheo and morphism come from the same root, you see–their combination is a crude tautology."

In the hope of making Morloc look small in the eyes of Davida Amalek, the fiddler was actually questioning the pedantic judgment of Axel Rathenius! I was amazed; it was as if a dwarf, in the hope of outshining another dwarf, had challenged a giant to a stamping contest.

"Not at all, Master Sphendon," I said, with deadly gentleness. "Morpheo and morphism may originate from the same root, but they make their subsequent etymological journeys by very different routes. Morphism refers directly to the process of shaping, but Morpheo's immediate reference is to the god Morpheus, whose kindly arms are supposed to rock us to sleep. The god's name, it is true, similarly derives from *morphe*, to shape, by virtue of the fact that he is imagined to be the bringer of dreams, and hence the shaper of sleep, but he is a distinct entity. His name is sufficiently distant from its origins to lend itself to *morphine*, a narcotic refinement of opium, whose function carries no implication of shaping at all. If the implication of morpheomorphism were no more than the *shaping of shapes*, then it would indeed be merely repetitious, as if one were to speak of sculpting a sculpture. What it actually implies, however, is more akin to the *shaping of sculptors*, and I must insist that the action of molding the mechanism by which dreams are made is by no means trivial. It is, in fact, a mode of secondary creativity by which the practitioner of the art intervenes in the natural process personified as Morpheus, in order to amplify and enhance its self-transformative effect. Such enhancement may be therapeutic–thus allying morpheomorphism with your vocation, Master Commonal, as well as mine–or oracular, but it is most certainly and quintessentially artistic."

Davida smiled, very prettily, but she was the only one present who seemed to enjoy my performance. The others didn't seem sure whether I meant what I said or whether I was indulging in mere obfuscation in order to make fools of them.

"Oneiromorphism," I went on, "does indeed imply *dream-shaping*, but morpheomorphism carries the more profound and more accurate implication of shaping the fundamental generator of dreams: collaborating with the natural mental endeavor that used to be symbolized as the god of sleep. A morpheomorphist does not impose a dream upon the dreamer, but rather allows the dreamer to make more and better use of his–or her–most intimate and powerful faculty. It is the purest art of all because it reaches beyond all matters of sensory apprehension to enter the substance of the soul. *Pure* art doesn't enter the soul from without; it emanates from within. Music, poetry, storytelling and painting can only stimulate dreams from far away, having been filtered through consciousness in a more-or-less haphazard manner; the morpheomorphist's work is far more finely focused and carefully co-ordinated. A concerto, a song, a dance or a painting appeals to many members of an audience simultaneously, and is therefore generalized; therein lies its vagueness and its turbidity as well as its popularity. The art of a morpheomorphist is always individual, always so precisely tailored that no one but its destined recipient could benefit from its administration; therein lies its clarity, and hence its purity."

"Well, no wonder it never caught on, then," Morloc Hyat exclaimed, more concerned with his own embarrassment at never having heard of something with which Tybalt Sphendon seemed familiar than he was with Tybalt's distress at having his casual misjudgment so comprehensively overruled. "You can't sell tickets to a performance like that!"

"All medicine," Fion Commonal observed, judiciously, "has its artistry. Surgery is the most intimate kind of sculpture, and the pharmacopoeia is a means of restoring the internal harmony that is lost when the humors are unbalanced–or, in more fashionable parlance, when the body is invaded by the germs of disease. In the same way, I suppose, music and painting have their science and their technology. What a difference the steel nib has made to the productivity of writers who would once have been condemned to scratch away with quills, forever in quest of keenness with the aid of a razor!"

"Yes, Master Commonal," Davida Amalek said, daring to cut him short. "We've heard that particular rhapsody before, I think–but it seems to me that what Master Rathenius says is far more interesting, as well as original. Do you think, Master

Rathenius, that the foundations of all the arts are to be found in the process of dreaming?"

"Where else?" I answered, spreading my arms wide.

"In the kind of mental discipline that brings order out of chaos," Tybalt Sphendon stated, firmly. "There is no beauty in dreams, which are mere detritus: residues of the work that consciousness does in refining daily experience into a coherent life-story. Dreams are excreta–fragments discarded by memory, which afflict us with their writhing as they fade away, striving mechanically but ineffectually to form meaningful wholes in imitation of the true self."

"Do you really think so, Tybalt?" Davida said. "I think there is beauty in dreams, and sublimity too."

"They are *waste*," Tybalt insisted. "Shards of experience shot like sparks from the fire of self-creation–or splinters chipped away from the block as the sculptor's image emerges, to use Master Rathenius' analogy."

"The analogy demonstrates the mistake you're making, Master Sphendon," I pointed out. "You're confusing the process with its by-products. Fragmentary dream-images aren't the whole of the dreaming process, although they're certainly evidence of its activity and sometimes offer invaluable clues to its achievements. They're far more meaningful, if properly interpreted, than you will credit; even if they weren't, they'd be firm evidence of the sculptor Morpheus at work, and the firepower of his armory. In the terms of your other analogy–whose implications you seem equally intent on misreading–sparks have a light and heat of their own, but they are symptomatic of a much greater and more powerful combustion. Dreaming is indeed the fire of self-creation–and morpheomorphism is a means of feeding fuel to that fire in order to control its temperature and the color of its flame."

"Mere wordplay," Tybalt said, furiously. It was one of his favorite phrases, although his scorn was unconvincing in the present instance. "Froth, like dreams themselves."

"It's a pity," said Ragan Barling, "that we can't put the matter to the test. When summer eventually arrives, artists of every stripe will flock to the island, but I've lived here longer than the rest of you–except, of course, Master Rathenius–and I've never actually met a morpheomorphist. I've heard rumors of their healing and prophetic work, of course, but the island attracts travelers' tales in almost the same profusion as travelers. Do you know any morpheomorphists personally, Axel?"

There was a mischievous glint in his eye; he had been on the island long enough to know perfectly well that I did, and where I went in order to consult her.

"Of course," I said. "One of the finest has been resident on the island for more than 30 years–longer than you, Ragan."

"I never heard of him!" Fion Commonal exclaimed, presumably more anxious for the implied omniscience of his position as Council leader than for the possibility of hitherto-unsuspected competition in the business of healing.

"*Her*," I corrected, mildly. I looked at Hecate Rain, rather ostentatiously. I wanted to draw her back into our little society from the distant wilderness to which her spirit had retreated.

"Oh," Hecate said, dismissively, "you mean the madwoman, I suppose? The one who lives on Snowspur Mountain, communing with the winds. Eirene Magdelana."

"I know *her*," Fion said. "A diehard believer in the pathetic fallacy, who thinks trees, stones and pools of water capable of emotion–and capable of dreaming, too, I dare say. She's your example of a pure artist, Axel? Not much of an advertisement, in my opinion."

"I would never venture to *advertise* pure art," I told him. "As I said, I much prefer my own art to be profoundly impure. Pure art requires too much of the artist. All pure artists go mad–don't worry, Master Sphendon, I foresee no danger of that for you–although their madness is a kind of artistry itself. Morpheomorphists, if they're effective, transform themselves as they transform others. In their own estimation, they become increasingly able to perceive the greater-than-human dreaming that shapes the sleep of the universe entire. The universe is far too vast to allow mere human interference, of course–the diseases of the cosmos are beyond the scope of any therapy we might devise–but its very vastness entrances those who can perceive it. As Davida says, there is sublimity in dreams, in far greater quantity and quality than beauty."

Davida smiled at me again, causing Morloc Hyat to frown. I wondered whether the time had come to paint a portrait of Davida, despite the fact that she was still awaiting her first considerable success as a player or composer.

"There never was a morpheomorphist who could cure herself–or himself–of any but the most trivial woes," I continued. "Eirene was once apprentice to Edom Sombre, whose father Lucian was the great pioneer of the art in the glory days of the last century. Lucian was more notorious than famous, I suppose, and had the reputation among superstitious folk of being an alchemist and black magician, but he and his son must have been great artists. Eirene had the misfortune to fall in love with her tutor, but it did no harm to the development of her talent–and she hasn't lost her artistry merely because she has gone mad. She might excavate your heartache, Hecate, if you would only give her the chance."

"What heartache is that?" Davida Amalek wanted to know. Until now, the disputants had not taken any note of Hecate's distress, but Davida had a woman's sympathies as well as an artist's and Hecate was a close neighbor of hers. The two of them were in the process of becoming fast friends.

"I have no heartache," Hecate said, sharply. "I saw something that dislodged one of Tybalt's shards of memory, which had fallen into a crack instead of being swept away with the other dust of experience. It's nothing–nothing at all."

"What shard?" Ragan Barling asked, quite mystified.

"The new lighthouse-keeper is someone Hecate used to know," I said, when Hecate refused to answer.

Ragan perked up at that. "Has Old Nick's replacement arrived?" he asked. "What an evil time to take up his post! Does he realize the danger he's courting?"

"Now, Ragan, I must ask you to be careful," Fion Commonal said. "It's all very well for you to harp on about the

91

ghosts of the *Haemon Redondo* in here, but the Council won't be pleased if you try to throw a scare into the new keeper or his sister. That would be most unkind."

"I've no intention of setting foot on Lucifer at a time like this!" the antiquary retorted, as if the idea were utterly horrific–although I happened to know that he had been there not six weeks before, chatting to "Old Nick."

Hecate had stiffened in her chair. "Is Phelim's sister with him?" she asked, faintly–too faintly, as it turned out.

"I do hope that Nicodemus Rham didn't say anything to the new man," Fion said, fretfully. "Rumor has it that he believes he's seen the crew of the *Redondo* many a time, just as distinctly as poor Dorothea Rosa saw the spectre of Conrad Othman."

"He's as mad as the old woman on Snowspur, then," Morloc opined. "It's the isolation that does it. I suppose. Hecate's old flame will likely go crazy too–but he has family, you say? That might help."

Nicodemus Rham, I knew, had had a family when he first moved to Lucifer. His wife had left him, though, unable to tolerate the barren rock, and had taken their children with her. It had hit him very hard.

"Just the sister, I think," the physician said. "No one else was mentioned at the Council meeting. No wife, at any rate."

I looked at Hecate, but now that her unheard question had been answered she seemed determined to give nothing away. She set her features in an unreadable mask.

"The sister will be company, though," Fion continued, "and she'll doubtless keep house for him as competently as any wife."

Hecate's mask proved brittle; it cracked as she loosed a hollow laugh. "Will she, indeed?" she murmured. She had spoken no more loudly than before, but every gaze abruptly turned in her direction, exerting more pressure than I had contrived to do. "Well," Hecate continued, in a stumbling fashion, "perhaps she is better now than she was when I saw her last.

Perhaps Phelim feels that the sea air will assist her convalescence."

"Something of that sort was said at the meeting," Fion Commonal agreed. "The sister's illness was mentioned. What was her name...?"

"Candida," Hecate supplied, when the physician hesitated–but she sounded slightly uncertain, almost as if she were hoping to be contradicted.

"Candida," Fion agreed. "She *had* been ill... but she's better now, apparently. There was a reason for their coming here to do with her condition, although I can't remember what it was, exactly."

"Perhaps she was in need of an expert morpheomorphist," Hecate said, casting a slyly venomous glance in my direction. "When I knew Phelim, she was in a kind of perpetual sleep or catatonia. She could eat and drink, mechanically, and sometimes moved about in the grip of dreams–even to the extreme of somnambulism–but she never woke up. She had not been awake for ten years and more when Phelim and I parted, and she was only 17 years old then. Perhaps the prince destined to awaken her came along at last–but if she's exiling herself to Lucifer's Light, he must have gone on his way instead of marrying her. She'll be 31 now, too old for a royal bride."

Hecate had never revealed her exact age to anyone, but I knew that she must be much nearer 40 than 30.

"I really ought to make him welcome, on the Council's behalf," Fion Commonal muttered, "and assure him that all these silly rumors about ghosts aren't to be taken seriously. When's the next full Moon, Ragan?"

"You won't be able to walk across the old causeway for three days yet," Ragan told him, "but you'd be a fool to try it even then. Go by boat, if you must. Hillbeck will take you."

"But I've seen you on the causeway yourself, Master Barling," Tybalt Sphendon put in. "It can't be as dangerous as all that."

"I suffer terribly from sea-sickness," the antiquary told him, stiffly. "I can't go out in small boats. Yes, I've risked the causeway—which is how I know that the tide returns more rapidly than one imagines, and the mists are improbably capricious. A boat is safer by far, if you have the stomach for it. I haven't."

I was the only person close enough to Hecate Rain to hear her murmur: "Neither have I, alas."

3

Hecate would say no more in the *Sprite*, but I pressed an invitation upon her as the party broke up and its members left the inn. She agreed to come to my house that evening; she refused to come for dinner, but said that she would arrive a little later, when she had had more time to compose herself. She promised that she wouldn't be late, although I assured her that I would wait up as long as might be necessary.

I offered her a lift home in my carriage, but she said that she would rather walk with Davida and didn't want to take me out of my way. Ragan hadn't brought his own carriage, since he lived only a few hundred meters away; he set off to walk with Fion Commonal, while Tybalt and Morloc ostentatiously went their separate ways, similarly on foot.

Jean-Jacques, my manservant, was a little put out at having had to wait outside the *Sprite* for an hour; I was usually more punctual in observing the hours at which I asked him to collect me.

"I'm sorry, Jean-Jacques," I said. "The company was larger and the conversation more interesting than I had anticipated."

"No ghosts then, sir," he observed. I had complained to him before about the awful fashionability of the current rumors.

"We passed over them quite rapidly, thank God," I said, "in favor of gossip about the new lighthouse-keeper. He's a former lover of Hecate's, apparently."

"I heard that old Nicodemus was expected ashore today," Jean-Jacques said. "He'll find it only a little less lonely, I'm afraid. Heard nothing about the new man at all."

"I must go to see him," I murmured, meaning Nicodemus Rham. "Hecate will be calling later, by the way–she'll make her own way to us in a hired carriage, but you'll have to drive her home. It might be late."

"Yes, sir," he said, meekly. "I'll make sure that the horses are kept ready for further labor."

The days were longer than the nights now that the equinox had passed, but the twilight did not linger when the sky was overcast, and the light was fading by the time we reached the headland. Luvah had already lit the lamps in the dining-room in anticipation of our return.

When my meal was concluded, I went into the library to read while I sipped a postprandial brandy. I was still there two hours later, when Hecate arrived in fulfillment of her promise. I was glad of the interruption, because the book–a romance of adventures in far Yucatana–was not living up to the hopes I had entertained of it.

We went into the dining-room, where the larger fire had been made up. Now that the table had been cleared and folded, it was effectively a sitting-room. I often entertained guests there, sometimes hosting concerts. There was a harpsichord set against the partition-wall; I made a mental note to invite Davida Amalek to play for a few select guests in the near future.

Hecate sank into an armchair on the far side of the hearth; under other circumstances, the languid gesture might have reminded me of old times, but there was more tiredness than ease in her relaxation. I poured her a brandy before taking to my own chair.

"It was all nonsense, wasn't it, Axel?" she said, a trifle plaintively. "It was all for my benefit, I suppose. Sometimes, I suspect that you're a great deal older than you seem, and that your corrosive skepticism is just an act devised to conceal your wizardry."

"If you're referring to my discourse on morpheomorphism," I said, "I suppose that it was intended to put a stop to Tybalt Sphendon's bad-tempered ramblings, by demonstrating their essential shallowness. There was no nonsense about it, though. Every word was true."

"I don't believe you," she said, baldly. "When I admitted that I knew the new lighthouse-keeper–that he had once been my lover–you decided to tease me. You may not be on the Council, but nothing that happens on the island escapes you. You knew Phelim's name; Fion must have told you about Candida, even though he seemed to have forgotten it himself."

"I can assure you that he didn't," I said, "and even if he had, I certainly wouldn't have concocted an argument about dream-shaping merely to remind you that your old lover had parted from you in order to minister to a somnambulist. You and I have been close enough to one another during these last seven years for you to know me far better than that. You can't possibly think that I'm like Tybalt, so ready to take offence if someone I've slept with turns out to have slept with someone else that I start hurling abuse in every direction. I'm your friend, Hecate, and always will be."

"I suppose you are," she admitted, not altogether graciously. "I'm sorry–it's ridiculous of me to suspect that your discourse on morpheomorphism might have been some kind of cryptic commentary on my relationship with Phelim and the nightmares that spoiled it."

I inferred that Candida Kracy wasn't the only one who had suffered from nightmares–and that Phelim had suffered the more, having carried their legacy into wakefulness.

"I don't like to see you wounded," I assured Hecate, "and I would never seek to increase the pain of any wound you suffered. I have as healthy an appetite for gossip as the next man, but any connoisseur of rumor will tell you that the appointment of a new lighthouse-keeper can't possibly qualify as an appetizing item of information, even if the man's sister was once a somnambulist. I knew that Nicodemus Rham intended to retire, but I certainly haven't been researching his successor. I knew nothing about Phelim Kracy but his name...until today."

I was, of course, hoping to find out far more.

Hecate was sufficiently chastened to remain silent for a full half-minute, and sufficiently distressed to swallow the last of her brandy without savoring it, but I was patient. I poured her another, and waited for her to tell me the story that she had never seen fit to tell me before.

"I'm still drunk from the wine I quaffed in the *Sprite* this afternoon," she said, to explain her delinquency in respect of the brandy. "I can't seem to take it in the quantities I once could. Old age, I suppose."

"It has nothing to do with age," I told her. "It's a matter of mood. Unbalanced humors, Fion would say. A disruption of the morpheotic flux, in Eirene Magdelana's language–that's a morpheomorphist's term for the dreaming process."

"A disruption of the morpheotic flux," Hecate repeated, pensively. "I suppose Phelim must have brought in a morpheomorphist at some time–for Candida, if not for himself."

Eirene Magdelana, I knew, had lived in Ormaux for a while, some time before she came to Mnemosyne–but it seemed highly unlikely that she could ever have been consulted by Phelim Kracy. If he was the same age as Hecate, or slightly older, he could only have been a child when Eirene was last in Ormaux.

"He would have expected failure, though," Hecate went on. "What you said today wouldn't have fit in with his views any more than they fitted in with poor Tybalt's. Except...."

"Except what?" I prompted.

"He might have liked the analogy you dismissed," she continued, after a pause. "The living sculptor Morpheus. Not a god, as such–Phelim was no better disposed towards gods than you are–but not a natural process like combustion either. Something active and alive. He thought dreams were living

97

things... not the fragmentary images, but the more substantial entities supposedly lurking behind them. You were happy to talk about sparks and shards struck by a sculptor's hammer, but Phelim would have been more likely to seize upon Tybalt's mention of *excreta*... although he might have preferred something slightly more grandiose... the sloughed skin of a snake, perhaps. In the opinion that he held when I knew him, the dream-maker part of us is like a partly-tamed animal, mostly untroublesome but occasionally prone to revert to a wild state that's essentially violent and dangerous... and sometimes deadly. Do you ever have bad dreams, Axel?"

"Rarely, nowadays," I confessed.

"Does that mean that you never needed a morpheomorphist, or that when you did, the treatment worked?"

"The latter," I confirmed, reluctantly.

"Eirene Magdelana treated you?" Hecate persisted. She had learned the art of guesswork from me, so she was correct. "When she first came to the island, or later? Later, I suppose–you can't be all that old. I hope that's not what drove her mad?"

"You're procrastinating, Hecate," I pointed out. "You came here to confide in me, so why waste time with silly questions?"

"Did I?" she retorted. "Well, I certainly didn't come in search of amorous consolation. I've known you too long for that. Being in your presence reminds me how old I am–but as long as I'm on the island, you'll always be here, won't you? If I live to be 90, you'll still be nestled in your shady corner of the *Sprite*'s balcony on warm summer nights, swilling absinthe as if it were nectar, looking out to sea with Lucifer's Light reflected in your eye. No matter–I'd been seduced by the Devil long before I met you, and was always content to make love with his minions. I'm a poet, after all, even though my muse isn't quite as demanding as Phelim's."

"Speaking metaphorically, of course," I said, suspecting the opposite.

"If dream-makers were indwelling pets," Hecate said, pensively, "a generous owner might accommodate more than one. Are our souls really our own, do you think, Axel? Are the aspects of us that become ghosts when we die really *us*, or merely our tenants... our possessors?"

"We don't become ghosts when we die," I told her. "If we see ghosts–and I don't deny that we sometimes do, or that your dear friend Vashti Savage hears them when she goes into a trance–it's because art gives us the ability to conjure them up within ourselves, by means of morpheotic flux. But the flux isn't independently alive; it's neither a predator nor a parasite; it's the greater and better part of our own selves."

"Is that Tybalt's ghost I hear, saying *mere wordplay*?" She was still procrastinating, but I could see that she was bitterly aware of her own cowardice. I had to give her time, and allow her to approach her anguish in her own way.

"No," I told her, sternly. "It's your own doubts in disguise. You don't have to trust anyone's word–all you have to do is think about it for yourself. Examine yourself, as objectively as you can. Study yourself. Come to your own conclusion as to what you are, and what you want."

"All I want, for the moment, is to stay drunk," she said. "Please don't tell me that you're out of brandy, Axel."

I got up meekly, and went to fetch another bottle from the cellar. I could have rung for Jean-Jacques, but it would have ruined the delicate intimacy I was trying to cultivate.

My cellar was usually a placid and welcoming place, even by candlelight, but as I went down the wooden stair shielding the candle's flame with my hand I heard something scurrying behind the wine-racks. I was mildly astonished, but I told myself that there was no need. The earthen walls were plastered, but plaster always cracks when soil stressed by the foundations of a house expands as rainwater seepage turns to frost; no human construction can be entirely safe from invasion when it extends into the bowels of the Earth, even on an island. I couldn't work out, though, whether the invader was more likely to be a large black beetle or a mouse–or an unusually light-footed rat–and I couldn't help wondering whether the talk of ghosts had contrived to infect my own imagination.

After collecting a bottle of brandy, I looked carefully around the racks, but saw nothing. I examined myself, quite objectively, and was astonished to find myself possessed by a strange sense of foreboding. Had Eirene Magdelana been present, she would undoubtedly have told me that the spirits of the surrounding Earth were trying to tell me something–not necessarily that I was in danger, but that something awful was going to happen, in my own house... something whose reverberations would extend even into the cool alcoholic gloom of the cellar.

I looked back again from the head of the stairs before I blew out my candle, but there was nothing to be seen from that angle save for row upon row of corked bottlenecks. There didn't seem to be any prospect of my running out of any kind of liquor for a very long time–but there was something definitely unsettling about the atmosphere of the cellar. When I breathed deeply, the cold air had a peculiar quality about it– not quite an odor, but a heaviness: an oceanic liquidity.

I'd told Hecate the truth when I said that I rarely had bad dreams nowadays, but she was my friend; while her dreams were disturbed, I was bound to sympathize with her plight. I hadn't quite realized how intense my involvement in her predicament had become.

I went back to the dining-room in a different mood. "Tell me about Phelim," I instructed Hecate, when I had replenished her glass.

"What's left to tell?" she countered. "You've deduced the whole story. I fell in love with him when we were neighbors in Ormaux, the way young and foolish people do. He didn't fall quite as far. He had bad dreams, and a sister who never woke up–even though her dreams seemed to be just as bad as his. It's remarkable how expressive a face can be with closed eyes. You'd have been very enthusiastic to paint Candida, I think, if you'd ever seen her walking in her sleep. She didn't often sit up, though, and she wasn't quite as vivid when she was lying down. Three mistresses were too much for poor Phelim–and his sister and his muse were far too much for me, even if they were by no means allied between themselves.

"Phelim liked me enough to try to spare my feelings, hopeless as it was. He told me to go, more than once, and not to come back. I took no notice. I stayed. When I did go, I went back, more than once. It was no good. In the end, I had to do as I was told. I didn't come to the island immediately–I went to the capital, and then to Mielle... anywhere but by the sea. Ormaux is such a busy port... everything there revolves around maritime trade. But I'd always lived by the sea, drawn my inspiration from the sea. I had to come back to the coast–but I didn't come to the island until I could hold my head up and put on an act... just like everyone else. I never imagined that I'd ever see Phelim again. I certainly never imagined that he would sail serenely past the harbor entrance, on his way to Lucifer's Light. If he's a poet still, it must have been his muse that brought him here. He'd never have come of his own accord. Are you ashamed of having known me now, Axel? Have I revealed my silliness, and forsaken my place in the foreground of your life? Have I faded away into the unfocused crowd?" Her tone was mocking, but she cared. She was artist enough to value my opinion as a connoisseur.

"Of course not," I said. "You'll always be unique." I was slightly disappointed, though; I'd hoped for more detail.

She got up from the armchair and began pacing back and forth across the hearth-rug. It was as if she really were animated from within by some stray and restless spirit that had invaded and disrupted the calm of her being. Her eyes flickered from side to side as if in search of something lurking in the margins of her field of view: something vague, supple and malevolent. It wasn't the brandy that was troubling her but something she'd consumed before coming to me: not wine, I guessed, but absinthe. What Eirene Magdelana called morpheotic flux always finds peculiar nourishment in a combination of wormwood and disturbing memories.

"The worst mistake you could make," I said, meaning it kindly, "would be to fall in love with a man like that for a second time."

"Do you think I don't know that?" Hecate retorted. "Do you suppose I'd have any choice in the matter?"

"Yes," I said, simply. "I know that you'll have a choice– but it may be difficult to exercise while everything you fear remains out of your line of sight." I had guessed by then what it was that she wanted from me, so I added: "Would you like me to go with you when you go out to Lucifer's Light?"

She pretended that it was my idea, and a surprising one– but the pretence was unconvincing.

"Would that be wise, Axel?" she said, softly. "I should face him on my own, don't you think?"

"It might make it a great deal easier for you if you had company," I said, "and it will even up the numbers, if his sister really is awake."

"She was never less than fearsome, even when she was asleep," Hecate admitted. "She demanded so much–but you'd be a match for her, Axel. You're a match for anyone, aren't you?"

"A discarded mistress of Morpheus," I murmured, "who thought she'd be forever in his arms... except that nothing lasts forever. Gods are fickle lovers, if myth is to be trusted. Perhaps she'll understand how you felt, if she really has been cast aside by her jealous lover."

"Perhaps she will," Hecate agreed, although she didn't seem to think that she would gain any benefit from that kind of understanding. "But I'm afraid–there, I said it! I've confessed to the man whose opinion matters more to me than anyone's that I'm afraid! It's a terrible thing to say, but I might need your help to face this ghost. I have nothing to offer in return, alas."

"You don't need to offer anything in return," I assured her. "Although, as it happens, you do have something. I'd like to paint you one more time, if I may."

"Because I'm haunted?" she guessed. "Did anyone ever tell you that you have something of the ghoul about you, Axel?"

"Of course. Who better than a ghoul to assist you in a matter like this? But assistance is all you need, not protection. You're stronger than you think, Hecate–much stronger. You might not have been a match for Candida Kracy before, but you are now. You could settle this matter by yourself, but I'll be delighted to go with you to Lucifer. Should I talk to Hillbeck, or would you prefer to wait until the causeway's properly exposed?"

"I'll wait for the causeway," she said. "I need time to prepare. If it were only Phelim... but to see Candida, awake..."

"Perhaps I'll be tempted to paint her too," I said, trying to make light of the possibility.

Hecate came to a halt then, her profile lit by the flickering firelight–and again I heard something scurrying behind the wainscot that probably wasn't actually there. "You will," she said, in a voice that had recovered a little of its usual confidence. "More to the point, she'll be tempted, too."

4

I talked to Hillbeck anyway, on the following day–ostensibly to ask him if he would come to ferry us home from Lucifer if Hecate and I walked across the causeway when it was next exposed, but actually in the hope of obtaining more information about Phelim and Candida Kracy.

Alas, the boatman had no talent for detailed observation. "Pretty enough," was his verdict on Candida, "but passing strange. As for him–won't last. Not the sort. Running away from something, I dare say, thinks a lighthouse is a good place to hide. 'Taint so."

"Did you say anything to them about the *Haemon Redondo*?" I asked. "Master Commonal doesn't want them bothered by silly rumors."

"Not my place to say anything," Hillbeck observed. "He mentioned it to me, mind. Asked me if I knew where the ship went down. How should I know? Have to ask Master Barling, I told him. He's the type to know about things that happened before anyone alive was born. Master Barling's been out to the rocks–though not as often as you have, sir–but he prefers to go out by the causeway too. I give him a flag to hang out, to summon me when he's ready to come back. I'll do the same for you."

"I thought Master Barling suffered from seasickness?" I said.

"Yes, sir, that he does, but not so bad he's willing to wait for the next low tide but one before coming home. Never get two in daylight, sir–not at this time of year."

After seeing Hillbeck, I set out on a much longer expedition, to pay a call that was somewhat overdue, of which my conversation in the *Sprite* had served to remind me.

Although it's the highest point on the island, Snowspur isn't really a mountain and is far more often capped with cloud than fallen snow. The exposure of the island to the weather-fronts moving eastwards from the ocean does, however, ensure that Snowspur suffers far more wind than any mainland ridge of comparable height. It's struck by lightning with remarkable regularity, twice or three times every year; no tree that ever struggled to extend its branches to the sky from the ragged peak survived unblasted for long.

Snowspur's peak was no place to build a house, but there was a hollow beneath an overhanging ledge, only a hundred meters from the summit, which qualified as a place of relative safety; it was there that Eirene Magdelana had established a home of sorts. She had improvised a series of walls beneath the ledge, compounded out of brick, loose stone, canvas, mortar and mud; they formed a chimerical edifice that was part hut and part tent. No sane person would have lived there, but no sane person did. There was only one man on the island who could instill enough composure in Eirene to enable her to remain coherent for an hour at a time, and only one who ever deigned to try.

A cold, damp April day was by no means the best time to make an ascent of the mountain, but I knew that the path leading from the road where I left Jean-Jacques to wait with the carriage was trustworthy and well-worn. Eirene walked up and down at least twice a week to obtain provisions from one of the farms nearby. She still had money lodged with the island's banker; I had no idea how much, but I presumed that her capital would last as long as she did.

Eirene was sitting outside when I arrived, in the early afternoon–not in front of her residence but on top of it, on the ledge that formed its narrow roof. The cloud had let the summit alone for once, but the wind was blowing keenly from the northwest–the direction from which a keen-eyed person could just make out the tip of Lucifer's Light.

"I knew you were coming, Axel," she said. "You've news for me, I think. I've been waiting a while, but the wind bade me be patient and the rain didn't care to let the secret out."

She could have seen me approaching simply by walking 30 meters or so around the shoulder of the mountain, but that wasn't what she meant.

"I've news of a sort, Eirene," I agreed, as I laid out the gifts I had brought on the bare rock: a freshly-baked loaf, a round cheese, a bottle of red wine and a phial of laudanum. She picked up the bread immediately, and began to break it piece by piece, feeding the morsels into her mouth and nibbling at the cheese in between. I uncorked the wine for her and she took a liberal swing. She offered me the bottle, but I shook my head.

"The voice of the air is faint at the best of times," she told me, between mouthfuls. "The spirits of the sea can only whisper, but their whisper is as clamorous as it is corrosive when they scent ripe flesh. There's ripe flesh in this, Axel, and flesh that's doomed to quick decay as well."

"Not mine, I hope," I said, although I wasn't entirely sure of the wisdom of saying so, given that it was almost a question. Questions tended to confuse her.

Fortunately, she didn't seem to notice. "They can't catch your scent," she said. "Your flesh has no odor, for creatures of that kind."

"There's a new lighthouse-keeper on Lucifer," I told her, wondering if his–or his sister's–might be the "ripe flesh" of which she spoke.

"I dreamed about him," Eirene admitted, furrowing her brow. "I dreamed that I knew him well, but I can't see his face. It's eclipsed by Edom's–but all faces have grown somber now that I'm lost." She sobbed abruptly, as she often did when pronouncing the name of her old mentor, but she didn't pause for long. "What have you made of me, Edom?" she whispered. "What have you made of our dreams? But the keeper's not the one... not the one who's still to come, whose flesh is ripe... Oh, Edom, Edom! It's my time too–I can't imagine that I'm safe, Axel, when the clouds can reach me. The clouds are the sea riding on the wind, and they have the sea's interests at heart as well as the sea's power to drown and wash away. Had I not ceased to care about the demands of the flesh, I might be afraid. Oh Edom, Edom! Was it always bound to come to this?"

Her mournful tone wasn't matched by any uncertainty in her actions. I watched her devouring the bread and the cheese, sucking on the mouth of the wine-bottle like a babe at the teat. I believed what she said, though. The demands of the flesh hadn't released their grip on her, but she had ceased to care about the kinds of rewards they offered to ordinary folk.

While I watched her, the wind seemed to be eating into my flesh despite the warm cloak I had wrapped around my upper body. The cold air I drew into my lungs as I breathed seemed strangely dank and stagnant, although it should have felt fresh and sharp. I knew that the sensation had to be illusory, but I had no idea why I was dreaming it, let alone why I was dreaming it while wide awake

"The lighthouse-keeper's name is Phelim Kracy," I told Eirene Magdelana. "He has a sister, who used to live in a perpetual dream–I think she has awakened now, though."

Eirene stopped eating, and sat very still for a moment or two. "Phelim," she repeated, eventually. "Yes, that was his name, Phelim. A thankless child, but... not as thankless as Lucian."

I presumed that she must mean Lucian Sombre, the reputed black magician: the father of her mentor, and the pioneer of modern morpheomorphology. I had no idea why she would describe him as "thankless." The more interesting datum seemed to be that she seemed to know Phelim Kracy's name. I had to be patient, though, and to hope that she would offer more information of her own volition before I risked prompting her.

After a while, she resumed eating, The food seemed to bring her down to Earth. She was nodding her head repeatedly as the information I had given her soaked into the deeper layers of her consciousness. "I knew that I knew him," she said, "although his face was confused with another's, and with Edom's. So he's coming here at last, a hundred years since the ship went down. Not chance, Axel. Not coincidence. The morpheotic flux is all astir; the sea and the rocks are dreaming, and Lucifer's dream has been Lucian's since Vyvyane went down. I knew. I knew I'd live to see the day, if not too many others. It's the clouds, you see... the somber clouds..." Except, of course, that it might have been the *Sombre* clouds.

My breath had caught in my throat, but I suppressed the question that rose to my lips. I waited until she had shoved Edom Sombre's image to the back of her mind and returned to the issue of present consideration.

"Phelim was a child when I last saw him, unformed by any dream," Eirene went on, eventually. "His mother Karenne was one of Edom's, one of Lucian's... one of the favored few.

I never ministered to her dreams as a healer might, alas... I never did. Bad woman, mother, healer... and mad."

"Phelim came here with his sister Candida," I said, keeping my voice as neutral as possible.

"No sister," Eirene said. "All alone. If I had been a *sister* ...no need, no need at all. Poor Lucian." She sobbed again, clearly in distress. I was still at a loss to know why; I hadn't come to upset her, or to find out more about Phelim Kracy. I had to agree with her, though, that it couldn't be chance, or mere coincidence, that she had known his mother. I didn't believe that the world dreamed, or that its dreams could be shaped by any god or healer, but I knew that there had to be a pattern here, of causes and effects.

I knelt down and put my hand on the old woman's shoulder. There seemed to be hardly any flesh upon the collarbone and the blade, but she wasn't starving. She was old–75 at least, I thought–and it was time alone that was shriveling the meat on her bones. She was still powerful, though, in her own way. Her hands hadn't much strength, but they certainly had power.

"They needed me," she whispered, "but they couldn't recognize their need, and I wouldn't. Bad. So he's come, has he... with his father following behind. Why? Running away? Yes, in panic–but panic sometimes leads us where we need to go... he's drawn, Axel, like a toy on a string. He'll come too, Axel, I know it. He'll come too, now. But the sea scents ripe flesh, and there's death and decay on the air. Bad... and mad. But music, too... music, too."

I didn't dare to ask for any explanation of the cryptic parts of this speech, although the puzzle seemed to be growing uncontrollably. Perhaps, in retrospect, it wasn't just the fear of making her even more confused that stopped me; perhaps I didn't ask because I didn't want to spoil the game. There had always been an art in the interpretation of Eirene's ramblings, and I was ever the artist.

I had guessed, of course, that there was a greater game afoot than Hecate's haunting before I set foot on the mountain;

now that I was here, sharing Eirene Magdelana's communion with the winds, I was perfectly certain of it. I was haunted too, and not by any mere emotional infection. It wasn't just to help Hecate that I had to go to Lucifer.

The cold had settled into my bones by now–but not lightly, as one would expect of mountain air. Whatever was welling up inside me was heavy. It was inside me, of course, even though it seemed to come from without. I was reacting to something–not merely something that was in the air, but something more profound. Unlike Eirene Magdelana, I had only a rudimentary morpheomorphic gift; the only dream-shaper I could influence very powerfully was my own, and the principal means by which I could do that was the application of my painter's eye, which often saw more than my con-sciousness knew. I knew now that I had seen something at the *Sprite* when Hecate saw her ghost–something contained in Hecate's frightened eyes, which had awakened the urge to paint her again. I had sensed something horrid; something that had to do, though I could not tell how or why, with the wreck of the *Haemon Redondo*. Hecate had sensed it too, although she had no more idea than I did as to what it might be.

There are puzzles that ought not to be hurried merely be-cause they might lose their savor if they were; there are others which must not be hurried because they are intrinsically stub-born and grow rigid rather than yielding. This one was stub-born. I knew now, though, that I had been moved by some impulse wiser than my conscious mind to introduce the topic of morpheomorphism to the discussion in the *Sprite*, almost as soon as Hecate had confessed that she had seen a ghost.

There was art in all of this, and purer art than my per-sonal taste could readily entertain.

"My friend Hecate Rain knows Phelim Kracy too," I told the madwoman of Snowspur. "She was once in love with him, but it ended badly. She never expected to see him again–but she came here, and he has come too, albeit belatedly. I think she knew, without ever admitting to herself that she knew, that he would come here one day... because of the *Haemon Redondo*."

"Even poets can be deaf to their inner voices," Eirene observed, as the food took further effect on her composure. "Your friend came here for her own reasons, I dare say–but in her dreams she must always have known that he... they... would come here one day for their own, even if he never told her his most precious secret. You must be careful of your friend, Axel. Phelim is his father's son. The ghosts can have no interest in her, but when ghosts rise, one woman's flesh may smell as sweet as another's... believe me, Axel, I know."

I knew that Hecate believed in the surviving spirits of the dead, even though I had tried so hard and often to persuade her of their non-existence–and I knew, too, that because she believed in such things, they had the power to hurt her. Phelim Kracy must believe in that kind of ghost too; a man who believed that the maker of his dreams was a living entity, afflicted by a parasitic muse, would hardly scruple to believe that the dead might return. But the *Haemon Redondo* had gone down a hundred years ago, long before Phelim and Candida Kracy–or their mother–had been born. What, I wondered, could its dead possibly have to do with them?

"Hecate feels a need to confront the spectre of her lost love," I told the morpheomorphist. "She's been waiting a long time, without ever letting her waking mind know that she was waiting. I've agreed to accompany her to Lucifer when the low tide next exposes the old causeway."

"You've no need to be afraid, Axel," Eirene said, with an anxiety in her voice that did not suit the words. "You were my last success, my last prodigy. How proud Edom might have been of the kind of work I did with you, had he not had Lucian's ambition to bear! You've made a peace with your dreams of which few men are capable. If you're careful, you can shield your friend. As for the others... they can never be safe. Lucifer's Light might be the worst place in the world for them, but it must be where they need to be. The Devil's waters haven't fed their addiction for a long while, and when the thirst for dissolution comes upon them, they're more avid by far than any earth hungry for dry decay, or any fire eager for cremation. Were they here with me they'd be no safer, for the sea and the air have a compact whose amity is thunderous cloud. I'm not safe myself–although that doesn't matter in the least, for there's very little left of me now but dreams, and whatever may become of my flesh I shall be part of the world's dream forever."

"Dreams aren't as real as that, Eirene," I said to her–although I knew how dangerous it was to risk challenging her. "They may be beautiful, sublime, even powerful, but they can't exist outside a dreamer. They're not material, let alone alive."

"Don't try to tempt me, Axel," she said. "You always try to tempt me, every time you come. You understand, although you pretend otherwise. Of course, they aren't material–but who cares about that? They're true. You know that very well. You come here with your bread and wine and cheese, always anxious for the fate of my flesh, but you know full well that the sustenance I offer you in return is more valuable by far. You pretend to be concerned for your friend, but you ceased to dream about her long ago. What you care about is the flow of the story, the color of the music, the mood and expression of the distant voice, the forlorn steps of the eternal dance of time and chance. You have an eye as keen as any I ever encountered, Axel, but your flesh has no odor in the elemental world. I think you were sent here to try me, but it won't work. You have no power of seduction over me. I was the one who helped you to shape your dreams, Master Rathenius. I know you better than you know yourself."

I didn't point out that she didn't know herself any longer, or that she no longer had sufficient clarity of mind, most of the time, to shape the dreams of a beetle or a bird. Her art was pure, now–powerful, to be sure, but entirely lacking in what Tybalt Sphendon would have called the ability to draw order out of chaos.

"I shall always be grateful to you, Mother Magdelana," I said, sincerely. "You taught me the folly of aspiring to purity, and the necessity of imperfection in art."

"Don't mock me, Axel," she said, grimly. "I could curse you yet, if I'd a mind to. Edom taught me more than you'll ever know! I have spirits at my beck and call that dream the very fabric of matter and time. I could curse you all, but I never would. Karenne Kracy was my friend once, in spite of all that I did not do, and I balanced her baby on my two knees. I wouldn't hurt a friend of yours, either, although you have not always shown your friends such consideration yourself. When I tell you that you have no need to be afraid, it's because I expect you not to play the fool. If you're determined to endanger yourself, I suppose, there's no better time than now–and no better place to start than Lucifer."

"I would never mock you, Mother Magdelana," I said, still speaking with the utmost sincerity of which I was capable. "I value your advice, as I always have."

"Well, you have it. I've been dreaming a great deal lately, and the wind has been insistent in its whispers. The dead won't be easily avenged, but they'll have their way. The sea will claim its due, in lives lost–but you'll be safe, unless you're reckless enough to endanger yourself. How's that for an oracle, Master Doubter? How close must I be to the world of the dead to cry its news so clearly? But you brought news to me that I needed, so it's only fair."

It was more than I had expected, although it was less than I now desired to know. I wondered whether I dared to risk a question–but I didn't know which of several carried the greatest risk, or might tell me what I needed to know if an answer were forthcoming. I decided to stick to my original intention. I moved closer to her, shuffling along on my knees, and I bowed my head. The cold in my bones shimmered like the surface of a Moonlit lake; I could see it now as well as feeling it, but it wasn't yet a ghost. It had no face.

"I need a dream, Mother Magdelana," I murmured. "I want to help my friend, and I need more insight to do it."

She cackled. "Liar!" she said. "You want to help your-self, as always. And why shouldn't you? You're a visionary, Axel Rathenius, and visionaries must dream, whether their visions turn to nightmares, or dissolve in the song of wind and water. Oh, Edom, Edom! Why shouldn't you offer yourself as a blade to cut, a swordpoint to penetrate, a brush to apply the color of the world? You'll see the dead soon enough, Axel–why shouldn't you do their work?"

So saying, she placed her hands on my head for a mo-ment or two; then, turning her body squarely towards me, she put her arms around me and hugged me like a son.

I was too comfortable to realize, for a few minutes, that she was weeping copiously.

"It's all right, Mother Magdelana," I said, when I did re-alize–easing myself from her grip as I said it. "I don't intend to lose you just yet to the wind and weather. It'll be summer soon enough, and you'll be warm again."

"I don't care whether my flesh is warm or not," she said, bleakly. "My soul is safe within the dream of the world. I shall see you once more, Axel. Once more, and once only. You don't have to be afraid. There really is no need to be afraid–unless you want to be."

5

Two days after my expedition to Snowspur, the spring tide retreated far enough from the northwest shore of the island to expose the ancient causeway that once bound Lucifer to the rest of the Empire's primary landmass, when the sea-level was lower than it is today.

After our loud discussion in the *Sprite*, the news had, of course, spread far and wide that Hecate Rain had once been in love with the new lighthouse-keeper and was determined to have a reckoning with him, but the only three people who actually came out on to the Knuckle to see us off on our adventure were Hillbeck the boatman, Ragan Barling and Fion Commonal. I told Ragan that I would like to see him some time soon, to pick his brains regarding the wreck of the *Haemon Redondo*; he seemed very pleased with my interest, and assured me that he would be glad to help. Fion, meanwhile, cast a skeptical eye upon the wreck-strewn causeway, and begged us to let Hillbeck row us out to Lucifer.

I pointed to the fishermen who'd taken their lines half way to the archipelago. "It's safe enough," I assured him. "I've been this way before, when the wind was brisker and the waves higher. The road won't last, of course, but I have Hillbeck's flag." I took the red-and-yellow pennant that the boatman had given me from the inside pocket of my cloak and displayed it to everyone. When I looked at Hillbeck he nodded, to assure me that he would come as soon as it was displayed, provided that the weather remained calm.

"Before nightfall," I promised him.

"It's safe enough now," Ragan told us, looking up at the placid sky, "but you'd best be careful–the weather can change in a trice, especially when the spirits of the deep are restless. The crew of the *Redondo* have forgotten nothing, forgiven nothing."

"We can do without that sort of talk, Ragan," Fion told him, sharply. "There's been too much of it lately, in the Council's opinion. The idea of holding a commemorative concert for the early visitors isn't bad, I'll grant you... but there's been far too much talk of vengeful ghosts."

"Don't worry, Master Physician," I said, making light of it. "Hecate and I have nothing to fear from the dead of the *Haemon Redondo*. No one now alive had anything to do with the disaster that overtook the vessel."

"The dead follow blood," Ragan stated, stubbornly. "Curses may be visited unto the fifth generation. That's a fact."

Hecate looked at him scornfully, but she said nothing. The antiquarian turned away from her gaze, pretending to be distracted by something lying near the water's edge, which he hastened to investigate.

So far as I knew, Ragan Barling was one of only a handful of islanders who'd been all the way to Lucifer across the causeway. Except for Hillbeck and other carriers charged with taking supplies to the lighthouse, no one had any reason to do so–and not everyone has my exotic taste in random excursions. Nicodemus Rham, alas, had had no real friends once his wife had departed, and Lucifer itself was no more than a weed-encrusted rock where cormorants and guillemots went to catch fish. I took leave to hope, though, that Phelim Kracy might fare better than his predecessor. Without friends and visitors, as Hillbeck had observed, he might not last long in his new occupation.

"What's that you've found, Ragan?" Fion Commonal asked. "Yet another priceless relic of the long lost past?"

"Alas, no," Ragan replied. "Mere litter, I'm afraid." He didn't bother to display his discovery, which looked like a small bag of some kind, but I saw that he put it carefully away rather than discarding it–which testified to the extent of his disapproval of people who dropped litter.

I took note for a second time of the fact that the line of fisherman drawn along the causeway extended only halfway to the island, to the jutting mass of Dead Man's Fist, and not a step further. My flesh, according to Eirene Magdelana, had no odor that the spirits of the deep could perceive; it was possible that the other islanders–even those who had arrived long after me–had no such confidence in their own undetectability... and yet, the causeway had been built to carry regular traffic in the days when the sea level was lower, before the *Haemon Redondo* went down.

I took Hecate's hand, and led her on to the causeway.

The route we had to follow wasn't much more than a kilometer in extent, but it wasn't an easy path to walk. The weed that grew over the narrow hump was dense and gelatinous; even though Hecate and I had taken care to put on solid boots with ridged soles, it was difficult to avoid slipping. It might have been easier had the causeway been level all the way, but its course was interrupted three times by jutting rocks, of which Dead Man's Fist was the most awkward. The pinnacles of the other two were below the surface when the tide was at its highest but at this low ebb all three presented awkward obstacles to be scaled.

"I can see why they call it Dead Man's Fist," Hecate said, as I helped her clamber over the obstruction. "It's easy enough to imagine a drowning man reaching beyond the surface one last time in search of the proverbial straw, only to close his empty fist on the prospect of oblivion."

"That's a poet's interpretation," I told her. "According to Hillbeck, it's called Dead Man's Fist because it's home to a thriving colony of alcyonarian polyps of a kind known locally as dead-men's-fingers. Why anyone would want to call something whose real name is as beautiful as *alcyonaria* by such a vulgar nickname I have no idea, but I suppose it fits in with the metaphorical sequence that represents the curling spur of land protecting the harbor as the Crooked Finger and the bulge in its middle as a Knuckle."

The interval granted to us by the tide was only 15 minutes more than an hour, and we needed almost every minute of it to reach and clamber up the black slopes of Lucifer, but we kept our footing. No siren eyes stared up at us from the water, tempting us to fall; no phantom hands grabbed us and drew us towards the treacherous edge.

The door of the lighthouse was opened to us before we arrived; our progress had been plainly visible, and we had been watched every step of the way by at least one pair of eyes.

Phelim Kracy wore spectacles, but they must have been ground by an excellent lensman, because he had recognized Hecate Rain while she was still some distance away and had obviously had time enough to conceal his astonishment, if not his embarrassment. He didn't seem pleased to see her; in fact, he seemed extremely miserable, and not a little fearful.

He wasn't as handsome as I had expected–one always expects too much when one hears of people with whom one's friends have been in love–but there was a certain elegance about his spare frame and lean features. He hadn't aged well, although I judged that he wasn't yet 40. His jaw and cheekbones were a trifle too obtrusive, and his slightly hollowed eyes also enhanced the impression that his skull had shed much of its fleshy covering. Were it not for his deeply anxious expression, he would have seemed far too ordinary to take a leading role in the life of a poet like Hecate Rain–or, for that matter, a minor one in mine.

"Hello, Phelim," Hecate said, while he was still staring at her from the threshold of his new abode.

"Hecate," he said, colorlessly. "I had heard, long ago, that you had come to the island. I didn't know whether you'd still be here. I could have asked Commonal, I suppose... and broken my journey from the mainland to call on you, or at least written to you to tell you that we were coming. I'm sorry."

"This is Axel Rathenius, the painter," Hecate said, without accepting the apology. "You must have seen his work, on the walls of fine houses, or in Myrica Mavor's gallery." She knew, of course, that he hadn't.

"I've heard the name, of course," Phelim said, extending his hand to be shaken–but he didn't move aside to let us through the door.

"My notoriety is undeserved," I assured him, as I took his hand. "In a world with a proper sense of value, my name wouldn't be known to so many people who have never seen my work."

"People on the mainland love to tell tales of the island, even as far away as Ormaux," he said, as if it were an explanation. He let go of my hand after exerting no more than token pressure. "The travelers who pause there like to pretend that they've been everywhere, and returned with a rich harvest of precious anecdotes. You're the stuff of legend, I fear, Master Rathenius–all the more so because you never visit the mainland. You were the only man who ever saw Claudius Jaseph's secret exhibition, they say, and the man who spyed on the revenant Conrad Othman as he made love to Dorothea Rosa."

It required all my reserves of politeness and fortitude to ignore the implication of the word *spyed*, and the delay in my reply was long enough to permit Hecate to take charge,

"Let us in, Phelim," she said. "We'll be prisoned here for quite a while, as you well know, and you can't possibly insist that we stay out here on the barren rock."

"I have a boat moored at the foot of yonder stone stair-case," Phelim said, pointing to the rough-hewn quay at which his supplies were landed when the tide was higher. "Master Rathenius and I can haul it to the water's edge, should the sea still be too low to float it. I'll take you back whenever you wish."

"We don't wish," Hecate said, not troubling to conceal her impatience. "Even boatmen who've lived here all their lives have trouble negotiating a course through the Devil's Rocks—I'd never risk them in company with a newcomer. When we're quite ready to go, Axel will summon Hillbeck."

Phelim Kracy obviously didn't like the assumption that Hecate, and she alone, would decide when we were "quite ready" to go. In the end, though, he stood aside to let us through. He had no choice.

I made my way into the familiar interior of Lucifer's Light. The ground floor of the circular edifice was unevenly trisected by partition walls, which separated a scullery and a storeroom from the principal living space. The living room seemed very cluttered; there was a massive oaken table, with four dining-chairs, as well as two high-backed armchairs arranged about the hearth. There was also a dresser, a sideboard and a crib—all left over from the days when Nicodemus Rham had been a family man. A spiral stair made of wrought iron ran around the interior of the shell, but only parts of it were visible; the greater part of its extent was obscured, either by the partition walls or the wooden ceiling, whose beams supported the floor of the bedchamber sandwiched between the ground floor and the lamp-room.

The table was laden with the remains of a meal: two bowls with spoons and three plates, two with forks as well as knives and the third heaped with fish-bones and oyster-shells. There was a half-consumed loaf, a half-full butter dish, several jars of miscellaneous preserves, a water-jug and two wooden cups. I knew before I stepped on to the hearthrug that someone would be sitting in one of the chairs, hidden by its high back.

I had sat in that same chair myself, drinking rum with Nicodemus Rham. I was far more eager to see its present occupant than Hecate was; when I moved to present myself, Hecate hung back, staying close to Phelim.

Candida Kracy met my curious gaze with an expression that I can only describe as indefinable. She was wide awake, and gave the impression of being very attentive. She was like her brother in some ways, although she wore her slenderness more comfortably, and the pronunciation of her facial bones was somewhat more refined. The flesh of her face was equally spare, but on her its insubstantiality seemed delicate, an impression aided by the translucent pallor of her skin. Her hair was white–not blonde, for it must once have been dark, but more perfectly white than I had ever seen on the oldest person I had ever met. It had none of the frailty or wispiness of ancient hair, despite its color.

I couldn't quite decide, during that first exchange of glances, whether I wanted to paint her or not. "Miss Kracy," I said, bowing. "My name is Axel Rathenius. Your brother has heard my name, but I dare to hope that you have not."

Her reply seemed a long time in coming, but the delay was caused by consideration rather than hesitation. "And why is that, Master Rathenius?" she asked. Her voice was smooth, not at all unpracticed. She had none of the uncertainty that might have been expected in someone who had slept from the age of seven to 30.

"Because he has only heard rumor of my actions, while he has never seen my work," I said, "and therefore has an ut-

119

terly false impression of me. I had rather you had none at all, until I make one."

I had no more opportunity to be gallant, because Hecate had gathered her strength and shouldered her way past me.

"Miss Kracy," she said. "I'm Hecate Rain. We've met before, although you've never seen me. I used to know your brother very well."

"Yes," the seated woman said, without any conspicuous hesitation. "He's often spoken about you. Forgive me for not getting up. I'm fully recovered, I think, from my long illness, but the journey here was exceedingly stressful. Although I'm perfectly well in myself, my muscles are not yet fully developed after their long indolence. Would you like to sit down?" She spoke freely and fluently. If she had only recently learned the language, I thought, she must have been a very apt pupil indeed.

"Thank you," Hecate said, as she took the other armchair. Phelim and I collected dining-chairs at exactly the same time, then embarked upon one of those curious contests of hastily-interrupted gestures as we negotiated over the available positions. In the end, I was able to place mine beside Candida Kracy's chair, leaving him no alternative but to station himself beside Hecate. In that disposition, I thought, it would be easier by far for us to divide into two parties of two when the time came, so that Hecate and Phelim could pretend a certain confidentiality while I distracted Candida.

For the time being, though, we remained an ill-assorted party of four, awkwardly unsure of where to begin the conversation. In the end, we settled for conventional banality, while we watched one another warily and tried to judge exactly where we stood in respect of one another.

"How have you been, Hecate?" Phelim Kracy asked.

"Quite well," she assured him. "The society of the island suits me. There are so many brilliant people here–it's a pity you'll have little chance to meet them, stuck out here with your light to tend. How are you?"

"Better than when you knew me," he told her, presumably without intending to be cruel. "Candida is much improved, as you see. We've been short of money, but we've never gone hungry. I was hopeful of obtaining a better position than this, but I know that I ought to count myself fortunate to have found it. I'm reluctant to expose Candida to all the hubbub and hazard of the world before she's ready... although we can't ever agree as to the extent of her progress."

"Have you written much lately?" Hecate inquired–wondering, I supposed, how his unruly muse was treating him.

"Nothing at all," he confessed, neither proudly nor ashamedly. "I've had far too much to do, since Candida's narcolepsy relented. She has had a great deal to learn, and life in a busy city like Ormaux can be very confusing. She will be much happier here, I think, at least for a while. She loves looking at the sea and watching the birds that use these rocks as fishing-stations, and we brought a great many books with us. The pause will do us both good, and allow us to collect ourselves." He seemed to me to be working very hard on his explanation–and Candida's languid eyes seemed slightly amused, as if she were savoring his performance. I couldn't believe, as I studied her, that she had come back into the world an utter innocent, with the knowledge and skills of a child; nor could I believe that Phelim was the decision-maker who had brought them here.

"Perhaps you'll start writing again, now that you have the benefit of relative quiet and solitude," Hecate suggested, more sarcastically than was necessary.

"Perhaps I will," Phelim replied, evasively. "When Candida is entirely ready for the complexities of society, we might be able to visit the island occasionally. The last keeper was a recluse, I understand, but it isn't strictly necessary for us to be completely isolated. The Councilman, Master Commonal, mentioned the possibility of appointing a deputy, who could relieve me at my post from time to time. In time, you may be able to see more of us–without the necessity of making that awkward passage across the causeway. I feared for your safety as I watched you–the weed is treacherous, as I have discovered while gathering shrimp and shellfish, and it becomes more treacherous as you approach the lighthouse. On the other hand, I never knew a place within easy reach of Ormaux where one could cast a net or a line from the shore and bring in such produce."

"You must be careful to cook it well," Hecate said. "A lighthouse-keeper can't afford to fall foul of a bad mussel. Wrecks have been caused by such accidents in the past. Perhaps that's why the *Haemon Redondo* went down a hundred years ago."

Phelim made every effort to control himself. I could see that he had steeled himself against the probability that Hecate or I might mention the *Haemon Redondo*, but he couldn't entirely conceal his sensitivity to the name. "No one knows why the *Haemon Redondo* went down," he said, trying with all his might to make the remark seem innocent.

His sister, on the other hand, didn't react at all; she had presumably heard the ship's name before, but it seemed to me that it was a name of no particular relevance to her. Even so, there was a subtle shift in the room's atmosphere.

Hecate didn't appear to have noticed Phelim's reaction, and didn't seem to know what to say next, so I took up the burden of the conversation's maintenance. "No one knows for sure why the *Haemon Redondo* went down," I agreed, "but there's no shortage of rumors just now, for all that it happened a hundred years ago. The lighthouse log was lost and no one seems to know what became of the keeper. Some say that he was ill, or drunk, that night–I've even heard it said that he was bribed to extinguish the light, while the islanders lit a beacon on the Knuckle to persuade the ship's master that he was still in deep water as he ran into the rocks. That last story must be false, I think. Any cargo carried by a ship that foundered on these rocks would far more likely be lost forever or washed up on the mainland than recovered by the islanders. I'm surprised that Fion Commonal should have taken the trouble to tell you about such ancient history as the *Haemon Redondo*." I knew, of course, that Fion had not–but I was curious to know who had.

"Oh, I knew about the *Haemon Redondo* long ago," Phelim said, affecting carelessness. "I heard the story on my mother's knee. My great-grandmother was one of the passengers lost, while my grandmother was hardly more than a child, and the captain was her husband's brother. The story was handed down through the generations because my great-grandmother was reputed to have been the custodian of the family fortune. If so, it must have been lost with the ship, although my mother could never tell me exactly what form it took. Gems, perhaps."

"More likely humble documents," I suggested.

"Some say that the ghosts of the people trapped in the wreck occasionally come up to haunt the rocks," Hecate put in, maliciously. "Perhaps you'll meet your great-grandmother, when the anniversary comes, and she can give you all the details."

I disapproved of that tactic, and turned so ostentatiously to face Candida Kracy that she had no alternative but to drag her gaze away from Hecate and meet my eyes. "I fear, Miss Kracy," I said, sternly, "that there has been a lot of foolish gossip about these imaginary ghosts. I can assure you that you are perfectly safe here from all supernatural harm. Incidentally, while we are on the subject of your family history, I was talking to someone only the other day who knew your father and mother."

"My father and mother!" The agonized exclamation came from Phelim, not from Candida, who seemed more interested than surprised. Again, I had the impression that Candida hadn't the slightest idea why her brother reacted so anxiously; her gaze was far from guileless, and I was still convinced that there was a sense in which it was she rather than her brother who was in control here, but whatever he knew–or thought he knew–about the wreck of the *Haemon Redondo* was his secret and his alone.

"Yes, indeed," I said. "She recalled bouncing Phelim upon her knees, when he were very small. You should be proud, Phelim–she was a great artist in those days, and a great healer too."

"*Who?*" Phelim demanded. The sources of his information regarding such matters as Hecate Rain's presence on the island and my petty dealings with allegedly supernatural forces clearly hadn't troubled to mention the hermit of Snowspur.

"The morpheomorphist Eirene Magdelana," I said "Your mother must have spoken of her."

This time, it was Candida who spoke, while Phelim showed every evidence of being genuinely confused. "I never knew my father or my mother," she said, quietly but not tremulously. "I must have seen my mother when I was a child, of course, but she died before I woke up. I have little or no memory of anything that happened before I went to sleep. Did you ever mention this woman's name, Phelim? I can't recall."

"No," Phelim said. "I never did. Master Rathenius, would you care to take a stroll with me? It would be very good for my sister to have a little female company for a while, if Hecate wouldn't mind."

I could tell that Hecate minded very much, and would far rather have taken a walk with Phelim herself. I was minded to refuse, and to suggest that he take Hecate out instead, but then I hesitated. I met Hecate's eyes with my own; I did my best to signal that her turn would come soon enough, but that it might be wise to let me scout the territory before she tested its borders.

Candida tipped the balance by saying: "I should like that very much, Miss Rain, if you don't mind."

Hecate wasn't one to prefer the company of her own sex, even though she was such fast friends with Vashti Savage–but nor was she the kind of person who could refuse a seemingly heartfelt plea. "I don't mind at all," she assured us all, not trying particularly hard to sound sincere.

6

Almost as soon as we were outside, Phelim Kracy said: "I wish you hadn't come here, Master Rathenius. It's too soon–far too soon. I thought we were safe from visitors, here of all places, until I felt the time had come to issue invitations. It's my fault, of course, for not having written to Hecate–but she would never have dared to cross that causeway alone, and I am amazed that you let her attempt it."

"I'll take due note of your criticism," I assured him, "and of your generous offer to accept a little of the blame yourself. Had you taken the trouble to communicate your feelings to Hecate, I dare say that she might have spared you the inconvenience of her presence–but you must have realized that, even if she dared not trust the causeway, it would only be a matter of time before she rode out in a boat. Don't be too disappointed–you probably spoke more truly than you knew when you said that a little female company would do your sister good. I can understand why the city might have been too much for her, but was it really wise to bring her to a desolate spot like this?"

"Our reasons for being here are none of your business, Master Rathenius," he told me. "My sister's welfare is none of your concern. You know nothing of her case, and I resent your entirely unnecessary attempt to protect her from what you imagine I might have told her about the ghosts of the *Haemon Redondo*. It was Hecate, not I, who brought up the subject of ghosts."

"That is not my recollection," I said, mildly.

"Oh, I don't count what I said to you on the step. I was talking about you, and what I'd heard of you. All nonsense, I agree. I'm glad to find that you don't take it seriously, and have no sympathy at all with these local rumors about the *Redondo* being deliberately sunk. I have none myself." He seemed to me to be a poor liar–and a rather desperate one.

"You must be careful, Master Kracy," I said. "The vocation of lighthouse-keeper can sound appealingly romantic while one is in a busy city, especially to a poet who thinks he might benefit from solitude in returning to long-abandoned work–but that is exactly the kind of person who should never take such a position. Nicodemus Rham was a solid and unimaginative man, who required years to go mad and begin releasing phantoms from the coverts of his imagination. You might not be so resilient."

"I suppose Hecate has told you all about my tendency to madness–the vampiric afflictions of my muse, the terrors that used to visit me by night. Well, I'm better now. As my sister has recovered, so have I."

"Is she fully recovered?" I asked. "If so, she must have made remarkable progress."

"Not entirely. Her muscles and sinews haven't fully recovered from their long wasting. She clings so hard to consciousness that I'm always afraid that she might precipitate a crisis, and slip back into permanent unconsciousness–but she is making remarkable progress. I dread the possibility of a setback, but... well, I must be strong for her sake, and I am. I'm very well, and determined to remain so. That's why I can't possibly resume the relationship I once had with Hecate. I had hoped that she might be... otherwise involved by now."

"She has been and is," I told him. "But some scars itch, even when they've healed. Sometimes, a tiny particle of foreign matter remains sealed up in a wound, ever liable to shift and stir the memory of past pains. If you're cold and careful enough you might set her mind sufficiently at rest that she won't trouble you again. She's resilient enough to bear it, and it might settle her mind. Your sister might not thank you for it, though, if she decides that she wants Hecate to be her friend."

"I told you–that's no business of yours."

"Is it not? Your sister and I have been properly introduced, I think. If she's to obtain a full life, she'll need more friends than you. You might be bound to Lucifer, but she isn't, and I'd be pleased to introduce her to island society–Hecate will serve as chaperone, I'm sure." His appalled expression was a joy to behold, but I didn't wait to hear his adamant refusal. "I think I'd like to paint her, if she'd like that–it might be very good for her to know that she is seen by other people and her beauty appreciated." To tell the truth, I hadn't yet made up my mind about whether I really wanted to paint his sister, but I thought he was behaving badly as well as slyly and I couldn't resist the temptation to upset him.

"I won't permit it," he said, forcefully–but there was a brittle quality in his firmness, which testified that he didn't have the power to prevent it, if she wished it. He looked away, out to sea.

The water was placid, except where the waves broke on the Devil's Rocks, where its grey turned to white foam. The rocks were easily imaginable as miniature mountains, their peaks whitened by bird-droppings and their lower slopes–which were gradually being swallowed by the returning tide–darkly forested with festoons of green and brown weed.

I was tempted to ask him aloud whether he really had the authority to reserve his permission, but thought it better to be diplomatic. "Has my notoriety painted such a terrible portrait?" I asked. "Do you think that I'm a villain, who would do your sister harm?"

"I don't know," he replied, brutally. "I certainly don't intend to take the risk. I'd rather you did not come here again, Rathenius–and I wish that you'd persuade Hecate to let me alone as well, if you can."

"Are you asking a favor of me, in the same breath that you insult me?" I asked, mildly.

"I don't mean to insult you," he said, unconvincingly. "I don't know you, and I'm perfectly prepared to believe that your reputation is exaggerated. Perhaps, when Candida is ready... but I must appeal to you to help me in this matter, and if you really are aggrieved at the notion of being thought a villain, I hope you'll oblige me. I beg you to keep Hecate away, and to keep away yourself, until I feel that the time has come to bring Candida to the island."

"You loved her once," I observed, mildly.

"Who?" he said–a remark of such extreme disingenuity that I was quite taken aback.

"Hecate," I said. "Or was she horribly mistaken?"

He blushed. "No," he admitted, eventually. "She wasn't mistaken. But things were difficult–as difficult as they are now, in spite of all the changes in our situation. I didn't come here to see Hecate again. Perhaps I'll be able to do that, some day–but not now. I should have written to her to explain, but I wasn't sure that she would take me at my word."

That, at least, was wise. Hecate wasn't the kind of person to be put off by explanations; it was a task that required the kind of tactical subtlety that came far more naturally to me than to a man like Phelim Kracy. On the other hand, I wasn't at all sure that she would need putting off. Now that she had seen her old lover in all his ill-tempered inglory, she might well be wondering what she had ever seen in him. I wondered what she might be making of her opportunity to provide Candida Kracy with "a little female company."

"Did you know that Eirene Magdelana was on the island as well as Hecate?" I asked.

"No," he said. "I've no idea who she is–and it doesn't matter. I've not the slightest desire to see some old woman who once bounced me on her knee. Perhaps she was once a friend of my mother's–but my mother has been dead for many years."

"Eirene hasn't forgotten you, by any means." I told him. "She had more than memory to draw on when I told her that you were here. Whether that means that she's been dreaming about you, or whether someone might have mentioned your name to her last time she went down the mountain for supplies, I don't know. She's quite mad, alas, but always strangely lucid in her madness. She talks to the wind, and hears the wind reply. She's heard talk of you in the air's babble–and even though the voice is really hers, there must be some significance in what it says of you."

"I doubt that," was Phelim's defiant reply. He sounded like Tybalt Sphendon accusing me of mere wordplay. "She hasn't seen me since I was barely able to walk, and I've never thought of her at all. There's nothing significant in the fact that we're both here–nothing at all."

"She might be able to help you even now," I told him. "She hasn't lost her talent for shaping dreams–if anything, it's grown along with her madness. She's not in the least danger-ous, and with proper assistance she might do a great deal for you and your sister."

"Thank you," he retorted, "but I've already refused your help and pleaded with you not to interfere. All we want–and need–is to be left alone. I shall explain that to Hecate myself, since you seem disinclined."

"Explain away," I said, generously. "Hecate is a good woman and a fine poet–she can see reason as clearly as any-one." It was my turn now to look negligently aside, staring out to sea.

Where, I wondered, was the shattered carcase of the *Haemon Redondo*? Where were the bones of her passengers and crew? Scattered over many a mile, I suspected. And yet... the air had a strange tang to it that was more than brine and rotting weed. There was an odor in it that I had never sensed before. It was certainly not a reaction to Phelim's leaden pres-ence, but it might have been a lingering impression made by his sister.

The dead won't be easily avenged, I quoted, within the private silence of my skull, *but they'll have their way. Alas, Eirene, the dead don't return, and they can only have their way if the living will act on their behalf–which I might even try to do, if I could only make sense of this mystery.*

Hecate Rain was, indeed, a fine poet, and a woman who could see reason. She had been sorely annoyed when Phelim and I had left her with Candida Kracy, but she hadn't wasted the opportunity. By the time that we returned, Candida was all a-bubble with excitement. Hecate seemed very pleased with herself, but as I looked down at the seated women I wasn't sure which of them had proved the more dexterous manipulator.

"You were right, Phelim!" Candida said. "I need female company. I need friends. Hecate and I shall be great friends, I think. She says that Master Rathenius is anxious to paint my portrait. Has he spoken to you about it?" Hecate had made that up, of course, but it had been a clever invention.

"He has," Phelim admitted. "I refused. You aren't ready. He understands, I think."

"Oh, no," Hecate was quick to put in. "Axel is a true artist. He understands that nothing must stand in the way of art. If you won't trust him to look after your sister with sufficient care and tenderness, you must trust me. I'll be glad to lodge her in my home–unless, of course, you would prefer that Axel came here to paint her?"

"I can't permit..." Phelim began–but Candida didn't let him finish.

"Your permission has nothing to do with it!" she said. "Hecate is so kind, so generous... I would love to accept her invitation. You said, did you not, that I need female company? I'm to be painted by Master Rathenius! Hecate tells me that his portraits are to be found in all the finest houses in the capital."

"It's not possible," Phelim said, trying to sound adamant, although his voice was reduced to a murmur. Clearly, it was possible, and seemed already to have become inevitable. His eyes were moving swiftly from side to side, in search of a way out of the web that Hecate and his sister had spun between them, but he wasn't quick enough to think of one.

"You must walk with me now, Phelim," Hecate said, sternly. "We haven't seen each other for so many years–we have a great deal to talk about, have we not?" She stood up as she spoke, and took the lighthouse-keeper by the arm. I doubt that he had ever seen her in such a commanding mood before, She had grown since he had known her.

"I don't..." he began.

Candida interrupted him again. "Oh, please," she said. "I do so want to talk to Master Rathenius. I must. And Hecate is right, is she not? You loved one another once, and only parted because of me. You must talk to her confidentially, make adequate amends if not a new start. You must, Phelim!"

I doubted that Phelim Kracy had ever seen his sister in such a commanding mood either. It annoyed him bitterly, but it was an annoyance he dared not show. He was supposed to have his sister's best interests at heart, and might even have convinced himself that he had. He was confused now, and knew that he had made a mistake in leaving Hecate behind with Candida. It seemed to me that he had done it because he couldn't face Hecate rather than because he believed that he could make an ally out of me; if so, he now had to pay the price for his cowardice.

Hecate steered him towards the door.

7

I sat down in the armchair that Hecate had vacated, and waited for the door to close again. The strange perfume that I had detected in the air seemed to have accompanied me into the lighthouse; it was more sensible now than it had been before. I wondered again whether it was an impression that Candida Kracy was imprinting upon me—if so, I thought, I would rather it let me alone. I didn't want to be possessed by any dream of hers, even though Eirene Magdelana had assured me that I had no need to be afraid... unless I wanted to be.

"Have you painted Hecate?" Candida asked, as soon as the latch clicked.

"Five times," I said. "I thought I had captured her in all her moods, but it seems that I was wrong."

"I should like to see those portraits," Candida said. She was relaxing now, but there was nothing slumberous about her renewed calm. "I must apologize, Master Rathenius, for my presumption. I told Phelim that you were anxious to paint me, but Hecate had no right to say that, had she? I should have asked you first."

"Hecate has every right to make promises on my behalf, in circumstances such as these," I told her. "I'm her friend–and now that I've met you, I believe that I am anxious to paint you. It would be a privilege."

"My brother doesn't want you to do it. He thinks you might seduce me."

"I might try," I admitted–although it hadn't seemed to me that Phelim was frightened of anything so trivial.

She smiled then, radiantly. "I'm glad," she said. "I might, of course, be too shy to be seduced. I've returned to the world a virtual innocent, so my brother tells me–a child, in spite of having lost the bloom of youth." It was obvious from her tone that she thought otherwise.

"You've lost nothing, Miss Kracy," I assured her. "But it's surely remarkable–is it not?–that you are not as innocent as your brother insists. Are you sure that you remember almost nothing of your life before you fell into your long sleep?"

"Quite sure," she said–but she followed it with a pregnant pause. I wondered if she might be tempting me to guess what she intended to say, but I couldn't. I still couldn't define the unfamiliar odor that weighed down the air, but it seemed curiously cloying, like an olfactory echo of the slick slime that lay upon the freshly exposed sea-wreck when Hecate and I set off to cross the causeway.

"I remember my dreams, though," Candida added, eventually. "The best of them, and the worst. I think I have been better educated by my dreams than I might have been by any school in Ormaux."

"Ah!" I said, softly.

It was impossible that she could have lived in her dreams as if in some parallel world, as rich in experience as our own–but what wasn't impossible was that her senses and her mind had been active even while she couldn't wake up or open her eyes, and that her dreams had been partly shaped by what she heard and felt. Even if she remembered nothing of her early life, her mind knew what sight was, and must have been able to add visual imagery of some sort to the sounds and other sensations she experienced without being fully conscious. In brief, it wasn't impossible that Candida Kracy had dreamed, prolifically and productively. If so, she must be a consummate artist, albeit of a very strange kind. One such as she might find it very easy to see ghosts–and to help others see them too, First, though, she would have to find a medium for her art: music, or painting, or poetry... or morpheomorphism.

I said none of this aloud; I simply savored the exotic texture of the atmosphere, and awaited further revelations. They didn't come yet–not, at least, in any form that I had expected.

"According to Hecate, you don't believe in ghosts, Master Rathenius," Candida said, suddenly tentative.

"I don't believe that the dead return, Miss Kracy," I said, carefully, "but I do believe in phantoms within. I believe in ghost-seers, and the power of art to help them see."

It was her turn to say "Ah!" Then she paused, as I had, before saying: "Do you think that your art might help me to see my ghosts more clearly, Master Rathenius?"

It wasn't a question I had anticipated, but it was certainly interesting.

"I was once enabled to see ghosts by another man's painting skills," I conceded, only a little grudgingly, "but music is usually more powerful in that regard. Since Conrad Othman perished, we've been a little short of true genius in that regard, but Davida Amalek has a talent that will surely mature as she grows older and wiser. At present, she might be a little too young, and a little too beautiful... but I mustn't judge her in the absence of evidence. She has been working on a new piece, I believe, and for all I know it could become her masterpiece–although I fear that she has fallen out with her accompanist. It might have to be modified for a new player, and perhaps a new instrument. Still, there will be concerts and

133

recitals aplenty when the summer visitors arrive, and they will begin to arrive very soon now."

"Is music, then, the most powerful of all the arts in the matter of prompting ghost-seers?" Candida asked.

I hesitated, but honesty got the better of me. "No," I admitted. "Morpheomorphism is more powerful still–but I'm not so sure now that I was wise to recommend Eirene Magdelana's therapeutic services to your brother. Given what you've just told me, it seems to me that you might be a trifle oversensitive to the shaping power of dreams. Music might be safer– and whether her compositional skills have matured or not, Davida is a fine player, even without the accompaniment of Tybalt Sphendon's violin. I might be able to arrange something even before the visitors begin to arrive..."

I shivered then, although I didn't know why. It was the kind of random sensation that sometimes caused a superstitious man to say that "a ghost has walked across my grave"– but I wasn't a superstitious man.

"I haven't yet had the opportunity to hear music of the highest quality," Candida said, thoughtfully. "I heard a great deal of it in my dreams, I suppose, but that was mostly voices singing, unaccompanied by instruments. Perhaps that's why I felt such a powerful desire to come here, to a place where great composers live and work. You've deduced, I suppose, that it was I who brought my brother here, not he that brought me?"

"The possibility had occurred to me," I conceded.

"And you've deduced, too, that I lied to him about the reason?"

"I couldn't know that," I told her, gently, "but it would have seemed far more than coincidence that he should come here, even if I hadn't been told that it wasn't."

"By whom?"

"By Eirene Magdelana. She said that the spirits of the sea had brought you, and I think she must have meant that they had brought you, not Phelim. She's mad, of course, but she's rarely wrong. When she speaks of spirits in the sea and spirits

134

that ride on the wind, I always have to reinterpret what she says in other terms, but I can't deny that she has uncanny abilities. I have no idea where their limits lie."

"Did she tell you that I'm in danger?"

"She implied as much," I admitted.

"From the ghosts of the *Haemon Redondo*?"

"From the avid spirits of the sea—by which, I suppose, she might have meant the ghosts of the *Haemon Redondo*, if the dead past really could return."

"The past isn't dead, Master Rathenius," Candida murmured.

"It isn't even past," I agreed. "The dead still exist, in memory and dream. You have no memory of your mother, nor of your great-grandmother, but that doesn't prevent your seeing them in your dreams... or hearing their voices, or sensing the pressure of their hands." I was guessing, of course, but I was confident.

"They woke me in order that I could come here," she told me. "They summoned me... but I can't see them clearly enough to understand exactly why. I know they're leading me, but I don't know where. I'm not even certain exactly who they are. Yes, my mother is among them... but the others I can't quite make out. My grandmother might be one of them, and her mother and grandmother too, but... I need to see them more clearly, if I can."

"If you'll forgive me saying so, Miss Kracy," I replied, "I think you're misinterpreting your experience. I don't say that dreams have no power to make demands, but that power isn't easily shaped by any human will, and it certainly isn't subject to the whims of the dead. When you see your mother in your dreams, it's not actually her that you see but your image of her. Whatever is leading you, it's no more a ghost of someone dead than it's the kind of living creature in which your brother believed when Hecate knew him. Perhaps, after all, you might benefit from the healing power of a morpheomorphist. Eirene Magdelana is mad, but she isn't powerless; if you need to be free of your dreams, it's possible that she can help you."

"Free?" she echoed. "I'm not in need of liberation, Master Rathenius–not at all. I may be summoned and I may be led, but I cannot be forced to do or be anything that I don't wish to do or be. I've been asleep too long, and now that I'm mistress of my fate I intend to remain so. If you really are eager to paint me, would you be prepared to start right away?"

We were nine days away from the centenary of the *Haemon Redondo*'s sinking; I wondered whether that was the deadline she had in mind, in spite of the fact that it was Phelim, not she, who had reacted guiltily to the mention of the wreck.

"I could," I admitted, "if that's your desire–provided that you can continue to overrule your brother's strenuous objections. Are you sure that you're strong enough?"

"It is my desire," she said, "and I'm sure of my ability to sit, if not to dance or climb mountains. Will you join Phelim in making difficulties, or try to bargain with my patience? I do hope not–I had thought that you might take my side in this."

I bend like any other man to the whims of lovely women, especially when they coincide with my own. "I shall be glad to take your side," I assured her. "I am at your disposal, Miss Kracy–but it won't be easy to persuade your brother to allow you to come back with us today. He's bound to play for time, given that he can't forbid you to go."

"My brother no longer has the power to decide my disposition," she retorted, flatly. "If I say that I will come today, he shall not prevent it. I can't be imprisoned here, given that the tide will expose the causeway a dozen more times before the Moon weakens. I shall be much safer going to the island in your company, of course–as he must understand."

"Hecate might be able to persuade him of that, if nothing else," I said, a trifle absent-mindedly. I was remembering yet again what Eirene Magdelana had said about there being no need for me to be afraid *unless I wanted to be*, and wondering exactly how far I did want to venture into this mysterious web of eccentric frustration and strange intention, if there should turn out to be any danger there. There was no contest, of course; having set foot in the labyrinth, how could I turn back without reaching the heart? I had, after all, been assured that my flesh was too cold to tempt the hunger of the stirring spirits while there were warmer and more succulent meats to feast upon. It wasn't as if I were capable of falling in love with Candida Kracy, in nine days or ninety, in the way that Hecate Rain had once fallen in love with Phelim Kracy.

"I'll do it," I confirmed, although it was hardly necessary. "I'll take you back this afternoon, if you wish, and I'll start on the portrait tomorrow."

She smiled again, in such a fashion as to convince me that I'd made the right decision. "Excellent," she said. "I'm in dire need of a pause, so that I might see how things will go once I'm free of Phelim's company. We've never been apart, you see–and I need to be apart, at least for a while, before I decide where I might or might not consent to be led."

I was surprised by this speech, but I was growing used to surprises. I wondered exactly what kind of dream-maker had Candida Kracy in its grip, and why it had woken her up after holding her in a closer embrace for so many years. I could hardly wait to begin painting her, in the hope that I might obtain more insight from the work.

"I wish that I had dreamed of you, Master Rathenius," Candida went on. "Alas, I never dreamed of great painters, or fine musicians, or clever poets. Mine has been a narrower world than yours, for all that it taught me. My brother would far rather I had never woken up–he thinks of dreams as living things, and believed me possessed by some kind of alien creature when I moved in my sleep. Now he wonders whether I am really his sister at all, or a monster in disguise. He used to think himself possessed too, when his so-called muse visited him, although she hasn't visited him since I awoke. I think he suspects that I might be his muse in borrowed flesh, who will become even more demanding in consequence. Sometimes, I wonder whether he might be right. Is it possible, do you think,

137

that my wandering spirit really might have been his muse, innocently plaguing him in intervals when it was displaced from my own flesh by rivals?"

"No," I said, firmly. "I don't think it's possible. But I do think that your brother might need help–and will probably need it all the more if you leave him here alone."

"I always intended to leave him here alone," she said, disingenuously.

I knew without asking that she had never told him so. That had been an element of the deception that had persuaded him to come. Phelim must have known that she had more reasons than she let him know, but he had his own secrets too. He had let himself be persuaded because he had thought that he would be alone with her, separated from the troublesome world and secure in their privacy. Fion Commonal and his fellows on the Winter Council must have mentioned the causeway when they described the post they were offering, but Phelim must have thought it too tenuous a link, and his sister incapable of contemplating such a difficult escape.

"Suppose I hadn't come here," I said. "Would you have come to me?"

"I wouldn't have known of your existence, Master Rathenius or Hecate Rain's kind disposition," she said, "but I would have done what I had to do. I think I would have found you... or someone like you."

"There is no one like me," I informed her, dryly. "Had you found another, you might have been direly disappointed. It will begin to get dark soon. I ought to put out the flag to summon Hillbeck, lest he decide that the light's too dismal to show him a safe passage through the rocks. In that case, we'd be stuck here all night."

"Go up to the light," she said. "You can drape it from the balcony. You'll forgive me if I don't come all the way with you–I must pack a bag, but I find the stairs difficult."

Perhaps I should have waited for Phelim, if only as a matter of politeness. Perhaps I should have gone to the door and called out to him, given that he could hardly be out of earshot–but I didn't.

I went up the spiral staircase all the way to the top. I hung the red-and-yellow flag from the balcony surrounding the lamp-room, on the shoreward side. I looked down then, and saw Phelim Kracy and Hecate Rain standing by the water-side, looking earnestly out towards the shore. They didn't glance in my direction, and I watched them for a full minute before it suddenly occurred to me to follow the direction of their gaze.

A long way away, on the Knuckle, there was some kind of commotion. A crowd had gathered on the rocky spur, and there were boats in the water. The tide was still inbound, but had almost reached its maximum.

Something, I guessed, must have been washed up–something ominous.

I was too far away to make out anything more than a blur of confusion. I couldn't distinguish any face or figure–but I was suddenly quite convinced that what had been washed ashore was a dead man, and that he was someone I knew. If it were also someone Eirene Magdelana knew, I realized, it might not have been the *Haemon Redondo*'s crewmen and passengers that she was talking about when she spoke of the dead having their way.

8

Hillbeck did not set out immediately to collect us, presumably because he had been detained by the crowd on the Knuckle, but he was eventually allowed to come. He set out boldly, even though the twilight was becoming dismal. In the mean-time, Phelim Kracy made his protests to his sister. He forbade her; he pleaded with her; he tried to reason with her–all to no avail. In spite of the fact that Hecate and I remained on the ground floor of the lighthouse while he ranted and railed at her on the other side of the wooden ceiling, we heard everything that he had to say.

All that Candida said in return was that the matter was settled. She had accepted Hecate's invitation, and mine, and she intended to follow her intention through. She was lying, I supposed. Her determination was no mere matter of invitations accepted and promises made–but she was also right to insist that he could not prevent her from leaving with us.

Candida finally came downstairs just as Hillbeck called out to us from the quay. The light of determination in her eye was somewhat steadier than her gait in the staircase; I lent her my arm for support as we made our way through the doorway of the lighthouse and across the dark surface of the rock.

Hecate, meanwhile, assured Phelim that we would look after his sister as well as we possibly could, and that she would be perfectly safe. I could hear her voice quite clearly, and appreciated the measure of steel that it contained. While we crossed the causeway, Hecate had still been nursing the ancient wound that Phelim Kracy's rejection had inflicted on her heart; now, in the space of a single afternoon, it had healed. Like Candida, she had obtained exactly what she wanted, and needed, from our collective encounter. What sort of wound Phelim had nursed as a result of his affair with Hecate I could not tell, but I suspected that he was the loser in that respect as well as in the other. As for myself... I had collected a few more pieces of the increasingly fascinating puzzle, but had not yet begun to glimpse the picture they would make up when properly juxtaposed.

As soon as we were settled on the benches of Hillbeck's vessel, I asked the boatman about the commotion on the shore.

"Man drowned, sir," he reported, laconically. "You knew him, I believe. Constable Clovis wants to speak to you as soon as I can bring you back."

"Who drowned?" I demanded, irritated by his taciturnity.

"Master Sphendon–the fiddler."

140

I had often referred to Tybalt Sphendon as "the fiddler" in my own private thoughts, but the label seemed infinitely more insulting from the mouth of a ferryman. I, after all, knew the true worth of Tybalt's talent. For all his obvious faults of character—which had become far more forgivable in consequence—Tybalt had been a first-rate violinist.

"Tybalt!" Hecate exclaimed, plainly distressed by the news. "Tybalt drowned!"

"Well," said Hillbeck, "maybe not *drowned*, exactly. Master Commonal will have the last word on that. Dead and adrift in the water, at any rate."

"Are you saying that he might have been murdered?" Hecate said, although it seemed to me an unnecessary question.

"Depends," said Hillbeck.

"On what?" I inquired, frostily.

"Is it murder if you're frightened to death by a ghost, sir?" the boatman asked, rather sarcastically—seemingly having had the nerve to take offense at my tone. "Come to that, is it murder if you're drowned by a ghost?" He was plying his oars with gusto as he spoke, but it occurred to me that his eagerness to return to shore might have more to do with catching up on the latest gossip than discharging his duty to his passengers. He did, at least, negotiate a passage through the Devil's Rocks with casual expertise in spite of the gathering mist, moving so skillfully through the treacherous waters that even Ragan Barling might have come through the experience without throwing up over the side.

"What has Tybalt's death to do with ghosts?" I asked, trying for Candida Kracy's sake to make my contempt clearly manifest.

"You didn't see his face, sir, or you wouldn't ask," was the boatman's triumphant riposte. "Never saw a drowned man so tormented in the features. And that wasn't all!" He paused, savoring his advantage.

"What else?" I asked—politely enough, since I had no choice.

"There was rope around his body, sir–not tight-wound, like as to have strangled him, but draped like weed and knotted too... and caught in one of the knots was something else..."

"Oh, get on with it man!" said Hecate. "We're not your grandchildren huddled round the hearth."

Hillbeck had the audacity to look at her as if he had been deeply wounded by her cruelty, but he gave up his telling detail with all the grace and dignity he could muster. "It was a small brass bell–a watch-bell. Too tarnished ever to sound again, I dare say, and encrusted with barnacles... but when the Constable scraped the barnacles off, the name engraved on it could still be made out."

"*Haemon Redondo*," I said, quick to deprive him of yet another excessively melodramatic delay. "How very convenient. A ghost that leaves its signature! Or a murderer... if there was a murder... who believes in the value of distraction."

Hillbeck was not in the least disturbed by the loss of his final punchline. "That's what the Constable said, sir," he announced, smugly. "As I say, he's very anxious to speak to you, Master Rathenius. Told me to fetch you *expeditiously*." He seemed to take great delight in the exaggerated pronunciation of the final word, as if its use were proof of his education.

I knew that there was no need to be afraid, unless I wanted to be. I didn't. "So someone told Constable Clovis that Tybalt and I quarreled in the *Sprite* the night before last," I said. "Fion Commonal, perhaps? I hope that he stressed that it was a disagreement about artistic matters, such as we have in the *Sprite* at least three nights a week. I would be deeply distressed were anyone to think that I could be goaded into violence by a disagreement of that sort. For safety's sake though, I ought to have an alibi. When did Tybalt die, do you think... in your capacity as an expert on the *drowned*."

Hillbeck was as immune to my sarcasm as I was to his. "Two days ago, by my reckoning," he said. "Maybe morning, maybe afternoon, but not the day before or yesterday. Fish had got at him, but they hadn't taken so much off his face that you couldn't see his *expression*."

"Where were you the day before yesterday, Axel?" Hecate asked. There was no amusement in her voice, but no suspicion either. She knew that I couldn't possibly have murdered Tybalt Sphendon.

"On Snowspur Mountain, or in transit between the mount and my home," I said. "My best witness for the time I was not with Jean-Jacques is, alas, a madwoman, but I must have been seen by a dozen field-laborers and shepherds as I went up the hill and came down. Even Constable Clovis cannot believe that I drowned a man on a mountain peak."

That was rather unkind of me, because Clovis was no fool. The Constable rarely made arrests in cases of murder, but that was no reflection on his deductive and inquisitorial skills. Most of the island's murders happened in the summer months, and the aristocracy always take care of their own affairs. No commoner would ever be allowed to arrest the likes of the Dellacrusca twins or the Duke of Alectryon's hired assassins.

"Davida will be desolate," Hecate observed. "If you will forgive me, Miss Kracy, I shall have to combine my duties as your hostess with my obligation to comfort a friend."

"Of course," was Candida Kracy's only response.

It occurred to me that Davida Amalek could not be as desolate now as she might have been in February, before she had transferred her affections to Morloc Hyat. It also occurred to me that I wasn't the only person who had been at odds with Tybalt in the *Sprite* two nights before, and that Morloc Hyat had been more stridently at odds with him than all the rest. I hoped, for his sake, that Morloc had an alibi at least as secure as mine; he was one of the few gentlemen on the island of sufficiently humble status that the Constable might arrest him, if he had a mind to.

When I had followed that train of thought to its destination, though, I realized that I had somehow set aside the real issue. If Morloc had not murdered Tybalt, and the ghosts of the *Haemon Redondo* had not, then who had? And why?

Suicide, I immediately decided, would be the kindest conclusion–but Tybalt Sphendon had never struck me as the

143

kind of man to commit suicide. Losing a lover might make him bitterly angry, but never suicidal.

Hillbeck was hauling on the oars with such awesome determination that we were already more than halfway to the Knuckle, and I wondered momentarily whether we might reach it in time to see the dead man's supposedly-tortured features–but even as I craned my neck to look over the boat-man's burly shoulder, I saw that all but the last remnants of the crowd had dispersed. The body had undoubtedly been car-ried off to Fion Commonal's house, where he would conduct the post-mortem examination.

Hillbeck made for the harbor entrance at the extremity of the Crooked Finger rather than the spot where the body had been washed up, so I never had a chance to examine the scene of the crime. Once we were past the Finger's tip the traffic became heavier; several small fishing-vessels were setting out for the night, and the *Merry Maid* sailed by us close enough to juggle us in her bow-wave and her wake. Our progress slowed, somewhat to the boatman's annoyance, but he finally made it safely to the jetty where his mooring was.

Constable Clovis was out on the quay, waiting for us to arrive, but I had no difficulty persuading him to take us into the *Rope and Anchor*–a relatively respectable fishermen's ale-house–in order that Candida might rest after the passage; it was by no means a salubrious spot, but its fire had already warmed the air, the chairs were well-padded and the smoke from its patrons' pipes had not yet accumulated into a foggy haze. The Constable persuaded the housekeeper to make a pot of tea for the ladies, while he and I sipped fortified wine.

We got down to business soon enough. It turned out, in spite of Hillbeck's hints, that Clovis had not been waiting to cross-examine me as his chief suspect. He wanted Hecate and I to tell him exactly what had passed between Tybalt Sphen-don and Morloc Hyat in the *Sprite* on the night before last.

We both assured him that our so-called quarrel had been a mild dispute about matters of aesthetic theory. When we were asked about the dead man's spoiled relationship with

Davida Amalek, we assured him that he had behaved with dignity under pressure, as befitted a man who had his art to console him, and that he had not given anyone the slightest reason to wreak violence upon him. I also took the trouble to point out that Tybalt was a powerful man, by the admittedly meager standards of our coterie–considerably more so, for instance, than Morloc Hyat–and that it was difficult to imagine anyone not blessed with Dellacruscan brawling skills deciding to start a fight with him, let alone succeeding in killing him in the course of such a contest.

Candida listened with interest to the conversation, patiently sipping her tea, and seemed slightly disappointed when the exchange of opinions came to an end.

The Constable admitted that my argument had the ring of plausibility, and apologized for troubling us. His eyes testified that his apology was sincere. Clovis had been the Constable for nearly 20 years, and there was a sense in which he and I knew one another well, although our paths rarely crossed. He wanted me to know that he was only doing his job. "Do you have any idea, sir, who might have wanted Master Sphendon dead?" was his final question, addressed specifically to me.

It was a good question, I had been racking my brains for inspiration on that score.

"No, I can't," I said, finally. "He was a man with a slightly unfortunate manner, but there was no harm in him. He was a good player, always a reliable and valued accompanist. If someone did harbor sufficient ill-will to kill him, I can't imagine why. I suppose the rumor's running along the waterfront that he was seized by ghosts and dragged into the depths?"

Clovis grimaced, and said: "People do talk, sir. Can't stop 'em, even when it's nonsense."

"No," I admitted. "It can't be stopped, even when the people saying it know full well that it's nonsense. It's a pity that the summer visitors haven't yet arrived, bearing likelier suspects by the score."

He only shrugged at that. The knowledge that this was a murderer he might be able to prosecute made it all the more necessary for him to make a case; his superiors on the mainland would expect it of him.

"Good luck, Clovis," I said, as we left the inn. "If there's any way I can help..."

"Thank you, sir," the Constable replied. "I must try to speak to Master Hyat now, if he's home yet." I inferred that Morloc had not been home when the Constable's men first went to look for him.

The night was well advanced by now, and the Moon was hidden by thick cloud. Although the quay was reasonably well supplied with lanterns, the roads leading away from the town would be pitch dark. The alehouse had filled up with customers, but they were all boatmen; I had to pay one to run and find me a carriage for hire to take Hecate home–or, as she now insisted, to Davida Amalek's house. The mission took longer than it should have done, but a man and a vehicle eventually appeared; it was a cart rather than a carriage, but it was clean enough and the horse had obviously had a great deal of experience trudging up and down the hill with cargoes heavier by far than two slim women. It wasn't until I began to give him instructions that Hecate realized that I didn't intend to accompany her.

"You could take the cart on to your own house when you've dropped us off," she pointed out. "It's not too far out of your way. Or is Jean-Jacques coming to meet you?"

"There's something else I need to do," I told her.

"Is it to do with Tybalt?"

"No–well, perhaps. I suppose his death must fit into the puzzle somehow. That bell from the *Haemon Redondo* must have been tied to him for a reason. I don't know who did it–but I do know someone who might know where the bell was before it turned up on Tybalt's body... among other things that I'd also be interested to know."

"Ragan Barling?" she guessed.

"Quite so. He might be at the *Sprite*, but I'll try his home first. Will you be able to see to Miss Kracy? I'm not sure that's she'll be able to walk very far once the carter's come away."

"It's only a short distance from Davida's home to my own," Hecate said. "Davida has no servant, but I know my neighbors well enough to be able to borrow a man to carry Miss Kracy between the two houses when we've made sure that Davida is all right... if Miss Kracy doesn't mind?"

"Not at all," Candida assured her, "And you must both call me Candida. We must certainly see your friend, if she is likely to be distraught. There'll be no need to hire a man to carry me; I'm perfectly capable of walking short distances."

"Please accept my apologies for leaving you, Candida," I said. "Come to my studio in the morning, as early as you like–or as late. I'll begin making sketches whenever you arrive."

"You're very kind, Axel," she replied. "I'll dream about you tonight–I feel sure of that. I think, perhaps, I'll dream of you every night, for some time to come."

The air seemed to thicken slightly as she said it, and I caught the faintest hint of the odor that I had perceived for the very first time that day, on Lucifer. It seemed to require an uncommon effort to draw the ponderous breath into my lungs.

I knew that Candida was already in my dreams, even though I hadn't closed my eyes since meeting her. Could she, I wondered, be a talented morpheomorphist without knowing it? When she offered me her hand, though, I kissed it politely. It wasn't the first time I had touched her, and whatever risk there might be in the touch of her hand I had already braved.

9

Once the vehicle carrying Hecate and Candida was on its way I set off in the other direction, moving along the waterfront until I came to the foot of the steep lane that led to the district in which Ragan Barling's house stood. It was some time since I had gone that way and I remembered the lane as a rather picturesque setting, whose charm outweighed its challenge. It did not seem nearly so charming in near-darkness–its street-lamps were few and far between, and were fuelled by very poor oil–and its gradient seemed a great deal more oppressive.

The district into which I climbed was a mixed one, where narrow undulating coverts of working-men's hovels huddled in clusters between larger and broader avenues lined with far better houses, which followed the contours of the hill with languid grace. Ragan Barling's house was a tall and narrow building wedged close between its smaller neighbors, with no alleyway connecting its frontage with the stables in the rear. Its upper story loomed up like a square head above broad shoulders, with two round windows whose resemblance to spectacled eyes was further enhanced by the poor quality of their glass.

I had called on Ragan before, but I had never been up to that eyrie, where Ragan hoarded the best part of his dubious treasure–the best, at any rate, in his peculiar estimation. He had conserved his inherited wealth by careful economy, but had never made the slightest attempt to increase it. In terms of merely commercial value, his cellar was probably the only part of the house that would have attracted thieves; like every true antiquary, he had a keen appreciation of old brandy.

He welcomed me into his hallway with the avidity of a man with gossip to impart, and took me through to a sitting-room that was too small to contain the clutter lining its walls. He sat me down on a high-backed chair and poured me a glass of red wine from a half-empty bottle that had been open a little too long. My eye passed over various display-cabinets with scant interest, but alighted on a rather fine harpsichord that stood against the far wall.

"That's new," I observed–meaning, of course, that it must be a recent acquisition.

"Oh no," he said, giggling, "it's very old. Probably the oldest on the island."

"Older than mine, certainly," I conceded. I could have said that practically everything he owned was the oldest of its kind on the island, but I didn't want to risk putting too much strain on his sense of humor.

He was eager to chatter, and seemed rather disappointed that I already knew all about the discovery of Tybalt Sphendon's body.

"They're saying that it was the dead of the *Redondo*," he whispered, in an oddly confidential manner. "You won't believe that, of course, but it's the explanation on everyone's lips."

I squirmed uncomfortably, although the seat of my chair was considerably less uneven than the moth-eaten velvet-upholstered armchair in which Ragan had seated himself, which had evidently molded itself over the years to fit his angular and ungainly body very snugly.

"Not everyone's," I told him, a trifle maliciously. "Constable Clovis is intent on interrogating everyone who quarreled with Tybalt in the *Sprite* the other day. He doesn't seem to be able to make up his mind which of us to choose as a chief suspect. I'd have been glad to oblige, but I was on Snowspur Mountain at the time Tybalt's body appears to have been put into the water. Do you have an alibi, by any chance?"

"Tybalt was my friend!" Ragan protested. "I received him in my house on many an occasion, as I have received you. He shared my antiquarian interests, to some extent, and he did me the honor of treating me seriously, as a wise and good consultant—which I could not say about everyone, Master Rathenius."

"That's a little unfair," I told him. "I'm here now to do you precisely that honor. It's your expertise as an antiquary that I have come, in all humility, to consult. I want to ask you about the *Haemon Redondo*."

He smiled broadly, as if he had known already what I wanted, and was delighted with the success of his anticipa-

149

tion–although it could hardly have been a difficult inference to draw. "You too!" he said. "I really am honored. I didn't know that you painted shipwrecks."

I was momentarily taken aback. "I don't want to paint the damned thing," I assured him. "I want to know why rumor of its dead is on everyone's lips–and exactly what the rumor has to do with Phelim and Candida Kracy."

It was his turn to be slightly flustered. "The new light-house-keeper?" he said. "Why... nothing, so far as I know. I thought you said that he came here because he was once in love with Hecate Rain."

I had said no such thing, but there was no point in calling attention to his habit of reading too much into what other people said. "So far as I can tell," I assured the antiquary, "Phelim Kracy regards Hecate's presence here as an awkward inconvenience. Indeed, so far as I can tell, he regards the mysterious excitement regarding the centenary of the *Haemon Redondo* wreck as a similarly awkward inconvenience–but his decision to come here is connected with the disaster somehow, however arcanely. He says that his great-grandmother was a passenger on the ship, and that her husband's brother was its captain. There was also vague mention of a lost family fortune–the stuff of popular romance, in all probability, but intriguing nevertheless. I was interested enough yesterday to ask if I might come to see you, but I'm doubly interested now that I've actually met Hecate's old flame and his enchanting sister. You're presumably the only man on the island who can cast any light on the matter of what actually happened to the ship. You're certainly the only one who has any chance of cutting through this pestilential fog of rumor to tell me what is actually *known* about the business." I didn't mention the matter of the bell found on Tybalt Sphendon's body; I intended to get to that later.

"Ah!" Ragan said, reveling in smug satisfaction. "*Known*, you say–as opposed to rumored. It's not so easy to distinguish the two at a hundred years' distance. There were written records, of course, but the businessmen of that era weren't such scribblers as their descendants are today. There's nothing in the island's ledgers, you know, because the ship was bound for Ormaux and was only driven to this shore by the storm. Her log was lost, alas. A man would have to go to Ormaux to find a copy of her bill of lading and a passenger list."

"I realize that," I said, "but I know you as a very serious and scrupulous antiquary, Ragan–no mere collector, but a true historian, whose insight into the past is clear and meticulous. You're exactly the kind of man who would have made such an investigation... and made copies of the documents to bring back here. That's why I've come to you, just as everyone else comes to you when they need to know about the island's history."

Flattery, in my experience, can get one anywhere if it is lavishly applied–even the topmost floor of Ragan Barling's house.

"You're right," the antiquary agreed, picking up the candelabrum from the table beside his armchair and standing up. He was trying to stand tall, but he hadn't the stature for it; even so, he had a certain legitimate pride in his stance. He was in his late fifties, but his hair was still black and his neatly trimmed beard hid some of the lines that time had graven on his face. He could still have been reckoned a handsome man, with a little imagination.

"So you did make copies?" I asked.

"I did. I have the names of all the *Haemon Redondo*'s dead. Were they to return, I would be able to greet them as old friends."

It seemed an odd thing to say, but it wasn't a good time to remind him of my skepticism. I let him lead me out of the sitting-room, into the hall and up three flights of narrow wooden stairs–which seemed considerably more treacherous than the wrought iron staircase that wound around the interior of Lucifer's Light–to the attic beneath the roof.

I hadn't left the island since the day I first arrived, long before, so it was many years since I had been in a museum, or seen an aristocrat's cabinet of curiosities; perhaps I might have been less discomfited by the sight of Ragan's multitudinous trophies if I had been more familiar with the habits of the mainland's collectors. As an artist, though, I couldn't approve of the atrocities of taxidermic expertise that crammed his dusty display-cases: fake mermaids compounded from monkeys and fish; sea-serpents created by the careful embellishment of conger eels; flying fish with birds' wings; eyes, beaks and tentacles allegedly cropped from the corpses of krakens. As for his collection of driftwood and bottles, culled from the tide-line over decades... well, the island's beachcombers must have been delighted to have him as a steady market.

Ragan did have some items of genuine interest on display, however, including some exotic shells, authentic sea-horses, and hundreds of small items that must indeed have been the shards of broken vessels: marlin-spikes, forks and shipwright's tools; sailors' chests and items of scrimshaw; shredded signal-flags and hammocks. There were even a few large items, which must have been far more difficult to salvage, including a brace of muskets and a small brass cannon. The display-cases into which these items were crammed stood cheek-by-jowl with narrower cupboards, one of whose doors stood slightly ajar. It was full of little bottles, each one bearing a hand-written label; most contained dried fruits, fragments of root or detached body-parts of vertebrate and invertebrate animals, but some were filled with treacly liquids.

There were several chests of drawers lodged against the walls beneath the slanting ceiling, and it was from one of these that Ragan drew out the documents to which he had referred. He didn't have to rummage for them; they lay on top of the drawer's other contents.

He set the candelabrum down on the chest and moved aside so that I could hold the papers to the light. They were, as he had said, copies made in his own script, but his hand was as skilled as that of any accomplished clerk and the lists were easily legible.

The bills of lading were uninteresting, given that the *Haemon Redondo*'s hold appeared to have been almost entirely filled with cotton and tea, but I looked more carefully at the record of her crew. The captain's name was given as Elgin Bayard, and it only required a rapid scan of the passenger-list to discover a Madame Vyvyane Bayard, who was presumably his sister-in-law and the mother of the anonymous woman whose daughter Karenne had married a Kracy. When Phelim had spoken of the "family fortune," I realized, he must have been calculating inheritance in a highly unorthodox fashion; Madame Vyvyane might have brought her own possessions into her marriage to Elgin Bayard's brother, but even in the days before the adoption of the New Imperial Code made the property of a wife automatically that of a husband, it would not easily have passed through two further generations to Karenne Kracy's children.

The name Bayard meant nothing to me. I was lifting my eyes to Ragan Barling, intending to ask what he knew of that family, when another name on the list caught my attention: *Lucian Embros*.

I had already scanned the name once without pausing, but some curious trick of the light or whim of perception made me see it slightly differently now... almost, but not quite, in reverse.

The great pioneer of morpheomorphism, the father of Eirene Magdelana's teacher, had been Lucian Sombre. Eirene had mentioned his name more than once when I had spoken to her two days before. Sombre was an anagram of Embros.

As the thought formed, it seemed as ridiculous as one of Ragan Barling's mermaids–but Eirene Magdelana had laid her hands on my head, weeping as she did so, and whatever else I might doubt, I couldn't doubt her ability to animate the shaper of my dreams. She had primed the arms of Morpheus within my intelligence, and there was no more coincidence in my sighting the name than there was in its presence on the page. I drew in a long breath, half-expecting the air to seem unnaturally heavy, but it didn't. I wasn't in Eirene's presence now, or in Candida Kracy's.

Ragan, who had become bored with my silent perusal, had idly looked aside, staring out of one of the windows let into the wall overlooking the harbor. It was poor quality glass, cut too near the center of a swirled puddle, so the image of the exterior world was warped as well as dark, but he was presumably well used to the distortion.

"Why," he said, softly, "there's someone on the causeway."

"What?" I peered out of the window, but I couldn't even make out the line of the Crooked Finger or the hump of the Knuckle. What I could see, though, was Lucifer's Light, shining like a huge Moon–and close by, like a tiny star dwarfed by the greater luminary, there was indeed a second and far more fugitive light.

I thought at first it was the cabin-light of a fishing-boat, but time enough had passed for the tide to go out again, and the causeway was exposed anew. I only had to study the movement of the light for a minute in order to be convinced that it was a hand-lantern, lighting the way across the causeway of some exceptionally reckless expeditionary.

Had the light been moving shorewards I would have had to assume that it must be Phelim, who had unaccountably deserted his post–but it was not. The lantern was headed in the other direction, towards the Devil's Rocks–which meant that it might, in theory, be anyone. What islander, though, would brave that path by night? It would require a very powerful motive.

"The man must be mad," Ragan whispered, amplifying my own conclusion, "to walk that way by lantern-light!"

"With murderous ghosts abroad as well," I murmured. "Is it Nicodemus Rham, do you think?"

"Why should it be?" Ragan asked, sharply.

"Can you think of anyone else who might want to go out to Lucifer at this time of night?"

"Old Nick would never go back," Ragan asserted, more vehemently than seemed necessary.

"If not him," I said, reasonably, "then who?"

The candlelight flickered suddenly as Ragan snatched up the candelabrum in a tremulous hand. "I don't know!" he said, fretfully. "You should go now, Master Rathenius. It's late, and I'm tired. Come back another time, at a civilized hour, and I'll tell you all I know about the *Redondo*. Everything known."

I was surprised by his abruptness. "But I wanted to ask you about the bell found on Tybalt Sphendon's body!" I protested.

"How should I know where it washed up, or when?" was his over-eager answer. "How should I know whether it ever washed up at all, or whether some phantom crewmen drew it from beneath the sea-bed to mark his prey?"

"I'm sorry," I murmured, reflexively. I realized that it really had grown quite late while I had been detained in the *Rope and Anchor* by the Constable and had then to toil up the hill to Ragan's house. He was fully entitled to hurry me—but I still had questions to ask.

"Lucian Embros," I said, pointing to the name on Ragan's list. "What do you know about him?"

"Nothing at all," Ragan said, immediately. "I've memorized the name, in case the vessel's dead should ever return, but I never heard it before."

"What do you know of Elgin Bayard, then—the captain, that is—and Vyvyane Bayard, his sister-in-law?"

"Sister-in-law?" the antiquary echoed. "Oh... you said that before, didn't you? Her husband's *brother*. I had always assumed—from the names, you understand—that she was his wife. But you might be right. I did look at some further documents relating to the captain, and he did have brothers. Look, Axel, I'm sorry, but it really is too late. I've had a trying day. Tybalt's dead, remember, and Davida..."

"What about Davida?" I asked, as he trailed off.

"She was supposed to... I don't suppose, now... I should have..." He seemed very disconcerted, and I wondered if he

155

had somehow jumped to the remarkable conclusion that the light on the causeway had something to do with Davida Amalek.

"Hecate has gone to see her," I told him. "She'll look after her. Candida Kracy is with her... an odd combination, I dare say, but I suppose Morloc will be there too by now."

"Morloc?" The candelabrum shuddered again, and one of the candle-flames went out; the other three were all burning low.

"Yes," I said, gently. "Morloc Hyat. Davida will be well looked-after. What was it that she was supposed to do, Ragan? Why are you so concerned for her?"

He turned around, moving towards the attic door with the light in his hands. I had no alternative but to follow him. As I moved past the cupboard whose door stood ajar, my shoulder snagged the catch and pulled it more widely open.

"Leave that alone, please!" Ragan snapped, as I glanced inside before closing the door again. "Davida was supposed to come to see me this evening. I've been... advising her."

"About what?" I asked, as we began to descend the precarious stairway. I wasn't ashamed to keep my hands pressed to the walls on either side of me, given that Ragan's body was shielding the candle-flame.

He didn't answer, but I guessed. *You too!* he had said, delightedly, when I told him that I wanted to ask him about the *Haemon Redondo*. He had jumped to the conclusion that I wanted to paint the wreck–which had seemed ridiculous at the time, but would have been far more plausible had I inferred that other artists had already approached him for similar reasons. Tybalt Sphendon, for one–and Davida Amalek. Obviously, the new composition about which Davida had been so secretive had been inspired by the upcoming centenary... or perhaps "inspired" was the wrong word, given that Davida was as ambitious to further her career as she was to make progress in her art. Had *she*, perhaps, approached Fion Commonal and the Winter Council with the notion that the event deserved commemoration, and that some kind of musical tribute might be in order? If so, she might have sought Ragan Barling's support for the proposal, under cover of requesting assistance with background information.

Real or imaginary, murderers or not, the ghosts of the *Haemon Redondo*'s dead certainly seemed to be very active. Was there anyone on the island, I wondered, whose lives had not been touched by their insistence on being remembered? They were obviously not prepared to let me alone, now that I had been tempted into their web. Alas, the more I struggled to see sense in the pattern, the more confusion I found.

We reached the ground floor safely, and Ragan ushered me to the door without delay. "Tomorrow," he said, "or the next day, I shall be only too glad to tell you all I know, Master Rathenius—but not now."

"I shall be busy tomorrow," I told him. "I have work to do. I'll come when I can, if I can't find out what I need to know from someone else... or I'll invite you to dinner, to return your hospitality."

I expected him to take the remark about finding out what I wanted to know from someone else as an insult, given that he was so very proud of his authority on such matters. It did indeed make him look at me rather sharply—and also rather suspiciously.

Ragan had found out quickly enough that he had jumped to the wrong conclusion, at first, when I came to him for information about the *Haemon Redondo*, but he was only just beginning to wonder why I had developed such a sudden and strange interest in the incident. He knew that I'd always treated the rumors of its vengeful dead with some contempt; indeed, he thought me a rather shallow person—as evidenced by his comment in the *Sprite* when I had first been invited to express my opinion as to which was the purest of the arts...

"Goodnight, Master Rathenius," he said, firmly.

"Goodnight, Ragan," I replied, reflexively. As he began to close the door on me, however, I remembered exactly what he had said when I had been invited to express that opinion...and I realized that it had not a feeble attempt at mockery at all.

It had been a feeble attempt to prompt me.

10

When the door was firmly closed between myself and Ragan Barling, I paused long enough to collect myself, and to give more detailed consideration to the question of why the sight of a light on the causeway might alarm him. Did he really think that it could be a ghost-light, carried by a revenant from the *Haemon Redondo*? Could he possibly imagine that Davida Amalek might have a reason for taking her research all the way to Lucifer? Or did he know something about the causeway that I couldn't, as yet, suspect?

I began to wonder exactly why Ragan had come out to the Knuckle with Fion Commonal to see me off that morning, as I set off on my own journey along the causeway to Lucifer. Considering that he claimed to know nothing at all about Phelim, he seemed to be taking a keen interest in the lighthouse-keeper's visitors. And yet, he had not been in the least reluctant to let me see the copies he had made of the sunken ship's documents. If he had been frightened of what I might find in them, he need never have admitted to having made them.

Clearly, there were more pieces missing from the puzzle than I had suspected–so many more, in fact, that I almost began to despair of ever fitting it together. One thing I couldn't doubt, however, was that it was the most intriguing puzzle I had ever encountered in all my years on the island.

If I had only had to go back down the lane up which I had come, I would doubtless have set out immediately, glad to have the gradient with me rather than against me. I knew, however, that if I went back down to the harbor I would only have to come up again on the far side of the town. It seemed that the best chance I had of finding a carriage quickly to take me home, given the late hour, was to make my way along the ridge of the hill as far as the *Sprite*. I set out in that direction, but I had only taken a dozen steps when it occurred to me to wonder whether I might do better to carry on up the hill to the livery stable just beyond the crown, where I could hire a horse.

While I was considering this option, I heard a door slam. I realized immediately that it was Ragan Barling's. My own eyes had adjusted well enough to the moonlight to let me see him clearly, but he had only just blown out his candles, and he didn't turn in my direction. Instead, he crossed the road diagonally and set off down the lane.

At first, I only intended to go back to the head of the lane so that I could watch his descent to the quay. By the time I reached it, though, he was already turning aside into an even narrower by-way densely packed with tiny cottages occupied by the families of deckhands and warehouse laborers. So far as I knew, it had no other outlet.

Consumed with curiosity, I moved as quietly as I could to the end of the secondary lane and moved into it. Lamps or candles had been lit in most of the dwellings, and few had curtains to shield their windows, so it wasn't difficult to see where Ragan had gone, and where he had paused.

He was peering into the lighted window of one of the little houses, with an expression of puzzlement on his face. After ten or twelve seconds, he turned aside and made his way back in my direction. Had he not been staring wide-eyed into a lighted room, he would certainly have seen me even though I quickly stepped aside into a narrow covert, but he was still slightly dazzled as well as deeply preoccupied.

He passed within arm's reach of me without having the slightest suspicion that I was there, then turned down the hill and resumed his descent towards the harbor.

I could have followed him, but I was more curious to know what he had been looking at, so I made my own way to the spot at which I had seen him standing. I looked through the lighted window just as he had.

Apparently, the occupant of the room had heard Ragan as he turned away, and had come to the window to look out. The two of us found ourselves face-to-face, separated by a pane of pooled glass no better than those in Ragan Barling's attic windows. In spite of the distortion, we had no trouble recognizing one another.

I was looking at Nicodemus Rham, whose retirement home this evidently was. Ragan Barling had obviously taken my suggestion that the man on the causeway might be Rham more seriously than he had let on–either that, or had wondered whether I might know something that he didn't.

The former lighthouse-keeper hurried to his door to let me in.

"Why, Master Rathenius," he said. "Come in, come in." The lateness of the hour clearly did not worry him–but that was hardly surprising, given that he had long been a man of nocturnal habits.

It was not entirely surprising that he should greet me as if I were his dearest friend; the causeway had never attracted many strollers, and few of those who had followed it to its end had bothered to call on Lucifer's sole inhabitant. Truth to tell, I had only done so myself in order to take a rest and beg a drink, although I had always been conscientious enough to bring my host a few light provisions by way of recompense.

Nicodemus was quick to pour me a drink now, assuring me that it was better rum than he had ever been able to offer me before.

"It's very kind of you to come, sir," he said. "I've very few friends, as you know, and although I was never lonely out on the rocks, I somehow seem to feel the lack of them now that I have so many neighbors packed so closely around me."

"I can understand that, Nicodemus," I said. "One of my own casual acquaintances lives just beyond the top of the lane there–Ragan Barling. Do you know him?"

"Oh yes–he came out to Lucifer to visit me on occasion. Wouldn't call him a friend, though, Not really *social* calls. Asked a lot of questions. Didn't seem to like the answers, neither–always trying to twist them, put words into my mouth. Never could figure out why."

"What questions?" I asked.

"Things I'd seen. Ghosts, mostly."

"And why didn't he like your answers?" Nicodemus Rham, I knew, was highly unlikely to have told Ragan Barling that he didn't believe in ghosts, or that he hadn't seen any. He did, and he had.

"Seemed to think he knew more about them than I did, though he'd never clapped eyes on them. The men and women who went down with the *Haemon Redondo*, that is. I seen them all, I suppose, although I didn't know their names till he told me."

"He told you their names?"

"Well, not all of them, I suppose. Anyways, I couldn't ever remember more than a few."

"Elgin Bayard?"

"Oh yes–and his wife. He was the captain, you know."

"I know. What about Lucian Embros?"

Nicodemus thought hard about that one, but eventually shook his head. "Don't think so," he said. "Might have forgotten. I knew the old captain, though–and his wife. Terrible, that... them going down together. Terrible thing... but I dare say it gave them some comfort to be together."

His eyes had misted with tears. I decided not to tell him that Ragan Barling had jumped to the wrong conclusion when he had copied the passenger list in Ormaux, and that Vyvyane Bayard had not been the captain's wife at all.

"Why didn't he like your answers, Nicodemus?" I asked, softly. "He believes in the ghosts, doesn't he?"

The old man looked sideways at me then, remembering that I didn't, and that he'd often been careful not to raise the subject when I visited him on Lucifer, in case I might think him too stupid and superstitious to bother with.

"Oh, he believes in them all right," Nicodemus said, pensively. "Though I'm not so sure he knows that he believes in them, if you know what I mean. It's *what* he believes, or wants other people to believe, that caused our disagreements."

It was all rather bizarre, but very intriguing–especially now that I had recalled Ragan Barling's crude attempt to interest me in constructing a defense of rumor-mongering as a fine art. Nicodemus Rham was no fool, despite his long isolation and lack of education. I was inclined to trust his judgment, no matter how peculiar it sounded. "What do you mean, Nicodemus?" I asked.

"He thinks they ought to be out for revenge," Nicodemus said. "He thinks they ought to be angry, with a hundred years having passed and no one brought to account for what happened. He thinks they ought to make themselves seen–to make themselves felt. At least, that's what he wanted me to think– but I know better, see? I know better, though I know you don't believe me."

"I believe that people can see ghosts, Nicodemus," I assured him. "I believe that people who need to see ghosts sometimes become expert seers. I believe you've seen the captain of the *Redondo*, and the wife who perished with him. I'll certainly believe you if you tell me that you see them very differently from Ragan Barling."

He didn't speak immediately, and he took a generous swig of rum before he did–but I was his friend, after all. He trusted me more than he trusted any other man on the island.

"They used to be bitter," he said, slowly. "Powerful bitter, and angry too. They used to hate what they were, what had been forced upon them. Might have done almost anything then, if a chance had come up at the wrong time to do something dark... but they didn't. They didn't. I don't say it was my doing, but I know it didn't do them any harm to have me to talk to, and probably did them some good. I never told them what to do, or how to feel, but I think maybe I helped them to see a little better what they might do, and how they might feel, now that they were what they were through no fault of their own. I never tried to tell them that it's a good thing to be a ghost, or to be lost at sea, but I think I helped them see that it isn't the worst thing in the world to be at peace, with the sea all around. I think you might understand that, Master Rathenius, because I think you're the sort of man who might be able to do something of that kind yourself, if the chance came your way. I don't know about your painting, but I think you might make a ghost-seer yourself, if you only had the trick of it. Anyways, it seems to me, who surely knows them better than any man alive, that the ghosts of the *Haemon Redondo* have grown a deal calmer over time, and far more content with their lot. They aren't angry, Master Rathenius. Not any more. They aren't about to come wailing and moaning on to the shore–if they come at all they'll come quietly, not disturbing anyone. They don't want any trouble. They don't want to make themselves felt. They just want to rest in peace, and maybe make a few more friends than they've had before–and that's not too much to ask, in my opinion. The captain's a good man, Master Rathenius. A good man. And his wife's an angel. They don't mean to do anyone any harm, and I can't see why Master Barling wants to see things differently, even if he is a poet."

It was, in its way, a very moving speech, once it had been put into its true perspective. I thought I understood every word of it–except, of course, the last.

"Poet?" I echoed. "Ragan's not a poet. He's an antiquary."

"Ah!" said Nicodemus Rham. "Not a poet at all? My mistake." He looked at me sideways again, not at all sure that I had fully grasped what he'd told me–but I had. He had been seeing ghosts for a long time now, and seeing his own plight reflected in theirs. It had done him no harm, and had probably done him a deal of good. I wasn't in the least surprised that he had been annoyed by Ragan Barling's slanted questions.

Perhaps, I thought, Ragan had been seeing ghosts of his own, whose influence had not been quite as healthy as that of Nicodemus Rham's kindly phantoms, even though they bore the same names.

"I'm sorry, Nicodemus," I said, "but it's late, and I'm a long way from home. I need to hire a carriage, or a horse. There's a livery stable over the hilltop, is there not?"

Nicodemus had no clock, but I only had to mention the lateness of the hour to make him conscious of it–and guiltily too. It didn't occur to him to wonder what I had been doing peering through his window at such an unlikely hour, because he was too busy regretting the fact that he had no spare bed to offer me, or anything that would serve in its stead. He insisted that he must bring his lamp and walk with me to the stable. I told him that it wouldn't be necessary, given that the night was clear and the Moon bright, but he insisted that the street was too dark for a man like me to walk alone. In the end, we compromised; I agreed to allow him to accompany me to the end of his by-way, where I could safely turn on to the broader and better-kept lane.

"I'll come to see you again, Nicodemus," I promised, as we left the house, "and you must come to me." I knew that he wouldn't, although I wouldn't have been displeased if he had; the island's customs gave me license to condescend, but conceded him none to presume.

Once we reached the end of the side street, though, my plans changed again. The brow of the hill was dark, save for a handful of nightlights burning in the upper stories of the better houses on the crown, but there were lights clustering on the quay down below. The waterfront was always lit, of course, and never entirely quiet, but there was a crowd gathering whose agitation could be measured in the sound of raised voices as well as the bobbing of lanterns.

A boat had just come in. I recognized it as the *Merry Maid*, one of the small craft that had interrupted Hillbeck's passage across the harbor several hours before. Doubtless it had a catch to land–but not the sort of catch that could be considered ordinary.

Nicodemus Rham, who was unused to the habits of the port, didn't realize that anything untoward was happening until I told him that I had changed my mind, and would head down the hill instead of up.

"Aye," he said, squinting in the hope of overcoming his myopia. "There's a carriage or two down there, right enough."

There were indeed two–but it wasn't the hope of a ride home that was drawing me like a magnet.

"Good night, Nicodemus," I said, as I set off down the hill at a run. It was a reckless pace, but I was fortunate enough to make the precipitate descent without slipping.

This time, I arrived in time to see the corpse, although it was a dubious privilege. I'd seen dead men before, including men who'd been pulled out of the ocean–and this one, like the other found that afternoon, could only have been in the water for two days and a half, at the most–but this was a man I knew and respected, and counted as a friend. To see him dead was bad enough, but to see his features so cruelly tormented, as if by some unnatural terror, was worse.

Pallid and frayed as its flesh was, the dead man's face was still horribly expressive; it forbade the conclusion that his death had been any mere accident–or, for that matter, suicide. The fact that his body was wrapped around by knotted rope tended to the same impression.

Constable Clovis, who had been examining the body with the care expected of him, looked up as I shouldered my way through the crowd. He wasn't conspicuously surprised to see me, but there was no suspicion in his speculative stare; I had not been promoted to the head of his list of suspects.

"Do you recognize this man, Master Rathenius?" the Constable asked. It wasn't a stupid question; he knew that I did, but was in search of formal confirmation.

"It's Morloc Hyat," I said. "Where was he found?"

"He was caught up in the *Merry Maid*'s nets northwest of the Devil's Rocks," the Constable reported. "I've sent for Master Commonal, but at a glance, I'd say that he must have been in the water at least as long as the other, wouldn't you, sir?"

"I never saw Tybalt's body," I told him, "and I'm certainly no expert–but I'm sure your judgment's sound."

Clovis got up then, and instructed the fishermen who had surrounded him not to touch the body until Fion Commonal arrived. When he drew me aside, the whispers started–whispers whose hushed tones could not conceal audible references to the *Haemon Redondo*.

"This is bad, sir," the Constable told me, unnecessarily. "One dead man is happenstance, but where there are two, there might be more–unless there's an explanation that only concerns the two."

I could see what he was getting at. Like me, he'd wondered wistfully whether Tybalt Sphendon's death might be a suicide–and now he was wondering whether Morloc Hyat's murdered corpse might provide a motive for that suicide. It was, after all, Morloc who'd displaced Tybalt in Davida Amalek's affections. If Tybalt had flown into a jealous rage and killed his rival, he might then have been mortified by anguish...

Except, of course, that it was all utter nonsense.

"I'm sorry, Constable," I said. "They were drinking together in the *Sprite* only three nights ago. They quarreled, to be sure, but their munitions were aesthetic theories and sarcasm. I can't believe that their contest escalated afterwards to actual violence, even in the absence of the other evidence."

"Their faces?"

"The ropes."

The Constable nodded, acknowledging that we were thinking along the same lines. "I had thought at first, sir," he said, "that attempts had been made to weigh the bodies down, so that they would not be found so soon, and that whatever anchor had been attached to Master Sphendon's body had merely come loose–but that sort of accident doesn't happen twice... and there's the matter of the bell."

He looked at me speculatively, inviting me to confirm once again that he was thinking along the right lines.

"And what did you find this time, serving as a badge rather than an anchor?" I asked.

"A flag, sir–a ship's signal-flag. Old, torn... been in the water a lot longer than the body. Maybe a hundred years."

"Give or take nine days," I agreed. "Or so it will seem to the superstitious."

"Will there be a third, sir, do you think?" That was what the Constable really wanted to know. His superiors on the mainland would not be too interested in one dead man, or even two–given that they were mere artists rather than men of rank– but an epidemic of murder was an opportunity for disaster... or, of course, for the making of Clovis' reputation.

"I don't know, Constable," I told him, truthfully. "I don't know what kind of game the man responsible is playing."

"Are you sure it's a man, sir?"

I carelessly took it for granted that the only alternative he could have in mind was a woman, but if I had realized sooner that even he was thinking in terms of ghosts, I would have given the same answer. "I'm perfectly certain that it's a man," I said.

"Do you have a particular man in mind, sir?" he asked, fishing for inspiration rather than a confession.

"Yes–but I can no more accuse a man without firm evidence than you can, Constable Clovis," I told him. "In any case, there seems to be one more person involved in this affair than I've yet encountered or fitted into the scheme, and he needs to be eliminated before I can be certain of the other. Do you know who it was that walked across the causeway to Lucifer a little while ago?"

The Constable raised his eyebrows. "No, sir," he said. "But if he's still out there, I can set a man to watch for his return. Whether he walks or summons a boat, I can find out who he is within the day. Should I question him about the dead men?"

"You have grounds enough to ask him for an account of who he is, and what his business was on Lucifer, if he isn't anyone we know," I said. "If you'd care to send a messenger to tell me the answer, I'd be interested... and I think I might then be able to help you further, whether he's your man or not. For now, I must get home. May I take one of the carriages that's waiting on the quay?"

The Constable glanced around. "Took an awful long time to get a cart out to the Knuckle this afternoon," he observed, dryly. "Doesn't take much to create an eager anticipation of further business, does it, sir? Please do—they'll only fall to quarrelling over which of them has the right to transport the body if you don't."

11

I took the better of the two carriages—not because Morloc Hyat had less need of comfort than I had, but because I expected to collect other passengers before I reached home. The driver was not in the least displeased to have my business rather than Fion Commonal's, and not merely because Davida Amalek's house—to which I asked him to take me in the first instance—was further away than the physician's. A body that has been in the sea for more than 24 hours tends to leak offensive fluids no matter how securely it is wrapped in oilskins. Even ghouls prefer to deal with the living if the fare is more-or-less equal.

"Nasty business, sir," the coachman opined, as his two horses made their patient way up the hill, untickled by his whip. "They say there's vengeful ghosts involved."

"The trouble with *they*," I observed, "is that they're always ready and willing to repeat whatever nonsense is put into their heads, the sillier the better. If you had lost your life in the wreck of the *Haemon Redondo*, why would you want to come ashore a hundred years afterwards to hunt down a violinist and a poet and scare them to death—assuming that you were capable of wanting anything at all?"

"They say that they were both working on compositions about the wreck, sir," the coachman opined. "That's what annoyed the dead, they say–such words as sacrilege and exploitation have been bandied about."

"Well, at least *they*'ve had a useful opportunity to increase their vocabulary," I said.

"And they say that Miss Amalek's been doing the same," the coachman added, dutifully. "If anyone were to be next..."

"It will be me," I assured him. "I intend to paint portraits of them all–the dead of the *Haemon Redondo*, that is, not *them*. I intend to demand that the shaper of my dreams shows me their faces in my next nightmare, so that I can make mental sketches, which I shall doubtless be able to convert into fair representations. I shall begin with the captain, Elgin Bayard, and then I shall produce a likeness of Lucian Embros. You've heard those names, I assume, on *their* lips."

"Never heard the second, sir–but the other has been somewhat bandied about. You'll be painting him with his dear wife, I dare say?"

"No, I won't," I told him, flatly–although I didn't care to explain why that would be ridiculous, in case the rumor returned on hasty mercurial wings to Nicodemus Rham. "I'll be painting him alone on his bridge, fighting the storm like the practical seaman he was, not knowing that Lucifer's Light had gone out."

"Will you paint a false light on the Knuckle, sir, as some say there was?" the coachman asked, curiously.

I mistook his motive for asking the question. "What makes you suspect it?" I countered. "Was your great-grandfather a wrecker, perchance?"

"Oh no, sir. Mine's not a local family, and we're not party to any of the isle's dark secrets–but I'm willing to take the word of those *theys* that say there never were any wreckers here, and that if anyone cared to check the almanac he'd realize that there was only a half-Moon the night the *Haemon Redondo* went down."

It was on the tip of my tongue to tell him that there had been a storm blowing that night, and that any moonlight there might have been would have been utterly obscured by black cloud–but then I realized what he meant, and why he was slightly mortified that I was treating him like an idiot. If there had ever been wreckers on the island, they'd have made sure to maximize the probability that any wreck they caused at the height of the tide would be re-exposed at the low-point, ripe for easy plunder. They wouldn't have chosen a night when the tides wouldn't have exposed the causeway to Lucifer on the following day.

I had already concluded, for slightly different reasons, that the rumor about the wreckers' light had to be false–but I had naively taken it for granted that it was an authentic rumor, in the sense than it was something the local people put about among themselves. The coachman's comment suggested that the opposite was true, and that its spread had generated enough resentment to prompt a search for evidence to the contrary. Ragan Barling's rumor-mongering was obviously not as artful as he liked to believe–but I still couldn't understand why he had been putting such tales about, let alone the more violent parts of his scheme.

"I don't suppose you happen to know who crossed the causeway to Lucifer earlier tonight?" I asked him. "Or whether a stranger has arrived on the island within the last three days?"

"I didn't know anyone had crossed the causeway," he replied, "but as for strangers... there's been traffic enough, even though none of the fancy yachts carrying the gentlefolk has yet set out from the mainland. Humble folk travel back and forth all the time. The new lighthouse-keeper arrived not three days hence, although he seems more gentlemanly by far than the man he's replaced. Mayhap he'll be the next to die, if he's the kind of man he seems."

He meant that Phelim's status as an artist had been manifest, even though he hadn't written a line in years.

"No," I said. "I've issued my own invitation to disaster–I expect it to be honored." And I remembered yet again what Eirene Magdelana had told me about having no cause to be afraid *unless I wanted to be*.

The coachman reined in his horses; I told him to wait for me.

Davida Amalek's house was dark, but I only had to rap gently on her door to obtain an answer, from Hecate Rain. We held a whispered conversation in the gloomy hallway; Hecate had a candle in a tray but the tallow was poor and the flame feeble.

"Have you abandoned Candida Kracy at your house?" I asked her.

"No," she said. "She's in the next room, keeping me company. I didn't like to leave Davida alone in the house, although she's asleep now. Candida seems more awake than ever, although I expect she's been keeping strange hours since she arrived at the lighthouse."

"I'll have to wake Davida up, I'm afraid," I said. "I have more bad news, and she wouldn't thank me for hoarding it till morning."

"What bad news?" Hecate demanded.

"It's Morloc. His body was probably fed to the sea shortly before or after Tybalt's, but didn't drift to shore. One of the fishermen found him adrift while hauling in a net."

"Did Tybalt kill him?"

"No more than he killed Tybalt. I believe I know who did, and how, but I'm not at all sure why. I have no proof that would entitle me to make an accusation, and there's a second strand to the plot that's become entangled with the first, whose implications I'm not yet in a position to calculate."

Hecate would not have accepted such an enigmatic speech without question from anyone but me, and might not have accepted it from me in any circumstances less awkward than the ones in which we found ourselves. As things were, all she said was: "Do you want me to wake her and tell her the news?"

171

"No," I said. "I saw the body; from you, it would come as rumor."

A door opened then, and Candida Kracy looked out. There was candlelight behind her, but it was as weak as the light in the hall and her silhouette seemed oddly vague. "Master Rathenius?" she said. "I thought it must be you."

"You'd better tell Miss Kracy instead," I said to Hecate. "Which room is Davida's bedroom?"

"There's only the one room on the second story, at the head of the stair," Hecate said, handing me the candle-tray she had brought to the door. "Take care, Axel–please."

While Hecate took Candida Kracy back into the room where they had been waiting, I went upstairs and knocked softly on the door at the top. There was no answer to my knock, but the unlatched and ill-fitting door swung inwards. The room was by no means tiny, despite the slanting ceiling, but there was no furniture in it, save for a capacious bed and a small shelf beside its head. A greater contrast with Ragan Barling's cluttered attic could hardly have been imagined.

Davida was asleep, her blonde hair distributed in glorious disarray across her pillow. In the uncertain light she looked more beautiful than she did by daylight, perhaps because her features were relaxed. It had never occurred to me before that she was perpetually strained and anxious, although the revelation wasn't surprising; she was an artist, after all. One day, I thought, I would have to paint her–but not now.

When I touched her shoulder, she awoke with a start, and sat up in panic. "Who is it?" she demanded. "Hecate?"

"It's Axel Rathenius."

"What are you doing?" She was blinking furiously as her eyes adapted to the light–although the candle-flame still seemed exceedingly dim to me. No longer relaxed, she now seemed fearful–as if the presence of a man in her bedroom could have only one implication, and that unwelcome.

"I'm sorry, Davida. I had to come. I knew that you'd want to know. A second body has been found. It's Morloc's."

Morloc was her current lover; Tybalt had been discarded. In theory, she should have been far more distressed to lose Morloc than Tybalt–but she didn't react as badly as I had feared. She had been Tybalt's protegée for a long time, and her relationship with Morloc was of a different order, as well as far more recent. In any case, the news of Tybalt's demise had depleted her capacity for further shock. A nightmare compounded is still the same nightmare–but it was a nightmare nevertheless, and Davida was possessed by a terrible distress.

"You must get up, Davida," I told her. "I don't think you should stay here alone, or even with Hecate for company. It would be best, I think, if both of you–and Miss Kracy too–came home with me. I think it might be the best way to ensure that no one else is hurt."

"No one else?" she echoed. "Do you think I'm in danger? Do you think I might be the next to die?"

"I don't know. Probably not–but I don't want to take the chance."

It was the simple truth. I had artistic reasons for wanting to gather all the threads of the puzzling plot into my hand, so that I might discover the extent and nature of their entanglement, but I really didn't want to take any unnecessary chances with Davida Amalek's wellbeing. It was, after all, conceivable that the coachman had been right, and that the murderer really did intend to execute all the people who were working on compositions related to the famous wreck.

"I have two good servants," I added, reassuringly, "and a house that can be properly secured. You will be safer there than you would be here, all alone in a dwelling whose locks and shutters appear to leave much to be desired. Hecate will certainly come, if I ask her, and Miss Kracy too. You'll be well cared for, and you won't lack for company."

Davida was confused, and unwilling to trust me–she was undoubtedly familiar with the less complimentary aspects of my reputation, and did not know me well enough to discount them–but she was also distraught. Locked in a nightmare, she had no wish to be alone in a house that had little protection against invaders. "Morloc?" she said, as if the news had only just filtered through to her consciousness. "Morloc's dead?"

There was authentic grief in her voice, but it didn't seem to me the grief of a woman passionately in love. Davida was an artist first and a woman second; Morloc Hyat had not swept her off her feet any more than Tybalt Sphendon had. In a spirit of self-indulgence, she'd forsaken an older consort whose patronage had reached the limit of its usefulness for a younger and more sensitive one, but she hadn't traded away her heart; it wouldn't break, even under the strain of the double loss. She was deeply distressed, but not mortally so.

"I'm sorry, Davida," I said, again. "Please allow me to help you, if only for a few days. You will be perfectly safe in my house–I promise you that."

She finally nodded her head; her features were no longer relaxed, but there was a plaintive quality in her renewed anxiety that was very appealing, hardening my resolution to paint her, when the time became ripe.

"I'll dress," she said. "Go down and wait. Please."

There was no hazard in doing as I was told. I nodded, and set down the candle on the shelf for her convenience. I groped my way down the stair and found the door to the room where Hecate and Candida Kracy were waiting. Quickly, I explained to them what I planned to do.

As I had anticipated, Hecate made no objection to coming home with me, although her own house was less than a hundred strides away. When Hecate agreed, Candida Kracy had no hesitation in following suit.

"This is a terrible place," Candida observed. "I was promised quiet and art, not murder and conspiracy. Perhaps, after all, I should have stayed on Lucifer with Phelim." She had been very enthusiastic to get away, but she certainly hadn't expected to find her first expedition away from her brother's side to be littered with murdered corpses. The doubt in her voice was genuine–but I couldn't be entirely certain, as yet, that she would have been safe on Lucifer.

"You arrived at a bad time, Miss Kracy," I told her. "Not entirely by coincidence, I fear–but I can't believe that there's any threat to you in this matter of the murders. By the way, was your brother expecting a visitor tonight?"

"A visitor?" she echoed. "No, of course not–the only person on the island who knows my brother is..." She had half-turned to glance at Hecate before remembering that I had told her of another.

"What visitor?" Hecate asked. "Who is it you suspect of having killed Tybalt and Morloc, Axel?" She ran the two questions together, as if it were obvious that they had the same answer–but it wasn't at all obvious to me.

"Someone crossed the causeway tonight, by lantern-light," I said. "It must have been someone brave, foolhardy or mad–or a stranger who had no idea how dangerous the passage would be. Tell me, Miss Kracy, apart from the friends in Ormaux who helped secure this position for Phelim, did he write to anyone else to say that he was bound here?"

"I don't know," Candida said. "He said nothing to me... but why should you think he might? This woman you mentioned before: Eirene Magdelana. Do you think she...?"

She trailed off.

"I doubt that it was Eirene," I said–but I knew that I couldn't discount the possibility. Eirene seemed to fear the spirits of the sea, but that wouldn't necessarily inhibit her from crossing the causeway, if she thought that they had granted her safe passage.

While I pondered the matter, I looked around the room. It was not uncomfortable, in its way, but it gave forceful evidence of Davida Amalek's relative poverty, and clear testimony of her sense of priorities. The furniture was crude and utilitarian; her most valuable possession by far was the harpsichord that stood against the internal wall. I compared it, automatically, with my own instrument and the one I had seen in Ragan Barling's house. Barling's was the oldest of the three, as befitted his antiquarian interests, and mine the most highly-decorated, but Davida's showed evidence of the most meticulous craftsmanship and care. It had been made with love, and kept with love–and I didn't doubt, although I didn't lay a finger on the keyboard, that it would be tuned to perfection.

My own harpsichord was always ready to be played, but that was because I couldn't bear to have anything in my environment that was faulty; Ragan, I suspected, must also have hired a tuner in the not-too-distant past–but Davida looked after her own instrument, as tenderly as if it were her only child... or her only *true* lover.

"You're being more than usually perverse tonight, Axel," Hecate complained. "I wish you would tell me what you're thinking."

I was saved from the necessity of improvising an elaborate excuse by Davida's appearance in the doorway.

"I'm ready," she said, and was swift to add: "You're very kind to take the trouble, Master Rathenius, and I thank you. I'm sorry if I seemed rude."

"Not at all," I said. "I'm sure that I should have seemed far ruder, had I been woken so unexpectedly with such bad news. Shall we go?"

When we were all four huddled in the carriage, the coachman's presence was a useful disincentive to further conversation. I welcomed the time to think, but tiredness had taken hold of me to such an extent that I could make no headway. I needed sleep–and I needed that precious interval when a refreshed sleeper returns by degrees to wakefulness, when the mind is at its most creative.

The coachman was inhibited in his turn by the presence of the ladies. There was no more talk of ghosts. He drove us to Hecate's house, where we piled even more luggage on the roof, and then he took us on to mine. The distance was not great, but the journey was long enough to seem wearisome; we all became impatient. Once we were home and the vehicle was unloaded, I paid the coachman off and immediately set about making arrangements for the accommodation of my unscheduled guests. My own room I gave to Davida, and the spare bedroom to Candida Kracy. I had a cot made up for Hecate in

176

the library, and took the couch in the studio for myself. I instructed Jean-Jacques and Luvah to go into town as soon as dawn broke to lay in extra provisions.

"Be careful not to wake us when you return," I told them. "We'll need to sleep as late as we can–but be careful, too, to lock the doors when you go. There's trouble in the town, and I fear that it might not be confined there."

I didn't bother to instruct either of them to pick up any gossip they could; they could be relied on to do that as a matter of course. If anyone in town knew the identity of the person who had crossed the causeway the previous evening, the Constable's questions would have shaken the news loose within an hour of dawn, even if no one had given the relevant information to the Constable.

12

I wasn't the first to wake on the following morning. I took my time over the process, in case the lingering intrusion of my dreams into renascent consciousness should offer me an epiphany of enlightenment, but I was disappointed. All that I recovered was the same sense of foreboding that I had felt before–although it was unaccompanied, this time, by the sound of vermin scampering within the walls.

I had to tell myself, as reassuringly as I could contrive, that at least I had both Candida Kracy and Davida Amalek safe under my roof, so that no harm could come to either of them from any source without my having an opportunity to intervene on their behalf.

The servants were still out, but Hecate Rain had made a pot of tea, and she brought it into the studio with two cups. She gave the impression of having been quite unable to sleep, but she had had the grace to wait until she heard me stirring before coming in. She knew as well as I did that the most creative interval of the day is the period when one emerges from wakefulness, one's dream-self having become lucid without having yet succumbed to the awful pressures of conformity–but that only increased her impatience for enlightenment.

"What is this all about, Axel?" she asked, without waiting for me to dress myself. I wasn't annoyed by her lack of respect for my privacy; we knew one another well enough to be above such concerns.

"I believe it's all about art," I told her. "I thought, briefly, that one aspect of it might be about infatuation and jealousy, but that can only be a tiny part of it. That aspect, at least, is about pure and impure art, and the haphazard entwining of their strands. I hope that the other might be more closely akin than it seems at present, else I should not be so sensitive to the whole. We might use the chimerical confusion, I think–and might even succeed in exploiting its energy."

"You do delight in teasing me, don't you, Axel?" she retorted, exasperated but not surprised. "I think that's why I was never able to love you the way I once loved Phelim–mercifully, as it turned out, since you could never have loved me even as much as Phelim did. Do you have designs on Davida, by the way, now that Morloc's out of the picture? She's quite pretty, I suppose, in her way."

"I'm flattered that you should think me such a perfect ghoul," I said, "but I didn't bring Davida here to seduce her, no matter what the symbolism of setting her in my bed might imply. I brought her here primarily to help and protect her."

"Protect her from whom? The murderer?"

"Of course."

"*Primarily* to help and protect her," Hecate echoed, cannily. "What's the other reason? Are you setting some kind of trap?"

"Yes," I admitted, "I believe that Davida's presence here should help me to reveal the truth of what happened to Tybalt and Morloc–and perhaps, by way of bringing down two birds with a single stone, the truth about Candida Kracy's mysterious urge to install her brother as keeper of Lucifer's Light. To do that, though, I need to know what effect yesterday's conversation with you had on Phelim."

"What effect it had on Phelim? Don't you want to know what effect it had on me?"

"I knew before we set foot on the causeway what effect it would have on you," I told her, frankly. "The wound he caused was healed at least ten years ago; you would have forgotten it entirely had the affair not been one of your formative experiences. The person you are now could not possibly love Phelim Kracy, despite the fact that the person you once were could not help it. I knew that you would only have to see him, and converse with him for an hour or so, to realize that he was merely a phase in your personal evolution, not a crucial opportunity lost. You've derived far more benefit, artistically speaking, from the fact that he broke your heart, than you ever could have obtained from a marriage. I understand your need to scratch the itch, but I always knew that once it had been scratched, it would never bother you again."

"You really are a monster of arrogance, Axel," she observed. "A veritable fallen angel."

It was a compliment of sorts. "Thank you," I said. "Now–what effect did your meeting have on Kracy? Has his wound healed?"

She thought about it for a few moments before replying. "I don't think so," she said, eventually. "He tried with all his might to put me off and send me away, insisting that there could be nothing between us... just as he did before... and he couldn't even begin to recognize, as you have, that there was no need. In his mind, if I may borrow your phrase, I still seem to be a *crucial opportunity* that he lost, or threw away. He knows full well that he made the choice himself–but that doesn't seem to have made its consequences any easier to bear. He still thinks, and perhaps always will, that when he gave me up he sacrificed his one and only chance of... would it sound absurd to say *redemption*?"

"No," I said, "it wouldn't."

"Do you think he came here, even though he can't admit it himself, because he couldn't keep away from me? Because his wound simply wouldn't heal, no matter how long he waited?"

It was slightly brutal, but I had to shake my head. "No," I said. "It was Candida who brought him here, and you had nothing to do with it. She doesn't know herself why she did it, but I think she realizes that the ghosts who are guiding her are phantoms of her own imagination rather than external forces. It's possible–probable, even–that the person whose presence on the island was crucial to the subconscious impulse is Eirene Magdelana, but Candida has no conscious recollection of the name or its significance. She has lived a very strange life, Hecate, locked away in a prison of dreams–but all the while she was there she was undergoing some bizarre process of preparatory rehabilitation. She wants to see her ghosts more clearly, in the hope of obtaining an explanation... although I suspect that she would be better by far if they could be laid to rest, or exorcised."

"And you think that your beloved morpheomorphist might be able to help, as well as holding the key to the mystery? But you said that she only knew Phelim as a baby, and never knew Candida at all."

"The point is," I said, "that she knew their mother and father–their true father."

"*True* father?"

"I doubt that they're the children of the man whose name they bear."

Hecate shook her head, unable to see the import of that allegation. "What has that to do with the murders of Tybalt Sphendon and Morloc Hyat, and the potential threat to Davida?" she asked, impatiently.

"Nothing material, so far as I can see," I conceded. "I believe that they're two entirely separate conspiracies–but they've become entangled because they both have a connection, however fragile and ridiculous, to the wreck of the *Haemon Redondo*. That was presumably accidental–but it does give us a chance to obtain a simultaneous insight into both mysteries, if we're clever enough."

"We? How can I help you, Axel, if you won't tell me anything? Do you really expect me to decipher all these cryptic clues?"

"I haven't yet deciphered them myself," I confessed. "I'm not hiding anything of which I'm certain, Hecate–I only hesitate over half-formed and potentially fallible conclusions. But what an opportunity this is for artists like us!"

Hecate would doubtless have complained that I was being utterly unreasonable, but fate was kind enough to arrange an interruption at that dramatically convenient moment. Candida Kracy came in, seemingly oblivious to her own lack of tact and my lack of clothing.

"I have been looking at your paintings, Master Rathenius," she said. "In my room, in the corridors, in the library... I went in to search for Hecate, of course, but when I deduced that she was in your studio, where the largest hoard of all must be kept... well, I can only hope that you will forgive me."

"Most certainly," I said. "I'm glad that you'll have something to distract your gaze while I make myself decent. Did you sleep well?"

"Quite well, thank you," she said–although I judged that Hecate might have been right, and that she had hardly slept at all. She didn't treat the remark about distracting her gaze as a joke; she did indeed absorb herself in the paintings that were resting on easels and stacked against the walls while I made the necessary preparations for another challenging day. Hecate was polite enough to watch her rather than directing her censorious gaze at me.

When Candida had finished her investigation, she declared that my portraits of Hecate were exceptionally fine.

"Only three of them are here," I told her, regretfully, "And not the best of them–but you'll see two better ones when you visit Hecate at home."

"Axel has always been exceptionally kind to me," Hecate admitted, "but his portraits of me are by no means his best. The trouble with an artist's home is that it accumulates the detritus of his work–the unfinished, the unsatisfactory, the unsaleable. His greatest efforts are directed into his most lucrative commissions, so his finest work is to be found above the fireplaces of every aristocratic mansion that was ever home to a lovely daughter. I always thought that his portrait of Dian, daughter of the Duke of Alectryon, was his masterwork– although the ones that Claudius Jaseph did of Dian and her sister Roxane are said to have been... more powerful." It was her turn to tease me; I didn't mind at all.

Candida Kracy, it seemed, didn't even notice the sarcasm in Hecate's voice. "I can't believe that," she said. "Perhaps I think that the pictures of you are the best because they're the only ones I can properly judge, having never met any of the other models. I would like to see your image of Davida Amalek... but not nearly as much as I would like to see your image of me. I am to be first, I hope–you haven't brought Miss Amalek here to sit for you, in order that she might be distracted from her grief?"

"Not at all," I said. "I must certainly paint Davida some day, if she is willing to sit for me, but now wouldn't be the right time. If she is to be distracted from her grief, her own art will serve the purpose far better than mine. My hope is that she will condescend to play us her latest composition–that we three, and perhaps two others, will be the audience for its debut."

"What others?" Hecate was quick to put in.

"Ragan Barling ought to be here," I said. "I don't know whether he gave Davida the idea for her subject, or whether she took it to him, but he's certainly helped her to research it and I think he may have done more than she realizes to shape it. He has a right to be here, and I wouldn't dream of excluding him. The other potential guest is, I fear, a matter of self-indulgence on my part. I should like to invite Eirene Magdelana. I've been trying to persuade her to visit me here for

182

many years, without success–but I think the time might now be ripe, and I think the subject of Davida's piece might tip the balance."

"What subject is that?" Candida asked, innocently.

"The wreck of the *Haemon Redondo*, I believe," I told her. "Centenaries mean nothing to the dead, of course, but they have an intrinsic appeal to artists of a certain stripe."

"And what stripe is that, Master Rathenius?" asked Davida Amalek, who had appeared in the doorway while my back was turned to it, so that I had been quite unaware of her presence–even though I should have realized that it was almost inevitable, given that fate was in such a whimsical mood.

I turned and bowed to her. "A Romantic stripe, of course," I said. "The story of the *Haemon Redondo* is so rich in tragedy and mystery–especially the way that Ragan Barling tells it. It's the perfect subject for a plaintive concerto... or even an oratorio. I'm very sorry, Miss Amalek, if I've presumed too much, or let my mouth run away with me. Please don't be offended–I've followed your career, and I know that you're ready to produce a masterpiece. I would be mortified to think that I'd allowed my artistic sensibilities to ride roughshod over your feelings. If you simply can't bear to play, then I wouldn't dream of trying to persuade you."

I'd made a great many hypocritical speeches in my time, so that one was never at risk of claiming any prize, but it was pure dissimulation from beginning to end. What I actually meant by artists of a particular stripe was artists of ambition, hungry for publicity: artists who might see the prospect of a centenary as an opportunity to attract more attention to their work than it would ordinarily command; artists, in brief, who might be vulnerable to Ragan Barling's suggestion that if only one were to make enough noise, the centenary of the *Haemon Redondo* might become a occasion for public recognition. There might, for instance be a hastily-organized but solemn ceremony of belated mourning to which the whole island might turn out, with music and poetry specially composed for the event: a nice occasion to greet the annual visitors in style.

Reputations could be made by events of that kind, especially by artists who, though poor and as-yet-unrecognized, really did have unusual ability.

"I can bear to play," Davida said, flatly. "I'd intended... but that doesn't matter now. Yes, Master Rathenius, I can play here as well as in my home, and I need to play. I'll do as you ask. Thank you for giving me the opportunity."

And the audience, I thought. *Small and select, but influential*. I was glad to discover that she had such confidence in my taste–but I also chided myself for my insensitivity. She was, after all, genuinely distressed by the loss of her two lovers. Perhaps she had been using them, just as she had been using Ragan Barling, but she wasn't a monster any more than Claudius Jaseph or Conrad Othman had been a monster; her affectionate feelings had doubtless been genuine, her pleasure in their love-making precious as well as authentic. If her distress could only be fed into her work rather than undermining it, her performance might be magnificent–but it wouldn't be without emotional cost. No truly great performance ever is.

"But when will you start to paint me, Master Rathenius?" Candida Kracy put in. "I'm truly sorry to be so impatient, but I have lost so much of my life to dreams, and I am terribly fearful of wasting time."

"I shall begin before noon," I promised her. "You must go with Hecate, so that she can help make you ready–and afterwards, Hecate, you must see that Davida has everything she needs. I will give careful instructions to Jean-Jacques and Luvah, to make sure that everything will run smoothly–they must have returned from market by now."

The three women accepted their dismissal graciously. It turned out that Jean-Jacques and Luvah had indeed returned from market, having arranged delivery of much that they could not carry.

"Well?" I said to Jean-Jacques, when we had settled more mundane matters. "What of the mysterious light on the causeway? Can anyone put a name to the man who carried the lantern?"

"No, sir," the manservant replied. "Everyone's been asking about him, apparently, but he's a stranger, and by no means a talkative one. I have a description of sorts, although I fear it won't be much help. He was tall, and his hair and complexion seemed to be dark, although both were hidden by a wide-brimmed hat worn at a tilt. His cloak hid his clothes as well as his figure, but he was a gentleman of sorts. Good boots, sturdy and well-made."

"Of sorts?" I queried.

"Can't be more accurate, sir. Not an aristocrat of the kind that comes here in the season, nor a man of law. Perhaps an artist like yourself, or a physician like Master Commonal, but I have no reliable clue as to that."

"Impressions can be more useful than they seem," I told him, "though sometimes treacherous. Where is he staying?"

"Not in any hostelry in the port, so far as anyone knows. But if he comes back across the causeway today, you can be sure that there'll be a thousand eyes looking out for him, to see where he goes."

"That's good," I said.

"Why?" Jean-Jacques asked. "Is he the murderer?"

"No," I said. "Not the murderer of Tybalt Sphendon and Morloc Hyat, at any rate. What crimes he might have committed before he arrived, I can't say–and as to what crimes he might commit before he leaves, I can only hazard the vaguest guess."

"Is the lighthouse-keeper safe?" the servant wanted to know. "There's a gale coming, they say–blowing straight towards Lucifer. There's ships at sea might need the light for guidance tomorrow night, if the Moon and stars are obscured and the wind drives them faster than they want to go."

I knew that *they* were far more reliable as weather forecasters than purveyors of tales of the supernatural. The weather was bright enough at present, but I knew how rapidly it could change.

"I doubt that any harm has come to Phelim Kracy as a result of the stranger's visit," I said. "I think the man might be his father. They've a family secret of some kind to protect, but they're more likely conspirators than contestants."

"A secret concerning the wreck of the *Redondo*?" the servant wanted to know.

"Almost certainly," I said. "But don't go adding to the stories that are flying around. I don't want any of your fancies clouding waters that are far too murky as it is. Be content to listen, and I promise that you'll have the whole story before a single carter or publican gets wind of it–provided that I'm alive to tell it."

"You're surely not in danger, sir?" was his smiling response to that.

"A man who knows too much is always in danger," I told him, without matching his smile. "The problem is that there are some people who yearn to know too much, and will not be stopped even when they know they're courting disaster. What we must remember, Jean-Jacques, is that fear is a stimulant, like absinthe–excellent in moderation, fatal in excess. It isn't that we shouldn't want it... but we need to know when, and how, to stop."

"Yes, sir," he said, as a good servant always does, even when receiving unwanted advice.

13

As soon as Candida Kracy was posed and I began to sketch, I was able to push everything else to the back of my mind. Whether some unconscious fraction of my being was still working upon the question of the double murder I cannot say, but I do know that the intensity of my concentration on Candida's features reduced the context of her story to the status of a mere frame–not utterly irrelevant, by any means, but marking the boundary of attention while evading any direct contemplation.

Except, of course, that it wasn't quite as simple as that. No matter how determinedly one focuses on matters of detail, the details in question never lose their connection with a greater picture.

I sketched lines, capturing shapes and curves. I turned my charcoal aslant to import shading, adding impressions of light and depth to the image. I reproduced appearances, as scrupulously as an expert hand and eye could contrive. I paid attention to what was there, and only what was there, with a view to its duplication in another medium: to the creation of a faithful simulacrum–but features are no mere shapes, and the expressions that haunt them are no mere muscular tics. The emotions that change the subtle deployment of the muscles of a face run deep–far deeper than the feelings that are their conscious correlates. Their efflorescence is buoyant, but they're rooted in the silt of memory and they draw their sustenance from the world of dreams.

I had never seen a face so strangely nourished as Candida Kracy's.

Before I took up my charcoal and my chalk, my pencils and my palette, I had only observed her with my eyes. I had seen her mask and her mystery as well as her beauty, but of what lay behind her mask I had caught only the merest glimpse. As soon as I involved my hands in the process of simulation, however, I was able to observe her with my whole intelligence, and my genius too. I was able to begin the work of penetrating her mystery, gauging the true extent and strangeness of her being.

I soon realized that the painting would be no masterpiece; she was not sufficiently comprehensible for me to capture her entire. I could not do her justice. No painter alive could have done her justice. Claudius Jaseph would not have been able to capture any but the faintest echo of her soul. But that was not to say that the painting would not be good, and precious, and fascinating.

Three nights before, I had sensed that my house was haunted, and had shaped the haunting in my mind as an elu-

187

sive creature scrabbling within the walls. Now, I sensed that it was haunted more elaborately than that, not merely by enigmatic irritants clawing at its fabric but by subtler and freer entities, more fluid and more ubiquitous–like the voices of the air and the clouds that murmured so insistently in Eirene Magdelana's ears. The odor that I had sensed on Lucifer did not reassert itself in my studio, nor did the air seem unreasonably ponderous as I breathed in and out, but I was still different in her presence, and my house was different too.

I wondered whether I had been wrong to accept Hecate's judgment that she had hardly slept at all rather than her own polite statement that she had slept quite well. Perhaps the two of them had very different notions of what it meant to sleep "well."

It was difficult to determine why her presence was so unsettling, in the absence of any precedent to which I might refer. Candida Kracy was far too solid to qualify as a ghost, but there was something within her that was infinitely more accomplished as a haunter. The shaper of her dreams had made her a gift, whose exact quality I couldn't make out at all, but whose power was undeniable. Perhaps, I thought, she was the raw material that might make a powerful morpheomorphist, with the right training... or perhaps she was something allied to that, but crucially unlike in one detail I was not equipped to distinguish. Eirene Magdelana would have known what it was, I supposed. Did Phelim Kracy know?

Phelim, I remembered, considered dreams to be living things, or very nearly. He also believed–as many poets do, especially unsuccessful ones–that he had a muse whose demands he could never fully meet and whose offerings he could never properly employ. His muse too was supposed–by him at least–to be a living thing, albeit one compounded from the substance of dreams. In some way, it was connected to his sister, but surely it could not be her, nor anything that had emanated from her while she slept...

I suppressed the reverie and tried to focus on the matter in hand. Candida had become too still, too statuesque. Such is the tendency of models whose determination not to spoil a pose has become too insistent.

"Tell me about your mother," I said. "Don't be afraid of ruining my work–I'd rather you relaxed than forced yourself to be too rigid. I have the lines of your face now; I need a little more of the life before I can think of applying color."

"I never knew her," she said, wistfully–and the wistfulness I seized upon, as a welcome resource. "I must have seen her before I fell asleep, and felt her touch while I lay in my long coma, but all I know about her is what Phelim has told me. She was very beautiful, he says, but careworn. She was no longer young when she gave birth to me, of course–Phelim is seven years older than I am–and I must have added more than my due to the weight of her cares. I wish I had been able to forge a better bond with her, to be a person to her rather than a slumberous enigma. I would have liked to be able to love her."

"And your father?" I prompted, as if it were simply the natural question to ask, given the nature of the conversation.

"He died while I was very young. His name was Nathan Kracy and he was a businessman–an importer and exporter of goods through Ormaux's port. I doubt that he was a successful businessman, although we were certainly never poor. Phelim always speaks of him as if my mother had married slightly beneath her–but as you know, Phelim has this notion that our mother's family once had some kind of fortune that was lost when the *Haemon Redondo* ran on to the Devil's Rocks."

She was no longer wistful, but she had a hint of perplexity about her that was quite piquant, which I appropriated as my due.

"I know that Phelim never mentioned your mother's friend Eirene Magdelana," I said, "but I wonder if, perchance, he ever mentioned Eirene's tutor, Edom Sombre."

"The name sounds familiar," she said, "but I don't think... could his name, perhaps, have been *Lucian* Sombre?"

"Lucian Sombre was Edom's father." I told her. "He must have been long dead by the time Phelim was born, although... I have begun to wonder whether he might have been on the *Haemon Redondo*, no matter how unlikely that seems, given that he must have cemented his reputation as a morpheomorphist more recently than a hundred years ago. What did Phelim say about Lucian Sombre?"

"Only that he was a wise man, who had tried to minister to his dreams. Phelim seemed to think that he had disappointed him in some way."

"Ah!" I said, as I finally obtained the enlightening epiphany of which I was in search. "I begin to see. If Edom Sombre ever had a son, what could be more natural than naming him for his famous father? There are two Lucian Sombres, and it was the younger one that your brother knew. Morpheomorphism must have become a family tradition. I wonder that Eirene never mentioned him... but I dare say she did, and that I mistook the reference, assuming that she was talking about Edom's father rather than his son. Her talk is so often confused that one gets used to forgiving references that make little or no sense. Asking questions only disturbs her."

"Why would you think that the first of these Lucian Sombres might have been on the *Haemon Redondo*, if he was still alive after the ship went down?" Candida asked.

"I saw the name Lucian Embros on a passenger-list that Ragan Barling had copied in Ormaux," I told her. "It might be a coincidence, but Embros is an anagram of Sombre. I'm too sensitive to such things, I'm afraid. Unless, of course..." I stopped, realizing where my tongue had led me while my eyes and hands were intent on capturing a very different image.

My model had no difficulty following the train of thought. "Unless," she said, "not everyone who was on the *Redondo* perished in the wreck."

"Quite so," I said."

"I should like to believe that," she said. "It would open the possibility that my great-grandmother had survived too— although it would create the mystery of why Lucian Sombre was travelling under a pseudonym... or why Lucian Embros changed his name."

My hand didn't tremble. I was at work. I was busy with my palette now, mixing colors. I couldn't tolerate any serious distraction–and yet, I knew that what Candida was saying wasn't really a distraction at all. There was something here that was part of the frame and boundary of the narrative, and of my portrait. Fortunately, she was an intelligent woman, considering that she had slept for 20 years through the greater part of her youth.

"Do you think," she said, "that the mystery had anything to do with the family fortune of which Phelim speaks?"

What was the expression on her face as she said it? I can't say; it was no expression I had ever seen before. What was she feeling as she cast that particular shadow of her inner self? Probably nothing, or very little; not all emotion is reflected in consciousness. But her dreams had been educated to a pitch of sensitivity far beyond those of ordinary men and women while she lay asleep, and they had a better grasp of that particular thread of the mystery than I had.

I tried, with all my might, to capture that expression on canvas. Alas, I failed. I was a painter, after all: the master of an impure art. I was a ghost-seer too, but only when perception forced itself upon me, making full use of my vulnerability. I was no morpheomorphist, no bearer of the arms of Morpheus. I didn't know the answer to her question, any more than I knew how to turn its supernatural flavor into mere color.

"Fortune," I observed, "can mean so many different things. Money, goods, luck, fate... all precious, perhaps, but not in the same way. And some things that are precious are not equally precious to all men, for which we must be thankful."

"Would you not prefer it if works of art were treasured by all men alike?" she asked–not because she had misunderstood the import of what I was saying but because she had understood it better than she knew.

"No," I said. "If every man were an artist, or a connoisseur of art, there would be no art. The essence of art lies as much in difference and differentiation as in craft and creativity. I prefer a world in which art is rare, and great art very rare indeed, and in which good taste is a privilege and a fine possession. There can be no true appreciation without envy—which is by far the most underrated of the deadly sins."

"Are you very familiar with the deadly sins, Master Rathenius?" she asked. "Hecate calls you a fallen angel—can she possibly mean it literally?"

"I wasn't with Lucifer when he was expelled from Heaven, if some such expulsion ever took place," I said. "I'm older than I seem, but not that old. Hecate knows my attitude to myths of that kind, though, and she is poet enough to choose her implications carefully. We all begin life in the paradisal womb, Miss Kracy, and are all cast out therefrom. Some come into the human world ready to adapt to its customs and conventions, its demands and domestications... others are not content to be delivered, and are indeed subjected to a kind of fall, into eternal dissatisfaction. Yes, Miss Kracy, I'm a fallen angel, just as Hecate is; I understand the deadly sins as a connoisseur. I'm an artist—and you, at least for the time being, are a work of art."

"Sometimes," she said, "I think that I have always been a work of art. Is that why I was so enthusiastic to be painted, do you suppose?"

"Yes," I said, "I think it is. But you must remember, Miss Kracy, that you need not and ought not be content solely to be someone else's work of art. While you were asleep, you were compliant clay, but now that you're awake you have the power to choose what kind of artwork you want and need to be. I think you did a brave and wise thing when you asked me to paint you—and I will do my very best to be worthy of your trust—but you must think of this as a beginning, a first hesitant step on a long road. You must seek out other artists, and other possibilities, if you're to discover what you might ultimately make of yourself."

At that moment, Davida Amalek began to play my harpsichord. At first she played a few notes at a time, testing the instrument. When she moved on from phrases to longer sequences she was hesitant, and she moved from one fragment to another as if haphazardly, making no attempt to deliver a whole movement. Eventually, though, she settled into her work. She played something that wasn't her own, for practice, and then she began to recapitulate familiar compositions, as if to establish a more intimate relationship with the instrument.

Eventually, though, she began to play parts of her present composition; I had no difficulty at all in recognizing them for what they were. She didn't begin at the beginning, nor did she play the parts in order, but the strains of that music suffused the entire house like insistent spirits–the exotic fumes of her inspiration. They spoke of the sea and the wind... but the flow of the notes was only slightly less than calm, methodical and unhurried even when the suggestion of a storm crept in.

I didn't want to listen attentively–not consciously, at least–but the music was by no means unwelcome as a back-cloth to my endeavor. As part of the frame rather than the focal point of my mind's eye it was far from inappropriate. Its rhythm didn't possess my hand, but my hand was aware of its melody, and felt a kind of harmony in its own work. Chimerical as the combination was, it was most certainly artistic. I was still convinced that Davida's story and Candida's didn't overlap in any material fashion, but they weren't discordant.

I worked on, unhurriedly but relentlessly, caught up in the moment and the endeavor, oblivious to everything but need. Alas, need is an enemy of unity and eternity alike; it always turns on itself eventually to become intrusive rather than immersive, demanding rather than satisfying, tempestuous rather than controlled.

Eventually, I set down the palette. "We must stop now," I said. "A portrait is the kind of task that requires intervals of refreshment. We must eat, and rest a while."

"May I see it?" she asked.

"If you wish," I said. It was my habitual response to that question, albeit a slightly uneasy one.

She came to stare at the work in progress.

"Is that what I really look like?" she said. "Are mirrors so slyly deceptive?"

"Yes to both questions," I said. Nor was I referring to any mere matter of image-reversal.

She turned away from the easel without further comment and glanced through the large double window–twin to the one in my bedroom, directly above, which looked out on the cliff. Even from the upper balcony she wouldn't have been able to see the whole array of the Devil's Rocks, because they were partially obscured by the edge of the cliff, but from the angle at which she stood she could see the top of the lighthouse where her brother was. The rain was lashing the tower now, and the clouds above were grey and low.

"Is there a storm brewing?" she asked.

"It seems so," I said. "The folk hereabouts have long experience of the weather, seeing omens and patterns within its apparent capriciousness that I can't perceive. The word is that we shall not see the worst of it until tomorrow night, but I shall be glad to get the provisions I've ordered safely stored away, so that we might be ready for the siege whenever it begins and ends."

I led her out of the studio but indicated that she should wait in the corridor while I went into the dining room. Hecate was perched at the table, watching Davida–who immediately looked up from the harpsichord and stopped playing.

"Don't let me disturb you," I said. "We can eat in another room."

"No," said Davida, curtly. "That won't be necessary. I was just getting the feel of the instrument. It will do. I'll play the whole piece for you tomorrow night, if you care to send out your invitations now."

"There's a storm coming," I said.

"I know," she replied. "I was hoping for a storm. I only hope that another will follow in its train, in time for the centenary performance."

"Do you think the Council will go ahead with that?" I asked.

194

"Why not?" she retorted. "Ragan promised me. He won't let Commonal back down now."

I nodded my head. "Very well," I said. "If the commemoration does go ahead, you'll certainly need to rehearse. I'll send Jean-Jacques to town while the rain's still gentle. He can go to Ragan's house himself, and pay someone a little nimbler of foot to tackle Snowspur. Ragan will come, I'm sure. As for Eirene... Well, she'll be safer here than exposed on the hilltop if the storm becomes violent, so it's possible that she'll break precedent."

"Ragan will come," Davida agreed. There was a note in her voice harsher than any my harpsichord was likely to produce under the pressure of her delicate fingers. She too suspected that Ragan had killed Tybalt and Morloc, even though she had far less evidence to prompt her than I had accumulated; perhaps she even suspected his motive, in all its tortured complexity.

"When Ragan told you his version of the fate of the *Haemon Redondo*, Davida," I said, "what did he tell you about the lighthouse-keeper?"

Davida seemed startled to be asked, but she answered readily enough. "He said that the lighthouse-keeper collaborated with the wreckers," she reported. "The keeper left his post–but when he found out that the ship had been carrying passengers as well as crewmen, and that it had all been for nothing because the cargo was lost, he went mad and killed himself."

"By drowning?" I queried.

"Yes. According to Ragan, he walked out to sea to join the *Redondo*'s dead–and now he's the most active of all the ghosts."

"That's what I'd deduced," I said. "Thank you–I think I understand everything, now. I believe we can settle the matter tomorrow night. You're right; Ragan will come. I can only hope that Eirene will come too, in case we have need of her healing hands."

14

Constable Clovis called at the house in the afternoon to ask questions of us all regarding the recent movements of Tybalt Sphendon and Morloc Hyat. Neither Davida nor I confided our suspicions about Ragan Barling, although I felt that mine had been confirmed when the Constable told us that both men had, according to Fion Commonal's autopsies, been poisoned rather than drowned. The tortured expressions on their faces had been a convulsant effect of the poison rather than terror.

"Does Fion know what the poison was?" I asked.

"He has never encountered it before, sir," Clovis said. "There are references in his books to natural venoms with similar effects, but their points of origin are the remotest parts of the Empire–the Austral and Transatlantic continents."

"Traffic from both regions passes through the port of Ormaux on a routine basis," I pointed out.

"Yes, sir," he agreed. "Incidentally, the man who crossed the causeway to Lucifer last night is named Lucian Sombre. I was able to talk to him when he returned this morning. He came here from Ormaux, having previously been travelling in distant regions, in search of Phelim Kracy, the new lighthouse-keeper–he is, apparently, an old friend of the family. He claims that he has never heard of Tybalt Sphendon or Morloc Hyat."

No matter how careful I was determined to be, I couldn't let the Constable think that I had set him off on a false trail. "Miss Kracy has mentioned him to me," I said. "He has no conceivable motive for murdering two of our local artists, and there's no reason to think he's lying when he says that he's never heard of them. I fear that you must look elsewhere for the culprit."

Clovis looked at me a trifle reproachfully, having con-cluded that I was not being entirely frank with him, and that I had taken advantage of him by asking him to find out about the man on the causeway for reasons unconnected with his investigation.

"On the day after tomorrow, Constable," I promised, "I should be able to give you more help–but I need to be perfectly certain that I don't accuse an innocent man. It's not too long to wait, I hope."

Clovis hesitated, but nodded. "There'll be no communication with the mainland for a day or two," he observed. "The fishermen say that the storm will be uncommonly violent. They expect a blustery night, and the wind will then get steadily worse from dawn to dusk... no one can tell how bad it will become thereafter."

"It will all blow over," I said. "Storms always do."

Davida went back to work as soon as the Constable had done with her, but I found it a little more difficult to do likewise. Davida's composition was effectively finished; mine had only recently begun. It took time to reimmerse myself in the play of color upon the canvas, but I settled eventually and began to make better progress. Alas, my lack of sleep was beginning to catch up with me; my hand and eye lacked a certain alertness and co-ordination. In the end, I decided that it would be better to wait until morning and put my brushes aside. Davida was still playing, albeit in repetitive snatches, determined to perfect the most challenging parts of her performance in time for the concert.

Ragan Barling sent a note to say that he would be glad to attend. There was no reply from Eirene, although Jean-Jacques confirmed that the message had been delivered.

We dined well, and drank a little too much. The conversation thereafter was poor by the high standards of my dining-room, but that was understandable. Davida was doubly preoccupied, and Hecate was subdued; Candida, by contrast, was excited by the prospect of seeing her portrait completed, and eager to release some of the energy pent up while she had posed. She became voluble, and moved around the room incessantly. Much of what she said was mere froth, but when a

197

gust of wind sent the rain hammering on the window she became suddenly troubled.

"I do hope Phelim will be all right," she said. "He has not been much alone these last 30 years, although I suppose he often hungered for better company. He has been too long devoid of good conversation."

"The ghosts will keep him company," Davida said, a little cruelly. "The dead often rise from the sea-bed, so I'm told, when the crashing waves disturb the mud in which they lie... and they make a special effort for centenaries."

It wasn't Candida who had provoked her bitter tone, but Candida didn't know that, and seemed hurt by it. "The spirits of the sea wouldn't hurt Phelim," she asserted, defiantly. "He's done them no harm."

"That's not what Nicodemus Rham thought," Davida countered, reflexively. "Phelim's only there because his predecessor fled, fearing that the dead of the *Haemon Redondo* might not know one lighthouse-keeper from another."

"Ragan lied when he told you that, Davida," I was quick to say. "I've seen Nicodemus, and he has no fear whatsoever of the ghosts of the *Haemon Redondo*. Indeed, he feels that they have done him a great deal of good. Were Rham's ghosts objectively real, Phelim would have nothing at all to fear from them."

I had intended to soothe Candida's sudden anxiety, but she understood me too well for that. She immediately took the inference that the only ghosts Phelim might see were those projected from his own dreams... and that was no reassurance at all. She bit her lip–but she said nothing, leaving the field open for Davida.

"What else did Ragan lie about?" Davida demanded–although she must have known that I was in no position to judge the full extent of his deceit.

"Perhaps *lie* is too strong a word," I said, reflectively. "It isn't easy for an antiquarian to summon up the past from a handful of relics, harder still when he yearns to make a coherent and meaningful story for the benefit of their own times. All history is fantasy, after all."

"I suppose the ship never went down at all," Davida said, contemptuously, "if there ever was such a vessel. Doubtless the whole thing's a myth."

"There was a shipwreck," I said. "No one doubts that. The problem arises in making sense of it. To understand history, one needs to understand the motives of the people who make it–and we rarely understand our own motives fully, let alone those of the other people we observe and consult. The dead are no longer available for observation or consultation, so we're free to conjecture and invent, whether we do so as historians or as ghost-seers. That's what I mean when I say that *all* history is fantasy."

"Do we need to understand anyone's motives to know why the *Haemon Redondo* was wrecked?" Hecate asked. "It was blown on to the rocks by a storm-wind, and no one could prevent it."

"According to Ragan," Davida said, "it was drawn on to the rocks by a wrecker's false light, when the keeper on Lucifer extinguished his own. Was that a lie, Master Rathenius?"

"There's no evidence at all to support it," I said, "and plenty to oppose it. If Ragan hoped to generate enough anxiety among the poor folk to make them see ghosts in every mist or cloud-shadow, he'd have done better to leave that element out of his tale, for he's stirred up some resentment by calling their ancestors wreckers. He did it, I suppose, to add an extra note of piquancy to the tragedy of brave Captain Bayard and his supposed wife... but that was a false inference too. Had he done his research more thoroughly, he'd have discovered that the Madame Bayard on the passenger list was married to the captain's brother. The problem with actual history is that it rarely provides the melodramatic pitch that poetry demands, thus tempting reckless embellishment."

"Poetry?" Hecate queried. "Ragan isn't a poet."

"Probably not," I agreed, "but he aspires to be. He wouldn't confide his aspiration to you or me, for fear of criti-

199

cism–but he confided it to Nicodemus Rham, when he tried to recruit Rham's support for his campaign of rumors, and he must have confided it to Davida."

Davida seemed mildly surprised. "I didn't think he was serious," she said, in a tone that I found wonderfully revealing.

"Ah!" I said. "I should have realized. You didn't think he was serious. You didn't think he *could* be serious... the ultimate insult. As I said to Hecate, I thought at first that this was all about lust and jealousy, until I realized that it was more likely to be all about art. I thought at first that Ragan had merely become infatuated with you, as foolish old men sometimes do become unreasonably infatuated with lovely young women, and that he only urged you to write about the wreck of the *Redondo* as a means of getting close to you... but that was only the lesser part of his foolishness, wasn't it? His desire to share a bed with you was always overshadowed by the hope of a more intimate collaboration. His final ambition was to add his words to your music. Tybalt's involvement–at every level– he could tolerate, albeit with difficulty... but Morloc was a different matter. Morloc was a poet. When you communicated the enthusiasm Ragan had fired in you to Tybalt, it was a minor tragedy; when you suggested that Morloc should also write about the *Redondo*'s fate, it was a mortal insult. Mortal, alas, for Morloc... and Tybalt."

Davida's response to this speech was outrage; she had already appointed Ragan Barling her chief suspect, but she had taken a simpler view of his envy. She would have preferred it had his motive been pure and simple lust. Candida, on the other hand, was surprised but uninvolved; she had never met Ragan.

Hecate reacted more forcefully than either. "*Ragan* killed them?" she exclaimed. "Why didn't you tell the Constable? And why on Earth did you invite him here tomorrow night?"

"Because all we have at present is a story," I pointed out. "A fantastical history, compounded out of inference and conjecture. I've seen Ragan's collection of exotica, including his cupboard full of arcane substances–whose poisonous inclusions are doubtless more effective than its supposed magics—but that's not proof. Unless he can be maneuvered into a confession, or trapped in a further attempt at murder, we have no basis for a further accusation."

"How, exactly, do you propose to maneuver him into a confession?" Davida demanded.

Hecate, who knew me better, said: "Who, exactly, do you expect him to try to murder?"

"The double murder was more performance than purposive crime," I said. "It's as redolent with melodrama as his rumors of the wreck–indeed, it's the very same melodrama, insofar as he tried, absurdly, to put the blame on the *Haemon Redondo*'s innocent dead. Hopeful artists are rarely content with anonymity for long. Given the opportunity to parade his awful ingenuity in public, I think Ragan can be persuaded to confess... and in the meantime, the person he'll come here to murder, obviously, is me."

"Why you?" Davida asked. "You're a painter."

"Indeed I am, and a great one. That's why Ragan was momentarily pleased when he thought I'd been inspired by his false rumors and improvised centenary to consult his expertise, with a view to painting the shipwreck; but that was before I took Davida into my house, and put her–literally, of course, rather than metaphorically–into my bed. Jean-Jacques will have mentioned the detail in passing, of course, when he took the invitation. Servants can be *so* indiscreet, and Ragan can't be expected to know that mine requires instruction before he lets things slip. Combined with the fact that Ragan, quite rightly, fears the progress of my own investigation of the circumstances of the wreck, and the fact that Davida will play her composition in full for the first time at my invitation, in circumstances of my choosing, while he is a mere invited guest...the sum would be motive enough, I suppose, even without the most important motive of all."

"Which is?" Hecate obligingly put in.

"The man must know, even if he is in denial, that he will ultimately be caught, tried and punished," I said. "As things stand, he has only murdered two minor artists of no great standing or accomplishment. Given that it will not increase his penalty, how can he resist the temptation to add a true genius to the list? How else can he hope to increase his notoriety enough to be remembered?"

Candida was the only one innocent enough to laugh. Davida seemed genuinely shocked, and Hecate merely shook her head in mock despair.

"If my calculations are correct," I told them, "he'll try to poison my glass, just as he presumably poisoned the glasses from which Tybalt and Morloc were drinking. I shall be quaffing absinthe, so I suggest that the three of you are careful to drink red wine. I shall give him abundant opportunity by continually turning my back on my glass, but Jean-Jacques will be observing it constantly–without so much as blinking, I hope–through a convenient peephole. As soon as the deed is done, and witnessed, the alarm will be raised. I had thought of asking Constable Clovis to secrete himself in Jean-Jacques' stead, or at least beside him, but I decided against it."

"Why?"

"Because an early arrest might cause us to miss out on the grand confession which Ragan will surely be proud to make once he realizes that he is caught. That's a performance I'm keen to see–and I'm sure that Ragan will want me in the audience, once he realizes that he has failed to kill me. It will, after all, be his last chance to make an impact as an artist."

"What about my performance?" Davida asked. "You don't propose to interrupt that, I hope?"

"I, too, can only hope," I said. "Ragan has been on the island a long time; I think he might be connoisseur enough to wait until you've finished playing before making his attempt to poison me–although I fear that I can't guarantee it. It's possible that he's mad enough by now to be capable of anything. That's one reason why I hope Eirene might come; she would be able to calm his madness, though not his murderous intent."

"She'll be too late, alas, to calm yours," Hecate murmured. She meant my madness; I've never been guilty of murderous intent.

"She did try," I admitted. "She told me very specifically that I would be in no danger, unless I wanted to be. Her powers as an oracle are quite remarkable."

"What's the other reason why you want the morpheomorphist here?" Davida wanted to know.

I hesitated–needlessly, as it turned out.

"That's for my benefit," Candida Kracy put in. "Eirene Magdelana knew my mother, you see... and she knows as much about the shaping of dreams as anyone. Master Rathenius thinks that Eirene might be able to explain to me why I recently woke from my long sleep... and why I went to sleep in the first place."

"I'm sure that she can," I said, quietly, "but I can't be sure that she will. Hers is the kind of art that brings madness in its train, and her own dreams have placed her at the beck and call of imaginary spirits. I think she needs to come here, for her own sake as well as Candida's, but I'm not sure that she'll be able to perceive her own need, or to act on it. Perhaps, in any case, it would be safer to take matters one at a time. There will be time enough to see to Candida's mysteries when we've trapped Ragan Barling in our cunning web."

"*Our* web?" Davida queried.

"It's ours now," Hecate told her. "Or it will be, as soon as we've taken the decision not to go home. You do intend to offer us the choice, Axel, I suppose?"

"You're free agents," I said. "If any of you would prefer not to be here when he arrives, I'll make your apologies to Ragan and improvise as best I can." I knew full well that none of them would want to miss any part of the performance.

"I shall be here," Davida said, grimly.

"In that case, I wouldn't miss it for the world," Hecate agreed.

"Nor I," said Candida Kracy. "It will add immeasurably to the pleasure I take when I look at my portrait in future years, to remember its making in such intriguing circumstances."

"Excellent," I said. "That's settled, then."

<h2 style="text-align:center">15</h2>

Ragan Barling arrived almost an hour late–some 15 minutes after nightfall–having been delayed in his journey by the weather. In possession of a carriage of his own, he had had no need to make a hopeless attempt to hire one, but his manservant had been even more insistent than a specialist coachman in judging that the steep slopes separating his home from mine were impassable by wheeled vehicles, given the force of the wind and the treachery of the mud and free-flowing water. Ragan had, in consequence, been forced to set off on foot; he was, of course, absolutely determined not to miss Davida Amalek's debut performance of *The Wreck of the Haemon Redondo*. His apologies were profuse, but I assured him that he had not held up the performance at all, our other expected guest not having arrived. I took his sodden topcoat and scarf, and placed them on the stand myself. I volunteered to take his bulky frock coat too, since it seemed more than a little damp, but he told me that he would rather keep it on and let the fire dry it out.

I seated him by the hearth and offered him a brandy to warm him, which he gratefully accepted. His chair was separated from mine by a small table, where my half-full glass of absinthe stood in tempting isolation. My chair was separated from Hecate Rain's by a similar table, on which her own glass stood beside a bottle of red wine; everyone else was drinking from that same bottle.

While Ragan wiped his boots and warmed himself, huddling next to the fire in his tightly buttoned and many-pocketed frock coat, I continued arranging the furniture, prattling to Hecate and Candida and wondering loudly where Eirene Magdelana might be.

When another half-hour had passed and Eirene still hadn't put in an appearance, I suggested that we ought to start. I apologized for the fact that the thunder was incapable of following the score that Davida had provided, but expressed the hope that its rumblings would not be too inapposite.

"It seems to be getting closer," I said, making eye contact with Ragan as I said it. "We're a little exposed, I fear, so close to the cliff, but I have a lightning-conductor mounted on the house in case we're struck. All the shutters are closed and all the bolts securely bedded, so we need have no fear that the wind will cause any breaking of glass or slamming of doors. We shall be a little chrysalis of sanity in a world of confusion, lost in the wonder of music while the spirits of the sea and air howl and moan and crash about like madmen."

Ragan didn't seem to be impressed, but he nodded politely by way of acknowledgement.

I went to the door then, and called out to Davida to tell her that we were ready. She came in promptly, and went to the harpsichord without glancing in Ragan's direction. Hecate had combed and bound Davida's hair for her, and her expression was admirably earnest; I doubted that she had ever looked the part of a serious artist quite so well, although she had probably been lovelier on occasions when she was more relaxed and emotionally liberated. She sat down, and began to play.

I must have heard every note in the piece three or four times over in the course of the previous 36 hours, so there was a sense in which what she played was already familiar, but I had never heard the piece as it was intended to be heard–as a whole, in linear progression from beginning to end. When I had heard its fragments before, moreover, I had been at work on Candida's portrait, and had not been paying any heed to finer details. To some extent, the composition had soaked into my unconscious mind sufficiently to ease the process of concentration that I now brought to bear, but that inattentive exposure had not spoiled the novelty of my immersion within the flow of the notes.

The piece lacked something, I have to admit: Tybalt's violin accompaniment, perhaps, or the familiarity of Davida's own instrument–or perhaps the unforced serenity that Davida would doubtless have brought to a performance free of thoughts of murder, entrapment and revenge. Even so, it was unmistakably a work of quality, whose further refinement might make it into a very fine work indeed. It was still raw, in spite of its wholeness, but I judged that it might well mature into the solid foundation of a great career.

I think Ragan Barling sensed that too. Alas, his listening must have been tainted by his own emotions–regret and remorse, I hope, as well as anxiety and murderous intent–and I knew that he would be unable to surrender himself to the music as he should. I was able to let it flow into me, to occupy and furnish my mind; he had to remain separate from it, conserving the secrecy of his irreparably wounded self.

Surreptitiously, even though I had resolved not to do it, I kept an eye on my glass. Occasionally, I took a sip therefrom–always pausing long enough to facilitate an interruption should one be necessary–but I didn't top it up. It seemed to me that if I waited until the piece were finished before refilling the glass from the bottle on the mantelpiece, and then leapt up to congratulate Davida and embrace her with a little too much honest affection, I would provide my guest with the perfect opportunity to execute his nefarious plan... always assuming, of course, that all my deductions had been correct and that he did intend to kill me.

The music was loud and insistent, as befitted a rhapsodic description of a storm, but its froth and fury were counterpointed by a plaintive melody signifying the plight of the ship caught in the gale. The delicacy of Davida's work was evident in the contest between the two, blatantly unequal but nevertheless sustained, every note clearly audible no matter what its register.

I found myself dreaming–lucidly, given that I was fully awake, but dreaming nevertheless. I found myself imagining, in spite of my better judgment, that the strains of the music were escaping the house, leaking through the shutters and the doors, over the sills and beneath the lintels, to mingle with the sounds of the storm, reproducing its own precise contrapuntal balance on a larger scale. I imagined an audience of animate spirits gathering, moving within and through the walls of my residence, where those blessed with oracular sight had been waiting and fidgeting for days, jostling for the privilege of bathing in the waves of sound.

I imagined, too, that echoes of the concerto were sounding even in the depths of the sea, where the dead of *the Haemon Redondo* rested in peace, undisturbed by the impotent violence of the waves... and I imagined that the dead, being human, responded far more avidly to seduction than they ever had to violence, stirring in their own eternal dream as the strains of Davida's composition reached them from afar, and caused them to remember....

To remember what?

Their terror, as the crew battled to keep the hull secure and the passengers huddled in their cabins?

Their unanswered prayers?

I hoped not. I hoped, if the dead were capable of the least vestige of memory, that they remembered the best quality of life itself... its aesthetic substance, its emotional resonance, its patient nourishment by the meat and wine of dreams.

I hoped, if the dead were capable of memory, that they were also capable of false memory: of nostalgia, and the kind of fantasy that reconstructed history into a coherent and meaningful pattern, a tale with a moral ending.

I hoped that, if the ghosts of the drowned men and women were to be seen at all, they might be seen as Nicodemus Rham saw them, not as Ragan Barling had perverted them: that they might be spirits with the power of consolation, who came in answer to loneliness and not in pursuit of horror or fear.

It was all possible; if, as Eirene Magdelana believed, there were a universal dream-maker helping to animate and motivate the cosmos, whose emotions really were expressed in the spin of the world and its patient progress around the Sun, in the random flares with which the Sun tormented its planetary flock, and in all the winds and ocean currents that stirred the surface of the Earth's living envelope, then the scattered atoms of the long-dead might indeed have retained some slight vestige of awareness of their former state.

If, as Eirene Magdelana dreamed, the whole of creation had to be pervaded by a morpheotic flux that was neither predator nor parasite, but only a consummate artist, it was possible that the strains of Davida Amalek's concerto might be reaching out through time as well as space, to excite the memory of the unlucky crewmen and passengers who had gone down with the *Haemon Redondo*–and also to soothe them, to reconcile them to their violent end by reassuring them that their history, like all history, was no more than a fantasy within a fantasy, a moment in a work of art...

Alas, I was not alone in allowing myself to be immersed and consumed in that indulgent fashion.

I had hoped, when I planned the occasion, that Davida's concerto might have an effect on Candida Kracy, of a kind which might assist Eirene Magdelana to unlock the secrets of her dream-built past. I had expected that the experience might be mildly troublesome as well as enlightening, but nothing I had been told of her history–by Phelim or herself–had given me reason to think that her nightmares were unduly terrible or violent. Even if she dreamed of the *Redondo*'s dead as Ragan Barling had tried to redefine them in rumor, I had assumed, she would suffer no more than any ordinary person would suffer from a bad dream.

My expectation and assumption were wrong; my hope was betrayed.

What the combination of the concerto and the actual storm awoke in Candida Kracy was far more monstrous than

Ragan's imaginary phantoms–and Eirene Magdelana had not come to help me deal with it.

I was first alerted to the problem by Hecate, who touched my arm and directed my attention to Candida. At that point, Candida seemed merely to have fallen asleep in her chair.

Davida's was not the kind of music that would ordinarily be capable of lulling members of its audience into a doze, and I realized very quickly that Candida's was not an ordinary sleep. Her expression began to change, so swiftly that within a few seconds her face had altered completely–and I do not say *completely* in any casual way, for I had spent the greater part of two days painting her face, and I knew it intimately.

The underlying bones and the fabric of Candida's flesh had not been transfigured, but the information of her flesh by life and emotion had caused the subtle muscles of her expression to undergo a remarkable metamorphosis. Hers was not the same face that it had been; it was not, in effect, *her* face.

Whose face was it? No other person's, that's for sure, nor any god's or demon's. Shaped by the morpheotic flux it must have been, but Morpheus himself it was not. That was the most awful thing of all–and it told me that I had badly underestimated the nature and extent of Candida Kracy's malaise. She had spoken of wanting to see "her ghosts" more clearly, meaning the ghosts of her mother and great-grandmother... but she had no notion of what kind of ghost she harbored in the remoter depths of her unconscious mind, or what kind of force.

She had, as I had innocently observed, no idea what kind of a work of art she really was.

The air in my lungs seemed impossibly thick and ponderous; my nostrils filled with an odor that was still unrecognizable but far more offensive than it had been before. I had to fight against the stench lest it render me numb... but I had the music to help; like the imaginary ghosts of the *Haemon Redondo*, I found strength and solace in the music–and I, unlike them, was still alive and capable of action.

I got up, and moved towards her, ready to lay my hands upon her, or to embrace her, no matter what danger there might be in such a move. I wasn't afraid, because I didn't want to be.

It occurred to me momentarily, as I went to her, that the mask which had taken possession of Candida's flesh might be Phelim Kracy's "demanding muse," of which Hecate had spoken–but I quickly put that conclusion aside. It might, in some sense, have been the counterpart of that mercurial mistress in Candida's unconscious, but if it were to be reckoned a force of inspiration, its art was far darker than any poetry that Phelim or Hecate Rain could ever have composed.

I saw, or felt, that this was a morpheomorphic muse, geared to an art that was immensely powerful in its awful purity–that Candida, however helpless she had been for the greater part of her existence, had the potential now to become a medium of awesome magic. Unlike Vashti Savage, who merely imagined that she could dream the voices of the dead into audibility, Candida Kracy had become a channel for something far less shadowy, far more active if not actually alive.

The storm outside was now directly overhead. Pulses of bright lightning forced their radiance through cracks in the shutters, and the staccato thunder became so abruptly insistent that the walls shook.

For a moment, I honestly thought that Candida might draw down the lightning–not to burn and blast us but to claim its power.

Then, as I reached out to her, I saw that Candida was fighting it–that she was by no means content to be possessed or displaced. I saw her own face trying to reassert itself... except that it was not so much her face as she might have seen it in a mirror but her portrait, which was not yet complete but had the ghost of its eventuality already within it. She had seen that image in the process of its formation, and she had seen herself in it, in a manner that I always intended to impose upon my sitters, if I could.

She had the power of my art to help her now, and the knowledge that my art had not yet finished with her, had not yet completed its account of what she might become, if only she could cling to wakefulness.

I drew back my helping hands, just for a moment; I knew they would be needed, but not until she had carried forward her own fight. My role was to be a supportive one.

It is a bitter thing to admit, but mine was by no means the more forceful art at work in that room, and in that mind. My art was horribly weak by comparison with the pent-up power of the *other*–but Davida's music had been more than a trigger. Davida's art was as weak and as impure as my own, but in this one instance, its rawness and its emotional edge were no imperfections at all. They chimed with something in Candida herself that had woken up when she did: a determination to be, and to become, what she intended rather than that which had been intended for her.

The monster, I knew, had no independent existence–yet. No matter what Phelim Kracy–or Lucian Sombre–might believe, it wasn't alive, any more than any ordinary dream or muse is alive... unless and until it could claim Candida Kracy's life for its own.

Candida surged from her seat and flung her arms wide, as if in an attitude of crucifixion.

My hands and arms were ready now; I caught her as her body became rigid with shock. I tried to enfold her in my embrace as Eirene Magdelana had often enfolded me. I tried with all my might to play the morpheomorphist and add the power of my dream-maker to hers, at the service of her struggling reason as well as her fugitive consciousness.

I knew that I wasn't attempting the impossible. The monster was, at that point in its nascent existence, something inspired rather than inspiring: a work of art rather than an artist. It was a work of art like none I could ever have produced or tolerated, perverted in some incomprehensible fashion into a kind of savagery, a kind of self-obliterating rage, but it was a work of art nevertheless. It could still be drowned out, painted over, rewritten... if only I had the authority, and the accompaniment.

"Play on!" I commanded Davida, as the fingers on the keys of the harpsichord faltered. Davida, at least, was amenable to my command, and she responded heroically. She played on, better than she had been playing before.

For a moment or two, Candida seemed similarly pliable; she relaxed into stillness within my enfolding arms–but then, without waking or even appearing to wake, she began to sing.

Again, I'm careful in my use of words. I don't say that she howled, screamed or wailed–I say that she *sang* her own improvised accompaniment, not merely to Davida Amalek's concerto but to the dissolving clouds in the sky: the spirits of the air and of the sea, whose raucous music was all around the house.

The others who heard Candida singing might have disagreed with me that it was singing at all, but I was holding her and I know what I heard, and felt. The air in my lungs was frozen solid; my nose and mouth were burning; my whole body was prickling; my ears were agonized... but it was all art, and I knew it. It was a *song*, which I could apprehend as a connoisseur, comprehend as a critic. The creature that was trying to possess Candida exerted its full repulsive force upon me, but I clung on.

I heard, and felt, the song of the lightning and the deluge: the voice of the vortex that is mistakenly called the *eye* of the storm, when it is really an avid, capacious and reckless mouth.

I heard, and felt that Candida was not only singing to the accompaniment of Davida's concerto and the greater storm without, but to some further accompaniment far beyond the bounds of the Earth.

I had always believed that all magic, however black, is art–but I had never been able to realize before how powerful black magic might be, if its art were sufficiently pure: untempered and unsoothed by the proper artifice of sensation, sanity and skill.

It was terrifying–all the more so because I knew that I couldn't contain or curtail it for long, and might not have been able to do so even with Eirene Magdelana's help. I cursed myself for having been distracted by mere matters of murder and criminal culpability–and I listened to the song.

In spite of my best instincts, I listened to the song that Candida Kracy didn't want to sing, and was properly appreciative of its potential for hideous genius.

Ragan Barling, I suspected, had harbored the secret ambition of having his words set to Davida's music to make an oratorio. Morloc Hyat had probably conceived the same idea, idly at least, while he made love to her. Neither of them, however, could ever have imagined anything remotely like the wordless anthem that Candida's *alter ego* added to Davida's music by way of complement and completion.

Anthem, I admit, is not as punctiliously exact as the other words I chose so carefully. Perhaps I could as easily have said *paean* or *battle-song*. There is no word in any Imperial language–let alone the composite *parole* that allows our multitudinous citizens to communicate, no matter what their native tongues might be–accurately to describe that unique and very particular work of art.

It did have the potential to be built into a work of genius, and I hadn't the power to stop it–but Candida Kracy did, with my support.

As soon as she perceived the quality of the song that she was being required to sing, she began, in spite of my restraining arms, to tear at her face and clothing with clawed fingers. It seemed to me, as I held her more tightly, that she was ripping at her very soul with imaginary talons. I had no alternative but to try to prevent her doing herself actual injury, and Hecate Rain supported me by grabbing the younger woman's flailing hands–but the real battle was the internal one.

Candida wasn't physically strong–her muscles had never had the opportunity to be trained while she slept, as her mind had been trained–but her sheer recklessness made her difficult to contain, after the fashion of madmen who appear to have the strength of ten simply because they've lost their normal reaction to resistance. Hecate was by no means frail, for a woman, but she had not strength enough in her two arms to control one of Candida's.

I had no alternative but to wrestle Candida to the ground, where she could be more easily contained by the mere weight of my body and held still until the fit relented. There was nothing I could do to contain that terrible voice; only Candida could do that. I knew, as I felt her struggling, that if this were only to be the first in an infinite series of battles, the war of attrition might be one that she couldn't win–but Candida was determined to fight it anyway. She was fighting with all her might, and not merely for her life.

She won–the battle, if not the war.

She reasserted herself, and the song faltered. Once it had faltered, as is so often the way with songs, it lost its way. It could not find the more distant accompaniment that had fed it for several minutes; and once Davida's music reasserted its priority, it lost its imperious quality and faded into something more akin to a threnody. The element of lamentation in it was Candida's own.

It didn't relent entirely for a few minutes more, but relent it did. The fit passed, and I felt certain, as I shared in her exhaustion, that the victory was secure, at least for the time being. No matter how weak she seemed as she lay helpless beneath me, she was stronger now than she had ever been before.

I could breathe again, although I was panting avidly; the air in the room was scented with woodsmoke and wine.

16

When Candida Kracy had finally become quiet again, Davida Amalek had stopped playing. The concerto's debut had been ruined–but as I caught Davida's eye I could see that her priorities were in order. Davida knew that there would be other, and better, opportunities to demonstrate her own artistry in less highly-charged circumstances.

Candida had slumped into such utter inertia that for three or four horrid seconds I thought that the price of her victory might be her life, but that anxiety was unjustified. When she opened her eyes, her gaze was determined. Her face was her own again, reflecting everything that I had tried to capture and preserve within my portrait.

"Why, Master Rathenius," she said, looking directly up into my eyes as if she were lying beneath me while I made love to her, "I have had the most frightful dream."

I would have found an answer, despite being a little out of breath, had Hecate not tapped me urgently on the shoulder to make me turn my head.

"Where's Ragan?" she asked, tersely.

My almost-empty glass of absinthe still stood on the little table where I had left it, seemingly unaugmented by any foreign substance–but Ragan Barling was no longer in his chair.

Davida leapt up from her stool, ready to play the hunter, but as I got up in my turn I held up my hand to instruct her to be still.

"Jean-Jacques!" I cried.

Jean-Jacques hurried into the room to assure me that my absinthe-glass remained unsullied, and to explain that I had given him such strict orders not to leave his post...

I cut him off with a forgiving gesture.

"My fault," I said. "I misjudged him. I'll make repairs, if it isn't too late. Help Hecate, please. Davida–leave this to me." Given that Candida seemed to be herself again, or very nearly so, I felt that I had a license to devote myself to matters of lesser importance for a little while.

I had to guess where Ragan might have gone, but it wasn't too difficult. Nor was it too late.

I came through the door of my bedroom just in time to see the antiquarian pouring liquid from a phial into the decanter of water that stood on the table beside the bedhead.

Ragan Barling looked up as I came in, far too late to interrupt himself or hide what he was doing. There was only a single candle burning on the bedside table, but its flame was bright enough to display his crime, and his knowledge of its exposure.

"Damn," he said, softly. "It seemed certain that the madwoman would keep you occupied for at least a few minutes more."

"Water, Ragan?" I said, closing the door behind me in order to make sure that Davida could not follow me. "Would it not have been far better concealed in the absinthe?"

"So it *was* a trap! Well, I'm glad that you made the mistake, even though you seem to have caught up with me regardless. The poison is tasteless, you see—water will hold it just as well as brandy, in this particular instance, albeit in no other." He giggled at the feeble joke.

"Except," I told him, "that I'm not sleeping here just now. I'm bedded down in my studio, Davida sleeps here—alone."

He was sorely annoyed by the observation that he had made the greater mistake, but that wasn't surprising, given his situation. He shrugged his shoulders, trying to make light of it.

"Oh, Ragan," I said. "What kind of artwork is that? You must have started off with honest affection in your heart as well as ambition. You must have dreamed of a true partnership with Davida, in every sense of the word. No matter how embittered you became as you perceived the hopelessness of your illusions, you've been on the island long enough to be sensitive to the quality of this adventure. If you had killed the woman with whom you set out to collaborate instead of your appointed nemesis, the tragedy would be tinged with farce, and your grand performance would be that of a foolish clown, not a man who could plausibly represent murder as one of the fine arts. You may not be a poet, Ragan, but you surely aren't such a philistine as that!"

He tried to laugh, more robustly than before but hoarsely and humorlessly.

"You always were a mean-spirited critic, Axel," he said. "You don't give me credit enough for the parts of my scheme that worked out beautifully. I don't believe you've understood its true complexity."

"I understand that you fell victim to its ridiculous intricacy," I told him, coldly. "I understand that you lured Tybalt and Morloc out to the Knuckle by promising them the sight of a ghost, and that you poisoned them there–with brandy I assume, given what you said a minute ago–because you had no other convenient way of delivering the bodies to the sea. I should, admittedly, have realized sooner that what you picked up when you came to bid farewell to me as I set off with Hecate across the causeway was Morloc's tobacco-pouch, which you had been unable to find in the dark–but I surely made up for that when I guessed why you were so discomfited to see a lantern on the causeway when I visited your attic.

"The tale you spun to Tybalt and Morloc was that the guilt-stricken lighthouse-keeper who extinguished Lucifer's Light for your imaginary wreckers had committed suicide by wading out to Dead Man's Fist when the water over the causeway was only knee-deep, and waiting there for the tide to return... a performance his wayward ghost repeated whenever the conditions were similar. Alas, Dead Man's Fist isn't called Dead Man's Fist by virtue of association with an actual dead man, but by virtue of its infestation by a few clusters of harmless polyps. That sort of improvisation, Ragan, is definitely inartistic–almost as inartistic, in my judgment, as haring off into the night to ascertain whether there really was a man on the causeway the night before last, or whether one of the ghosts you had invented had actually come to haunt you.

"It was bad work, Ragan, from beginning to end. Do you know the worst of it? When I sent Jean-Jacques to find out whether anyone knew who the man on the causeway was, he came back saying that *everyone* had been asking–not Constable Clovis, not Ragan Barling, but *everyone*. That's the public's measure of the individuality of your work, Ragan–what will they think when they hear that you walked into my trap even though you knew that it had been set for you?"

"But you miscalculated it," he protested. "It would have been your fault if Davida had ended up dead in your place."

"I have my murderer," I pointed out, "and I've prevented his third murder. Oh, Ragan, why could you not be content to be a connoisseur?"

"You, of all people, can ask me that?" he said. Then my own plan went wrong again, as he drew an antique dueling-pistol from the inner pocket of his far-too-capacious frock coat and pointed it at me.

I was alone with an armed man who had come to murder me, with a closed door at my back. Even I, on occasion, am guilty of momentary failures of artistry.

"Aren't those things supposed to come in pairs?" I said, trying hard to sound suitably contemptuous.

"So they are," Barling replied, scornfully. "Had you not been such a precious fool, Rathenius, I suppose you might have made a tolerable antiquary."

"Have you ever fired such a weapon, Ragan?" I asked. "I have—and I can assure you that they're by no means as reliable in reality as they are in melodrama. I've witnessed duels in which the combatants blazed away half a dozen times at 20 paces distance, without ever scoring a hit."

"So have I," he said, "but you're only six paces away, and you'd have to come a great deal closer to take it off me." So saying, he backed away from the bed towards the big dou-ble-window. The window-frame had a catch and a door-handle, but it also had bolts set at the top and bottom.

I hoped that he might not have noticed both the bolts, but he had; he drew them back without taking his eyes off me. I knew, though, that the closed shutter would be far more diffi-cult, if not impossible, to open from the inside. There was a bolt on the outside that ought to be closed; because the room was on the first floor it had to be closed from within rather than without, but the loophole that allowed that to be done was itself covered by a sealed flap that would not be easy to manipulate one-handed.

I knew that Barling intended to shoot me, or at least to try; he was only waiting until his escape-route was clear before firing his weapon. The sensible thing to do was to maximize the distance between us, in order to make the most of the possibility that he would indeed be unable to aim the barrel accurately. I was, however, tempted to wait where I was until he began to struggle with the shutter, so that I could surge forward as soon as he seemed sufficiently distracted.

If things had worked out that way, I could easily have been killed.

They didn't.

To my extreme astonishment, once Barling had released the internal lock, the shutter swung open very easily–as if it had not been secured outwardly at all. Apparently, the external bolt had not been shot. I cursed Jean-Jacques for his carelessness, even as I said: "It's a long jump, Ragan, and a dangerous landing. You might hurt yourself."

Barling opened his mouth to reply, but he didn't get the chance. A long arm snaked in from the balcony to close around his neck. Another grabbed the wrist holding the gun and wrenched it violently upwards. Taken entirely by surprise, Barling couldn't even hold on to the pistol; it was wrenched from his hand and then brought down, butt-first, upon his head with sufficient force to knock him out.

Jumping, yet again, to the wrong conclusion, I uncursed Jean-Jacques delightedly. I was just about to congratulate him on his ingenuity when I saw that it was not Jean-Jacques at all, but an intruder, who had disarmed my would-be murderer–an intruder who reversed the gun in his hand so as to take hold of the butt and place his finger on the trigger, as soon as Ragan had slid unconscious to the floor.

"Master Rathenius, I presume," the newcomer said. He was tall, but his face was hidden by a broad-brimmed hat pulled down low to shield him from the wind and rain. His cloak was black.

"Lucian Sombre?" I guessed.

Mine, I think, was by far the more considerable feat of deduction, but he didn't seem impressed. "Constable Clovis has obviously been here," he remarked. "Don't worry, Master Rathenius, I mean you no harm—in fact, I believe that I might just have saved your life."

"Only because you were lurking on my balcony like a sneak-thief, ready to invade my house," I pointed out. "If you hadn't drawn the bolt, he would have been stuck inside, too fearful to shoot—and if you mean me no harm, why are you pointing that silly gun at me?"

He looked at the dueling pistol then, rather critically.

"You're right," he agreed. "It *is* a silly gun." He threw it down on the bedcover, and took another from inside his cloak. "This one," he observed, "is far more modern. It's called a revolver. Have you ever seen one before?"

"No," I admitted.

"It can fire six bullets from a rotating chamber. It brings an entirely new dimension to the art of dueling. On the other hand..." He moved forward to the bedside and picked up Ragan Barling's gun again. He seemed to be weighing the two—not to compare their virtue, but their various roles in a new scheme that was busy hatching in his skull.

I figured out what he must be thinking without undue difficulty. If he were to shoot me with Ragan's gun, Ragan might make a very convenient scapegoat. Even if he shot me with the other, it might be worth planting the revolver on Ragan, in the hope of shifting the blame. Presumably, he had spoken the truth when he said that he had meant me no harm, but that didn't mean that he wasn't prepared to be flexible, if he didn't get what he wanted. I wasn't prepared to give him what he wanted, so the situation was still dangerous—more so now than when poor Ragan had been wielding a single gun.

"I'm not alone in the house," I told Sombre, hoping that the thought of having to carry out a massacre might put a stop to his flight of fancy.

"I know that, you fool," he said. "Why do you think I came?"

"I'm not talking about Candida Kracy," I retorted. "I'm talking about my two servants, Davida Amalek and Hecate Rain. You have no quarrel with any of them. Would you really kill five people in order to get your hands on Candida? Do you really think that you could make Ragan Barling take the blame for that?"

He thought about it for a few moments. "I could try," he said, meaning that he could still make an attempt, however unconvincing it might prove in the long run, to set up Ragan Barling as the Constable's chief suspect for whatever might transpire here. That answered the other question too, asserting that while his present mood endured, he would stop at nothing to lay his hands on Candida. Why was the need so urgent, I wondered, given that he could presumably have laid his hands on her so much more easily before she came to the island, and would doubtless have had better opportunities had he consented to wait?

Playing for time, I said: "Your interest might be understandable, whether you are Phelim's father or brother... but to act so precipitately, and so violently... that I don't understand."

I was genuinely mystified; I had not anticipated any of this. In my mind, Ragan Barling had been cast as the play's only murderer; the second strand of the plot had not seemed nearly so melodramatic. I had not anticipated Candida's song, either; clearly, the prize at stake–or the prize that had been at stake before Candida won her internal battle–was larger than I had imagined.

I had scored a hit when I used the words *father or brother*. Sombre knew that the Constable couldn't have given me that information, and that Phelim certainly hadn't. He stopped weighing the mismatched guns in his two hands, and became even more hesitant.

"Who else have you told?" he said, ominously.

"Too many," I lied. "Constable Clovis, Fion Commonal... I also told them that your similarly-named grandfather, Edom Sombre's father, was travelling on the *Haemon Redondo* under an assumed name, but didn't go down with the wreck because he'd already left the ship. Did he kill Elgin Bayard before he left, by the way? Is that why the ship ran on to the rocks–because the captain was not there to help save her?"

That certainly gave him pause–as did the gentle rap on the door behind me.

"Sir?" said Jean-Jacques' worried voice. "Are you all right, sir?"

"Don't come in, Jean-Jacques," I said. "Just get the shotgun from the cellar, and make ready to defend the women."

He was a good servant; he knew better than to say anything but "Yes, sir," whether he intended to obey the order or not.

"How can you know all that?" Lucian Sombre asked me, momentarily helpless in his new confusion, even though he still held both the guns.

"I talked to a man who's on intimate terms with the ghosts of the *Haemon Redondo*," I said. "Not to mention the antiquary who lies unconscious at your feet. If he hadn't taken me up to his attic, by the way–a very rare privilege–we would never have seen your lantern as you made your way across the causeway to see Phelim. Ragan was sufficiently startled to wonder whether one of his imaginary ghosts might have materialized in answer to his call... but I knew better."

"Then, I might not feel so ashamed if I do have to shoot you," Sombre said. "But first, I think you'd better precede me down the stairs, lest your man should really be lying in wait with a shotgun. We'll have to make sure, won't we, that he can't shoot me without shooting through you?"

I still couldn't understand why he had come here so hastily, or why he seemed suddenly prepared to do anything at all to get his hands on Candida Kracy without the least delay. What, I wondered, could justify taking such an appalling risk?

Had he known in advance that Candida would suffer the kind of fit that had just taken hold of her? Had he assumed that if and when it happened, the other features would be permanently etched on her face? If so, what did he want with the entity that Candida might have become—and might have repelled only for the time being?

It was on the tip of my tongue to tell him that the crisis had come and had passed, and that Candida had prevailed—but then I guessed, rather belatedly, what it was that had brought him here in such a hurry, and why Phelim had been so eager to fall in with Candida's plan to get away from the people and places they knew, in the hope that he might hide her until his father—their father—arrived.

"She's pregnant, isn't she?" I said. "It's not her you're anxious to secure, but the child. You didn't want to risk anyone finding out about the child, because they'd be sure to guess who the father was—and once they began to investigate, they might even be able to discover what kind of child it was supposed to be."

I wished that I were able see his face, but it was too well shadowed. The candle was in entirely the wrong position.

"It's not the first time, is it?" I went on, speaking softly now that I was sure of my ground—my intention, after all, was to persuade him that his situation was hopeless, and that there was nothing any longer to be gained by abduction or murder. "In fact, it's the fourth. Her mother Karenne was your father's subject before she was handed on to you, wasn't she, just as Vyvyane Barling and her daughter were your grandfather's? The family fortune of which Phelim speaks so ruefully wasn't contained in bullion or documents... it was in the flesh that played host to a hereditary somnambulism. Nor was it entirely lost when Vyvyane lost her life, although your father and grandfather seem to have had a great deal of trouble endeavoring to recover it... and haven't yet quite succeeded. In fact, you must almost have given up hope. Almost... but not quite. When Phelim realized, and sent for you, the hope surged up again. But why, Lucian? *Why?*"

He curled his lip in what seemed suspiciously like contempt. "You have no idea," he murmured, "what *power* a child like that... not merely to see the future, but to dream the dream of the universe entire..."

I was disappointed, but not entirely surprised. Now that I had met and measured the man, I could not be surprised. "Power," I echoed. "Not art at all, then. I had hoped that it was all about art, not power, but I am ever in the habit of thinking too kindly of my fellow men. The urgency is not so puzzling, now. Art requires patience, but the prospect of power is a different and purer kind of greed. How your father and grandfather must have suffered, under a spur of that sort! Unto the fifth generation... Except that Candida has a choice that none of the others had, because Candida *knows*. Candida could fight–and she did. If only you'd been downstairs, instead of lurking here, you'd have seen that fight. Could you hear the song, Master Sombre? Or was it drowned out by the thunder of your own ambition? You're too late, I fear–too late!"

"You don't know what you're talking about, you meddling imbecile," Sombre said. "I ought to shoot you anyway. Perhaps I will, once I've got the girl."

He took two steps towards me–thus creating the space for someone else to come into the room just as he had done, having climbed up to the balcony in exactly the same way.

Yet again, it wasn't Jean-Jacques. Jean-Jacques was downstairs, waiting patiently with the shotgun, ready to defend the household.

"No, Lucian," Eirene Magdelana said, sounding perfectly sane in spite of the wind that was billowing in the curtains behind her. "He's right. It's over. At last, it's over."

The man in the hat half-turned, his hands moving wide apart as he kept the revolver trained on me while pointing Ragan Barling's pistol at the newcomer.

"And who the *Hell* are you?" he complained.

"Don't you know me, Lucian?" Eirene said, by no means untenderly. "I rather hoped that you would. I'm your mother."

17

Eirene Magdelana reached out to her son with both arms and stepped forwards, clearly intending to embrace him.

Lucian Sombre could have shot her, but he didn't hesitate even for a split second before raising the barrel of Ragan's pistol so that it pointed harmlessly at the ceiling. He allowed his mother to place her arms around him, beneath his upraised arms. Her right remained horizontal as it enfolded him, but the other bent at the elbow so that she could place her left hand on the base of his skull.

She had held me in the same fashion; I knew how powerful the grip could be, in spite of its seeming lightness.

He relaxed, and so did she. The moment seemed perfect, and infinitely elastic. Years of separation and denial collapsed into the crack in time. While I hardly had time to blink an eye, they slipped into a dream whose appearance was half a lifetime. They were both artists, capable of directing and sculpting the morpheotic flux; they knew how to make the most of that miraculous moment, and they did.

At least, I hope they did.

The storm was still overhead, but no lightning-bolt had lashed out for a minute or more. One descended now, splitting the fragment of sky that was visible to me through the open window. I was too far away from the open window to see Lucifer's Light, but I knew immediately where the bolt was headed.

The artificial light in Phelim's lamp-room must have gone out, but the white glare of the lightning drew a dazzling line through my visual field, stunning the receptors in my retina. Such light as I perceived thereafter was certainly illusion, but its implications were not unreal.

It seemed to me that the lightning's electric blaze descended through the body of the lighthouse to Lucifer itself, and then struck out across the sea, not merely turning its surface to a sheet of white but illuminating the depths, bringing instantaneous day to the silent darkness where the scattered remnants of the *Haemon Redondo* lay.

Then, it seemed to me, the light came ashore, surging up and over the cliff until it came with a rush upon my house. Diluted now, it was no longer capable of blasting stone or setting wood ablaze; it climbed instead to the open window in which Lucian Sombre and Eirene Magdelana were silhouetted, and flowed into their bodies like a flood that was no longer light at all, but the pure substance of dreams.

They were both magicians, capable of shaping the morpheotic flux, but they operated as such by permission of a force that was infinitely more powerful. It was not a god, nor a solution of ghosts, but it was not and could not be impersonal, for dreams are not merely the sustenance but the very fabric of personality.

Mother and son, who probably had not seen one another since Lucian had been weaned from Eirene's breast, were reunited in more than sight or flesh. Their bodies remained separate, touching one another without any particular force or fervor, but their minds were fused and their emotions seamlessly combined.

They had both been mad, each in a distinct and idiosyncratic manner, but when the shapers of their dreams were exerted to intervene in their common plight matters of sanity and madness became irrelevant. Dreams have a logic of their own.

Eirene was weeping. So was her son. They were not unhappy; they were ecstatic. The music of the storm had entered into them—as had the music beyond the storm—but they were not tempestuous within; they had found, instead, a precious and preternatural calm. Even so, Eirene was weeping; this was not a new beginning but a closure, a final settlement of something that had begun a hundred years ago—perhaps to the day, given that whatever had happened between Vyvyane Bayard and the first Lucian Sombre must have come to its climax some time before the *Haemon Redondo* had foundered on the Devil's Rocks.

After a while–I can't tell how long–Eirene moved her arms again, releasing the body of her son. Lucian Sombre slowly toppled sideways, his knees crumpling and his torso sprawling across the bedhead. His hat fell away from his head, revealing his face to the candlelight.

I was surprised to see how old he seemed, although he had perforce to be 15 or 20 years younger than Eirene. Jean-Jacques had said that he gave the impression of being a dark man, but his hair was more white than black now, and his features were ravaged by wrinkles and liver-spots. I still didn't know for sure whether he had been Phelim's brother or father, or both, but the family resemblance was abundantly clear and the detail no longer seemed to make much difference.

I couldn't help wondering whether I might be looking at some strange fleshy echo of the *first* Lucian Sombre–and whether, in some strange way, they were *all* figments of the same dark dream: both Lucians, Edom and Phelim too.

I am older than I seem, and I could easily imagine that Lucian Sombre was also older than he seemed, having won his own costly longevity by darker and different means.

Edom Sombre's experiments in somnabulism had evidently involved Karenne Kracy in exactly the same fashion as Eirene Magdelana, but how much further they had extended I couldn't estimate exactly. Here was an instance in which the sins of the father really did seem to have been inherited by the son, not once but three times over–but that inheritance had not solved the problems or ended the frustrations that had bedeviled the First Lucian Sombre.

I stepped forward and put my hand to Sombre's neck, feeling for a pulse. I couldn't find one.

He hadn't been murdered; I won't say that he'd been healed, but he hadn't been carelessly slaughtered as Tybalt Sphendon and Morloc Hyat had been slaughtered, any more than he had committed suicide. His had been a relatively natural and peaceful death: an ending that was not so much fated as belated, having been held in long but mysterious suspense. I knew, now, why Eirene Magdelana had been gathering her strength and refining her power for so many years on top of Snowspur, in spite of the fact that the process was driving her mad.

I could only suspect, at that moment, that Phelim Kracy was also dead–killed by the literal fraction of the lightning-strike that had hit Lucifer's Light. If so, I thought, the male line of descent extending from the first Lucian Sombre was now extinct... unless, of course, Candida Kracy was carrying a son and not a daughter.

"I had hoped that you would come to my concert, Eirene," I said. "It was a special occasion."

"I heard the music," Eirene assured me, "and I heard the song–but I had to see Lucian first, before I attended to Karenne's daughter. There is an order to be observed in these matters, no matter how chaotic dreams may seem. Oh, Edom, Edom! What have you done? Why could you not..."

The grief took her voice away. I knew that it wasn't only the face of her son that she saw upon the bed but the ghost of her old lover. Even Phelim, who must have been something of a disappointment to his father, had been able to cast that kind of spell on Hecate Rain.

I stepped forward and prised the two guns out of Lucian's clutching fingers, one by one. Then, I called out to Jean-Jacques. He took his time in arriving, having positioned himself downstairs exactly as I had commanded, with a shot-gun at the ready.

"Barling is still alive, I think," I told him. "Make sure that he's secure. Constable Clovis can collect him at his leisure. That little phial he still has in his left hand must contain some remnant of the poison that he dripped into the decanter by the bed. Preserve them both carefully; they'll be firm proof of his guilt, if any is to be required. The other man can wait, I think–but make sure he's quite dead, just in case. Store him wherever it's convenient."

"Are you and the lady all right, sir?" Jean-Jacques inquired, casting an inquisitive glance in Eirene's direction. She didn't look well at all, but that was because she was so pale and distraught, and because her clothing, being soaked through, was clinging to her body in a very unattractive manner.

"Perfectly all right," I assured him. "More to the point, how is Miss Kracy?"

"Asleep, sir–but troubled, I suspect, by a nightmare. Miss Rain and Miss Amalek brought the cot from the library into the dining-room in order to lay her down more comfortably. They're with her."

"I think I might soothe that nightmare now," Eirene said. "I shall need your help, Axel–I'm a little drained just now, as you can probably tell by the fact that I'm making so much sense."

"She can't dream the child away," I said, although I wasn't at all sure. The pregnancy couldn't be far advanced, and there was abundant scope for a miscarriage. I was attempting to discover whether that was Eirene's intention.

"She shouldn't even try," was Eirene's verdict. "The object of morpheomorphism is not to obliterate but to transfigure. Dreams are the fabric of our being; the destruction of their produce always leaves us diminished. It's not the child that's the problem–the problem is the dream that preoccupies it even in the womb."

I recalled what I had said to Candida about some of the unborn being ready to be delivered, while others were only ready to fall. I also remembered what Hecate had told me about Phelim's analogy between the maker of dreams and a half-tamed animal, still poised on the brink between domesticity and wildness. On the whole, I preferred my representation.

"The destruction of our dreams diminishes us by leaving us artless," I murmured, by way of clarification rather than correction. "You're right–the problem isn't to obliterate, but to transfigure, to temper dangerous purity with exactly the right combination of impurities. If only it were as simple as it sounds."

Jean-Jacques had already set about following my instructions. Eirene moved out of his way, and I beckoned her to the door. We went downstairs to the dining-room, where Hecate and Davida had indeed installed Candida Kracy on the cot which I had given to Hecate; it was longer than the dining-room sofa, and far easier to transport than the heavier one in my studio.

As Jean-Jacques had said, Candida did indeed seem to be in the grip of a troublesome nightmare. She was moving her head from side to side and her eyes were busy behind their closed lids. Her limbs were twitching, her fingers rippling on the counterpane as if they were trying to play a harpsichord.

"Do you, by any chance, have some spare clothes with you that might fit Eirene?" I said to Davida Amalek.

"Not good ones," Davida admitted, blushing slightly. "Even the better ones have not been laundered."

"No matter," I said. "Luvah will find something."

I called Luvah, who merely nodded in response to my request—but Eirene didn't leave the room with her immediately.

"I think you should complete your concerto when we're ready, my dear," Eirene said to Davida Amalek. "I'm truly sorry that you were interrupted. Will you be able to play?"

Davida was puzzled, but she nodded meekly. Eirene nodded too, and went after Luvah in order to change into dry clothes.

"Where's Ragan?" Hecate demanded. "Did you...?"

"I caught Ragan in the act of poisoning the water decanter beside my bed," I told her. As Davida's eyes grew wide, I was quick to add: "He didn't know, of course, that Davida had exclusive use of my room. I was his intended victim. He's in safe hands now—Jean-Jacques will make sure that he gives us no trouble until we hand him over to the Constable."

"Why did you send Jean-Jacques for the shotgun?" Hecate wanted to know.

"There was a second intruder. He won't give us any further trouble either. I'll tell you the whole story later–but Candida still needs help. The respite she won before was briefer than I hoped. She must be our first priority."

"What second intruder?" Hecate demanded, determine not to be put off.

I sighed, but bowed to necessity. "I believe that Candida is pregnant..." I began.

"By *Phelim*?" Hecate was scandalized.

"Yes. A belated twist of fate, I think. I deduce that Phelim and his father had made numerous attempts to impregnate her long ago–although I doubt that Phelim's involvement began until he had concluded his affair with you, and may have been the reason... At any rate, Phelim's father–and Candida's too–was not Karenne Kracy's husband but a man named Lucian Sombre, the son of Edom Sombre and the grandson of the other Lucian Sombre, who was the great pioneer of morpheomorphism. Their serial incest was no mere perversion, but an attempt to conserve and concentrate some hereditary virtue that Lucian Sombre detected in Vyvyane Bayard–fortunately or unfortunately, the fertility of their couplings seems to have been reduced in consequence. By the time Phelim guessed or found out that his sister was not barren after all, he and she were already *en route* here. Phelim must have sent word to Lucian to come as swiftly as he could. If he had been able to keep Candida on Lucifer... Well, I suspect things might have worked out badly for all three of them, given that Lucifer's Light was struck by lightning a few minutes ago."

"What!" Hecate didn't know whether to rush from the room in search of visual confirmation of what I said, or to wait for the end of the story. Had she still loved Phelim Kracy, she would doubtless have chosen the former course. She didn't.

"Instead," I went on, "Lucian followed her here, hoping to get Candida away before his troubles were multiplied by scandal–a prospect which must have seemed all the more urgent when he was questioned by Constable Clovis. He brought a gun to aid him, but he didn't want to hurt anyone... and the story had one remaining twist for which he was not at all pre-pared. Eirene, his mother, has spent a great deal of time on Snowspur purifying her own dreams and repairing the damage done to her by having once been party to Edom Sombre's scheme."

"What scheme?" Hecate demanded, mystification sharp-ening her tone.

"Eirene can provide the details, if she cares to," I said. "The bare bones of it, I think, are that the first Lucian Sombre fancied himself a new kind of alchemist, He was obsessed with the secrets of eternal life and the transmutation of ele-ments... not the chemical elements, in this case, but the ele-ments of the soul. He hoped, by means of an alchemical mar-riage, to produce a very special child–a medium far more powerful than the likes of Vashti Savage–and to provide him-self with the means not merely of a sort of resurrection, but of the acquisition of a new kind of power. He found a suitable subject in Vyvyane Bayard, but she was married. This is pure guesswork, but I think she was only allowed to travel abroad under the watchful eye of her husband's brother, which proved to be not watchful enough from her husband's viewpoint but rather too watchful from Lucian Sombre's... At any rate, whatever happened aboard the *Haemon Redondo* set in train a chain of betrayals and tragedies that recurred, in one way or another, with every daughter born to that female line, until..."

I was interrupted at this point by Eirene Magdelana's return. She was by no means flattered by Luvah's second set of clothes, but she was dry and the color was returning to her cheeks. Jean-Jacques came in with her to report that Ragan Barling was secure and that Lucian Sombre's corpse was safely stowed away in the cellar.

"Has Lucifer's Light been struck by lightning?" Hecate asked him. "Has the tower come down?"

"The light has gone out, Miss," he replied, "that's all I know. Pray that no ships need its guidance."

"Miss Amalek," said Eirene, "will you play again, now?"

"I might not be at my best," Davida muttered–but she knew that it didn't matter. The point was to finish what she had started, as best she could. None of us, I suspect, was really at his or her best just then–not even me.

Eirene sat down on the bed on Candida Kracy's left side, and indicated that I should take a similar station to the girl's left. I did so, and matched Eirene's moves in taking the patient's left hand in my left hand, and placing my right hand on her left temple. Hecate, meanwhile, looked on apprehensively.

Davida began to play, taking up her piece at the exact point at which she had left off. She had only a few minutes to play–four at the most–but there was no need for any recapitulation or prelude. Although Candida had ceased to sing, the music had not entirely let go of her dream. The notes played by Davida were merely a catalyst; the true author of Candida's continued distress was the storm beyond the storm: the disturbed power of Morpheus.

18

As soon as I heard the music start, I was part of it. I was no morpheomorphist, in any practical sense, but I was an artist. Even the most impure artist is capable of distilling his genius when the need arises–and Eirene Magdelana was the purest artist in the world just then. Just as she had fused her mind with Lucian Sombre's she now formed a trinity consisting of herself, Candida Kracy and me.

I dreamed Candida Kracy's dream. I met the monster that was distressing her.

The monster was not her child but something parasitic upon her child: something terrible. I have said, time and time again, that the dead do not return, and that what ghost-seers see is a reflection of something within, made manifest by artistry. I have also said that whatever makes our dreams has no life of its own, but only shares in ours. I hold to both those propositions now—but the first Lucian Sombre had been determined that the dead could and should return, not as ghosts but in the flesh, in blood, bone, brain and instinct, and he had been similarly determined to create new life and new force within that renewed flesh. He had believed that a man resurrected might be more than a man—all the more so if he had a pliant instrument to complete and complement him: a slavish empress whose morpheomorphic power might render her completely mad, but capable in consequence of working miracles.

Lucian Sombre was dead, but I met him again in Candida's dream—not, this time, as an old or middle-aged man but as disembodied idea avid to *be* and to *become*, which needed flesh to accomplish its ambition. He had no face or form, nor even a shadow, but the raw material of dreams needs no such imagery to do its finest work.

It was I who made images, by way of defense; it was I who painted portraits on the walls of my inner world, to fill it and protect it.

I dreamed that I painted Eirene Magdelana and Candida Kracy, Hecate Rain and Davida Amalek—and what paintings they were! I painted a self-portrait of a kind I had never attempted before, not flattering in any vulgar sense but aspirational nevertheless; I painted the better person that I might perhaps have become in the best of all possible worlds but never would or could in the tawdry copy that is actuality. I painted people I could have loved, in worlds far better than ours but not that best of all possible worlds—and regretted, if only for a while, the impurities of my character that prevented my loving anyone so well in the spoiled simulacrum of materiality.

I was a better painter in that dream than I had ever been or could be, and was not surprised by the discovery. The reach of dreams is never limited by mere practicality.

At the same time, I dreamed as Eirene Magdelana dreamed, in the language of the wind and the sea, surrounded by a host of spirits. I lived in her madness, and saw the artistic limitations of sanity, restricted by conformity and morality, logic and induction, color and form. I gave my force, my life, my consciousness to Eirene, so that she might shape the other part of our dream that was Candida Kracy's strange sleep and siren song.

At the same time, I saw the world as Candida Kracy had sensed it, unseeing, and reconstructed with the aid of her memory of sight. It was an exceedingly peculiar world, from an artist's point of view, but I am not entirely the tradition-bound representationalist that my particular interests suggest. I understand other vocabularies of sensation. I know the myriad ways in which the world may be transformed by an imagination that collapses three dimensions into two, and refuses to respect the limitations of focus and perspective, lines of sight and demarcation. The world of Candida's dream was a world by which I could be intrigued, and tempted... and a world in which I could work constructively, in harness with Eirene Magdelana.

We fought the monster that we could not see, and we slew it. We saved Candida Kracy's child from the jaws of that disaster, and we saved Candida Kracy's inner world from permanent corruption. I don't say that we set everything to rights absolutely and forever, for she had a long period of spiritual convalescence ahead of her, but I do say that we put an end to the progress of the disease that had been planted within her, and prevented the possibility of any further spread of its infection. We gave her mind the opportunity and the space to begin the process of healing itself, without fear of any reverse.

Then, the concerto ended. The storm, having passed overhead, began a long march across the mainland, where its vortex would eventually fill up and exhaust its fury. As for the vortex beyond the vortex... that one sucked up a great deal that had littered our world for far too long–including, if one cares to think in such terms, the ghosts of the *Haemon Redondo*.

Afterwards, I slept. So did Eirene.

235

Hecate confessed, when I awoke and found her waiting beside me, that she had been afraid for us. She was afraid that we might both have been infected with Candida Kracy's sickness, having drawn the poison out of her only to suffer it ourselves. We assured her that we hadn't.

"What have I missed?" I asked, when I realized that the light was not the day after the concert but the one after that, and that the last vestiges of the storm were long gone. I was in my own bed; the window was closed but the shutter and curtains were open, displaying a benign blue sky.

"Phelim's dead," Hecate told me. "The shock-wave of the lightning that put out the bolt must have stopped his heart before his body burned along with everything else within the tower's walls. Mercifully, no ship came to grief on the Devil's Rocks. Constable Clovis has Ragan Barling safe in the town jail; he's confessed to killing Tybalt Sphendon and Morloc Hyat, and is preparing a defense on the grounds that the double murder was a crime of passion born of his illimitable and enduring love for Davida Amalek. Fion Commonal has consigned Lucian Sombre's body to the morgue, having declared that he died of entirely natural causes. The summer visitors are beginning to arrive at last, but there'll be no Council-sponsored celebration of the centenary of the *Haemon Redondo* wreck. Davida won't lose out, though–news of her concert here is the rumor of the moment. Nobody has the least understanding of how her music contributed to the death of Lucian Sombre–or, for that matter, who Lucian Sombre might have been–and no one knows or much cares how her music contributed to the salvation of the dead lighthouse-keeper's sister and lover, but it all works to the advantage of the rumor-mill. Davida will be famous soon, the sensation of the season. You, of course, have been relegated to a minor role in the affair; you are, after all, a mere fixture whose potential for gossip was exhausted long ago. I, alas, am in the same category. Davida has gone home to prepare for celebrity, but I–loyal friend that I am–stayed to assist your servants in caring for you."

"I'm grateful to you for that," I said.

"Then again," she added, more truthfully than was strictly necessary, "I'm not quite ready to be alone, having lost so many friends and seen so many strange things in such a short space of time. Despite your heroic attempts to explain it all, I'm not sure that I understand a fraction of what happened here."

"Is Candida still here?" I asked.

"Of course. Where else has she to go? She's in mourning for her brother, but she's also impatient to see her portrait completed. She had no idea that she was pregnant, by the way, and still isn't sure whether to believe it. Time will tell, I suppose, if Fion Commonal can't... there's been no evidence of any miscarriage."

"If she miscarries," I told her, "it'll be an accident of fate. Eirene and I did nothing to harm the child—quite the opposite."

"What did you do?" she demanded, having no idea.

"We ministered to the shaper of her dreams," I answered. "We soothed its wrath into benignity, its madness into reason. With luck, her sleep will be natural from now on, and she will never sing again as she sang last... I mean, the night before last."

"I suppose I shall have to take your word for that," Hecate said, "Although it sounds like the kind of magic that you usually treat with the utmost skepticism."

"It doesn't matter what you or I believe," I said. "We're dealing with the fabric of dreams here—there is no objectivity in dreams, even though they shape us more powerfully than anything external to our being. They're all illusion and delusion, with nothing in them to be seen, heard or felt but the images we donate."

"If Tybalt Sphendon were here, he'd call that mere wordplay," Hecate observed.

"And he'd be half-right," I countered. "Wordplay it is, but there's nothing mere about it; without wordplay, how could we formulate or understand our world? If morpheomorphism is the purest of the arts, wordplay is surely the purest of the practical sciences."

"Well," she said, "if I had ever feared that you wouldn't wake up as the same person you were before you went to sleep, I could set my doubts to rest now."

When I had breakfasted–an urgent business, given the length of time that I had been asleep–I went to see Eirene, who had also woken up. Candida Kracy insisted on joining the meeting–which meant that Hecate refused to be left out, so it was a more complicated encounter than I had planned.

"I must go back home," Eirene told me. "The spirits of the air are awaiting me, and we haven't much time to complete our business. Did I tell you that I'm dying, Axel? Will you see to it that I'm buried at sea? The ground is so hard and unforgiving, and the spirits of the earth are kin to the spirits of fire, bent on dry combustion. Edom's dead, you know–my only love. Not for the first time, either, but perhaps for the last. It's time to join him, to dissolve into the sea and to be dispersed across the world, to the limits of the Empire and far beyond. He loved me too, Axel–you have to understand that. Karenne had the remnants of the treasure, but I was the one he loved: his pupil, his partner. Karenne's children were supposed to be his prodigies, but I was his protegée.

"It's not over, you know... it never will be over, while there's treasure in the world. But there'll be peace here, for a while, on the island. That's the secret of the island, isn't it, Axel? It's a haven of peace. The storms blow in from the sea, but they always blow over. The art remains. The art and the air. You'll see that I'm buried at sea, won't you, Axel? Edom too. He has to go back to the sea, because he cheated it once. We don't want to desiccate in hard, dust, stern and unforgiving ground. Best that we vanish, don't you think? The merciful current will carry us away with its tearful flood, mourning us as we dissolve. Poor Edom! He never could become *one* ...but how many people can? We all carry our ghosts within us–except you, Axel, of course. You paint them. Very wise, very sane, very..."

She trailed off.

"She's hurt, isn't she?" said Candida Kracy. "She helped me, but she hurt herself."

"She was like this before," I assured her. "She's relaxed again, that's all."

"Pity," Hecate said. "Candida and I were hoping to get her version of the story. We're not convinced that yours makes a lot of sense."

I tried not to be offended, but it wasn't easy. "What have you told Candida, Hecate?" I asked.

"It's Hecate who thinks that it doesn't make sense," Candida was quick to say. "To me... well, I haven't had Hecate's education. She told me that Lucian Sombre was Phelim's father, and mine too–that he used my mother, and me, in some kind of experiment in somnambulism, which worked better on her than me, in that she had two children and never fell finally asleep. He and his father collaborated in the use of my mother and grandmother, just as his father than grandfather had collaborated in the use of my grandmother and great-grandmother. Again and again and again, always hunting for a result they never quite achieved..."

"I helped," Eirene Magdelana said. "Forgive me, child, but I helped. I would have done anything for Edom, no matter what. I betrayed your mother, child. Forgive me, please."

"I forgive you," Candida said. "You saved me, after all. You saved me from that dreadful sleep, and from... well, I can't exactly tell, but *something*. Something inside me that I'm better off without. Perhaps no more than a nightmare... but certainly no less. When you've slept as long as I have, you can't be reassured that something's *only* a nightmare. Nightmares are real–more so than reality itself. So, thank you for that. It *is* gone, isn't it?"

"Yes, child," Eirene said. "It's gone. It needn't ever come back... unless you want it to."

That phrase again! Why did it never seem quite as reassuring as it ought to have been.

239

"I suppose you're my grandmother," Candida said, "if Lucian Sombre really was my father–and grandmother to my own child, as well as great-grandmother."

Eirene laughed at that.

"It's a fine history," I said. "Personally, I believe every word–but we mustn't forget that all history is fantasy, no matter how closely and carefully we witness its unfolding."

"Be careful not to get too carried away with your own inventions, Axel," Hecate advised. "Remember what happened to Ragan Barling." She could be very cruel at times–but I forgave her. It was a day for forgiving.

Eirene did go back to Snowspur, the following day. I resumed work on my portrait of Candida. I completed it on the hundredth anniversary of the wreck of the *Haemon Redondo*– which was, by coincidence, the day when the workmen began to reconstruct Lucifer's Light, determined to have some sort of functional beacon in place before disaster struck.

My image of Candida Kracy was an excellent portrait, but I felt that I had failed in its making–not so much because Candida had changed significantly during the course of its completion, but because there was another portrait too fresh in my memory: the one I had painted in my imagination while I was under the influence of Eirene Magdelana's morpheomorphic power, in a world that was not ours, unbounded by the limits of practicality. That had been a different Candida, but I couldn't separate the two in my mind, or in my art.

Eirene was found dead on the top of Snowspur a week later. Her funeral was the fifth I had attended in ten days, after Tybalt Sphendon's, Morloc Hyat's, Phelim Kracy's and Lucian Sombre's. It was the one that drew the smallest crowd– unsurprisingly, given that it was held on Lucifer, from which the body was to be released into the sea–but Davida Amalek was there as well as Hecate and Candida. So was Nicodemus Rham.

"It's good to see you, Nicodemus," I said, while we stood together afterwards, having raised our bowed heads again. "How are you?"

"Very well, sir," he said. "They've asked me to come back to Lucifer, to help tend the makeshift light. I said that I would, of course. A matter of duty. I didn't know there'd be so many people here. I wish my house were in good enough repair to offer you places to sit and something to drink. Was the lady a great friend of yours, sir?"

"Yes, Nicodemus, she was," I said. "And I think she might be a good friend to you, if only you could contrive to see her. I must tell you all about her, so that you'll recognize her ghost if you meet her. I'd like to think that I could come to you for news of her, occasionally."

"Well, sir," he said, "it's not for me to say whether she'll come or not, but I'll certainly keep a lookout, if you want me to. She'll come alone, I suppose?"

"No, Nicodemus, I doubt that she will. Her son is with her, you see... and perhaps her husband too. They all have gifts, although they might not always have been wise or virtuous in making use of them. Perhaps you might be good for them, if they only have the chance to learn from your example."

"I doubt that, sir," the lighthouse-keeper said, with sincere modesty. "Is the young lady all right?"

He nodded in the direction of Candida Kracy, who was standing near the water's edge, staring into the lightless depths into which Eirene's body had disappeared. Hecate Rain was close beside her; they might have been sisters.

"Yes," I said. "She has nothing to fear, at present, and everything to learn. Life will be exciting for her, in a way that you and I can hardly imagine, for quite some time to come. It will be an excellent summer, Nicodemus... an exceptional season." I glanced at Davida Amalek as I said it; she too was facing the other way.

"I think it will, sir," Nicodemus said, assuming that I was referring to the weather. "You never can tell when another storm will come, until it's only a day or two away, but I seem to feel it in my bones that there won't be one along for a little while now, until the light is shining steady and bright every

241

night. I'll sleep easier in my bed when it's all finished. Safe in the arms of... what was the old saying, sir? I've quite forgotten."

"It doesn't matter, Nicodemus," I assured him. "It's only wordplay."

Brian Stableford has been a professional writer since 1965. He has published more than 50 novels and two hundred short stories, as well as several non-fiction books, thousands of articles for periodicals and reference books, several volumes of translations from the French and a number of anthologies. He is also a part-time Lecturer in Creative Writing at King Alfred's College Winchester. His novels include *The Empire of Fear* (1988), *Young Blood* (1992) and his future history series comprising *Inherit the Earth* (1998), *Architects of Emortality* (1999), *The Fountains of Youth* (2000), *The Cassandra Complex* (2001), *Dark Ararat* (2002) and *The Omega Expedition* (2002). His non-fiction includes *Scientific Romance in Britain* (1985), *Teach Yourself Writing Fantasy and Science Fiction* (1997), *Yesterday's Bestsellers* (1998) and *Glorious Perversity: The Decline and Fall of Literary Decadence* (1998). His anthologies include *The Dedalus Book of Decadence (Moral Ruins)* (1990) and *The Dedalus Book of British Fantasy* (1991). Reference books to which he has contributed include the Clute/Nicholls *Encyclopedia of Science Fiction* (1979; 2nd ed. 1993), Neil Barron's *Anatomy of Wonder* (2nd. ed. 1981; 3rd ed. 1987; 4th ed. 1995) and *The Cambridge Guide to Literature in English* (1988; 2nd ed. 1993).